Chasing Mr. Wrong

Praise for Chasing Mr. Wrong

I had the honor and pleasure of reading an advance copy of Anastasia Alexander's new novel, *Chasing Mr. Wrong*. Zoey is a spunky heroine who has fallen on hard times in both her personal and professional life. To add to the complications, her meddling sister slips her a love potion in hopes of getting Zoey to fall for her sexy neighbor, who has complications of his own with his parents trying to arrange a marriage for him. The novel is fun, funny, and full of heart. Not only is it a feel-good romance, it's also a book about the importance of empowering oneself.

Karen M. Bryson, *USA Today* best-selling author

So are relationships all about destiny, with their success formula written in the stars? Or is finding a good match a matter of science and strategies? *Chasing Mr. Wrong* is a surprising, clever, and both lighthearted and heartfelt tale of Zoey's launch of her business, "Relationships Done Right." She has competition from Reynesh, plus, her sister can't help but interfere, and then there's that "maybe" Mr. Right. Read it. Trust me—Zoey and her very modern network are great fun.

Virginia McCullough, author of *The Jacks of Her Heart*

Gosh, I love the title of *Chasing Mr. Wrong*. Haven't we all chased Mr. Wrong at some point? Here is a short version of the story: Fresh off a divorce and jobless, Zoey is sure she can find Mr. Perfect, but her sister slips a love potion into the coffee. Let the games begin! What a fun read. Highly recommend.

Lana McAra, best-selling, award-winning author

Destiny versus self-made? A timeless question that is explored in the most surprising way. *Chasing Mr. Wrong* is an endearing enemies-to-lovers tale with a twist I never saw coming.

F. K. Isley, avid book reader

An Absolute Joy! Three things that make *Chasing Mr. Wrong* stand out are: 1) the cross-cultural aspects and the characters' differing views. Having spent a significant amount of time in India and living abroad, I really appreciate the diversity in this novel. This adds much depth to this wonderful love story; 2) as a divorcee and life coach, I completely identified with Zoey, and it was a joy and relief to watch her grow into a strong woman; and 3) and I saved the best for last . . . the twist at the end absolutely sets this romance apart from the crowd. This was very well done. *Chasing Mr. Wrong* made me laugh a lot and brought tears to my eyes. The characters are amazingly crafted and fun. This is an absolute must-read.

Lynne Hill-Clark, Psy.D., best-selling author of *A Woman's World* Series

Chasing Mr. Wrong features a heroine who is quirky and full of heart, and you can't help rooting for her. *Chasing Mr. Wrong* has it all—humor, sister drama, romance, motorcycles, fun twists, and, of course, a dreamy next-door neighbor.

Tiffany Walker, avid book reader

Chasing Mr. Wrong features Zoey, fresh off a divorce, unsure of herself and very naïve but determined to find Mr. Perfect. At the top of her list, (yes, she has a list) is Disneyland. If Mr. Potential Perfect doesn't like Disneyland, he's scratched off the list. Her quest for the right man receives unasked-for help when her sister slips a love potion in the attractive neighbor's coffee. What follows is a story filled with sister drama, humor, romance, and an unconventional hero who offers something more than beautiful teeth and a handsome bod. With his help, Zoey learns how to fend for herself. Watching Zoey evolve from a naïve young woman unsure of her place in life to a confident, self-assured fighter who can make her own decisions was very satisfying. *Chasing Mr. Wrong* is a quick feel-good read where the sparks are intense, the banter snappy, and the sister bonds are strong. You'll keep reading with a smile until the last page.

Lorraine Norwood, author of *The Margaret Chronicles*

Such a fun play on science, destiny, and self-discovery with a heroine you can't help rooting for. This clean sweet post-divorce romance is a refreshing read.

Sara LaFontain, author of *The Corbitt Calamities* Series

A riveting tale. *Chasing Mr. Wrong* beautifully weaves the complexities of modern love with irresistible storytelling. An absolute must-read!

Marta Lane, author and creator of *Trust Your Words*

Chasing Mr. Wrong

A NOVEL

Anastasia Alexander

NEW YORK

LONDON • NASHVILLE • MELBOURNE • VANCOUVER

Chasing Mr. Wrong

Published in New York, New York, by Morgan James Publishing. Morgan James is a trademark of Morgan James, LLC. www.MorganJamesPublishing.com

Proudly distributed by Publishers Group West®

Publisher's Note: This novel is a work of fiction. Names, characters, places, and incidents are either products of the author's imagination or used fictitiously. All characters are fictional, and any similarity to people living or dead is purely coincidental

Disclaimer

As a writer, I acknowledge that Indian culture is diverse and multifaceted, and it is impossible for one person who is not from that culture to represent it fully and accurately. However, I have made a sincere effort to be as culturally sensitive and accurate as possible in my writing. I traveled through India with the University of Arizona and tour guides trying to grasp some of its treasures. I am grateful to have had the opportunity to work with an excellent sensitivity reader, Vidhi Mohan, who helped me navigate the complexities of Indian culture and ensured that my representation was respectful and authentic. I hope that my writing will serve to educate and inspire others while also honoring the rich traditions and cultural heritage of India.

Morgan James BOGO™

A **FREE** ebook edition is available for you or a friend with the purchase of this print book.

CLEARLY SIGN YOUR NAME ABOVE

Instructions to claim your free ebook edition:
1. Visit MorganJamesBOGO.com
2. Sign your name CLEARLY in the space above
3. Complete the form and submit a photo of this entire page
4. You or your friend can download the ebook to your preferred device

ISBN 9781636983189 paperback
ISBN 9781636983196 ebook
Library of Congress Control Number: 2023945340

Cover Design by:
Rachel Lopez
www.r2cdesign.com

Interior Design by:
Christopher Kirk
www.GFSstudio.com

Morgan James is a proud partner of Habitat for Humanity Peninsula and Greater Williamsburg. Partners in building since 2006.

Get involved today! Visit: www.morgan-james-publishing.com/giving-back

To Anna and Lexi.
Thank you for your hugs, kisses, and always being there.

Author's Note

Although the traditional way to spell *ex*, as in a former spouse, is "ex," in this novel, it will be spelled *X*. Why? The *X* looks so much bolder, stronger, and the way it *should* be spelled. Most who have an *X* understand the visual satisfaction of the pronounced, much-earned *X*.

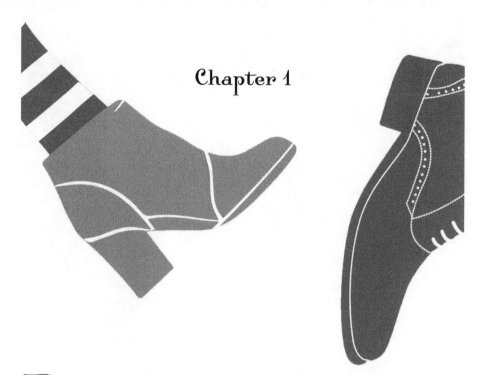

Chapter 1

Rarely, if ever, does a woman become divorced and receive a dozen roses on the same day from the same man. Only a few hours after my lawyer's phone call, the flowers arrived on my front porch in all their glory. They weren't even dead. Sending a bouquet of black flowers, I understood. But red?

It was like he was suggesting we made a mistake by breaking up, which we did not. Damion had fallen out of love with me about ten minutes after we got married. Maybe ten minutes before. But whenever it happened, the love vanished. Poof—gone like magic.

My part—I thought he was Mr. Perfect. After all, he was cute and paid attention to me, and I believed that after I said "I do" under the California sun, that would continue. Silly me.

His part—he thought he could actually talk me out of wanting kids. Didn't work. I just cried more often and offered to babysit whenever I saw a neighbor with a child. No one ever took me up on that.

I stared at the flowers and the unopened card. Heat crawled up my neck. Hopefully, my neighbors weren't watching a single woman, a divorced woman, a free woman . . . alone . . . just standing there.

Pressure to get back to my homework for my long distance-learning program finally compelled me to snatch the card. But before I could read it, a loud sports car jolted up my driveway.

My upscale older sister, Tiffany Marie Woodland, had arrived. The star of the family. She held the beauty and grace of a runway model and could pull off wearing brand-name clothes without a wrinkle or stain. How she did that was a mystery I doubted I'd ever crack.

I waited for her to park and approach me, half holding my breath. She strolled up in her outrageously high heels clicking on the sidewalk. Her eyes locked on the roses.

"Who are those from?"

I swallowed a lump in my throat. "No one." I wrapped my fingers around the card to hide it from her prying eyes. "Land more big deals at the bank?"

"Of course." Her face lit up. "Brought in $100,000 just today."

I picked up the roses and headed into my house. "Impressive."

"Zoey," I heard her call toward my back. "Tell me about those flowers."

There was a reason she was an all-star at the bank. She was more unrelenting than a hungry mosquito by a swamp.

"Who could it be . . .?" Her voice trailed off as her brain ran through possibilities. "Your lawyer?"

I said nothing.

She shook her head. "No, you wouldn't be hiding that . . . Nor would you hide a friend. Only people romantically interested would send *red* roses."

I hustled into the kitchen, set the flowers on the counter, and noticed her ever-common raised eyebrow. To avoid her eyes, I picked up a box of lentil crackers on my counter. I had left them out unopened, not having gathered the courage to try them yet, just like I wasn't quite ready to try on my new life.

Wanting to stay in motion, I slid open the pantry door. I studied the disheveled shelves. The new me was going to be on top of things—organized and healthy—which meant I had to rid myself of the cans containing evil MSG destroying everyone's health. And I needed a system for where things belonged.

I pushed dusty—probably expired—chicken soup cans to the side to make room for the new, improved food—lentil crackers.

"Tiff," I called out, "the lawyer rang. It's official. I'm divorced." My voice wavered.

"It's about time." She hunted for the card in the roses. "That man is a menace." She gave up. "Tell me about these." She eyed the flowers like it was some big secret, and I was obligated to explain.

I pushed a few boxes around on the pantry shelf. Pasta noodles tumbled onto the floor from an opened bag.

"Tell me."

"Damion."

Tiffany slapped the counter. "You're kidding."

"Wish I was." I opened the lentil cracker box, then turned to see my sister's face reddened.

"That's priceless. What a piece of work." She drummed her fingers against the counter. "You just received a call from your lawyer saying you were officially divorced—what, yesterday?"

This morning at 9:23 a.m. to be exact, but I wasn't going to correct her. Instead, armed with an open box of lentil crackers, I offered Tiffany one by shaking it.

She retreated like I was giving her poison. "Why?"

I shrugged as if it didn't really matter and popped a cracker into my mouth.

"You're not getting back with him, are you?" She gave me a judgmental questioning expression.

The cracker caught in my throat. "Of course not," I said through the crumbs. "It's taken me seven months to get the divorce." Pressing my lips together, dry crumbs still in my mouth, I handed over the note.

Here's to our first year of marriage.

Her eyes traveled over his handwriting, then to me. "What's that supposed to mean?"

I finally worked the cracker down my throat and swallowed. Lentil crackers didn't have the satisfying crunch of real potato chips. They were bland and had a terrible aftertaste. But I had to do things differently, even if I didn't like it, so I could create the life I wanted. That meant following the rules, including eating healthy food that tasted like gnawing on cardboard.

"It's some kind of hint to get you back," my sister concluded.

"I don't know. It's confusing since we were married for three years, not one." I popped another cracker in my mouth.

"Maybe he's trying to make you feel guilty for leaving him. It isn't working, is it?"

I grabbed a napkin from the holder on the counter and spat the crackers into it. "No." I brushed at my lips to knock off the remaining crumbs. I might cave with Tiffany all the time, but that didn't mean I'd cave with Damion. Well, at least not anymore.

"It's time for me to claim my life," I declared, sounding stronger than I felt.

My sister headed toward the fridge. I flinched—another lecture would soon be coming. Three, two, one . . .

She opened the door and stared at my expired brown eggs, wilted spinach, years-old ketchup, almost-gone jam, and the remaining bare shelves.

"Zoey!" Her nose tilted up.

Yep. There it was. I sat on a kitchen chair.

Her eyes were wide, and her mouth had fallen open. "You can't go on like this."

Damion owed me a token alimony check soon, but that wouldn't go far. The lawyer bills were daunting, and I hadn't figured out how to make money quite yet. But if I told my sister, she'd get all up in my business.

I rubbed at the grease on my fingers. "Working on it."

She sighed. "How much money do you need each month to survive?"

I sank low into my chair. "I'm not a banker like you."

She set her jaw tight. "That's not the point—"

"Stop," I snapped. "I have it handled."

She quirked her perfectly arched brow.

"In fifty-eight days, I will graduate from the Rules-Based Relationship Coach Program."

"And?" She rolled her hands.

"And I'll make money," I said flatly. "I can hold on until then."

Her eyes locked on mine. "Ah. Do they show you how to make money?"

"Well, um, they teach you the rules of relationships are actually a science, and if you follow them . . ."

"But the money, Zoey. What about the money?"

Feeling my face heat up, I mumbled, "Um, we aren't to that part yet."

"What about making money now? Why put it off?"

"Uh . . ."

My sister didn't get it. I needed to know the rules, follow them, and then presto, I'd have a loving husband and four kids and a white picket fence. There would be no need to worry about money like we did as kids with Dad gone and Mom drunk all the time.

Tiffany studied me like she was examining a math problem that needed to be solved.

She didn't believe I'd stick to my new career as a coach just because I have a slight history of not sticking to things. Okay, maybe a whole lifetime. But sometimes, it takes a person a while to find themselves.

But lucky me, I finally have found myself—or maybe more like the answer. Science would find me my perfect match, and I wasn't going to give up on that.

"We-e-ell," Tiffany drew out the word, "to be a coach, you need to dress so people can trust you. So, makeover time!"

"Forget it," I snapped, feeling a knot in my belly. "Not going to happen."

Tiffany flipped her brown hair to her back in a condescending way. "Sweats and a ten-year-old T-shirt won't cut it, Zo."

I inspected my stained shirt. She might have a point. "I'll figure it out."

She chuckled. "Heard that before." She waved her hand at my attire. "You look like a tent." Her nose curled. "You can't go out into the business world like that if you want anyone to take you seriously."

I glanced at my outfit. It was baggy and—okay, stained, and yeah, more like a street bum than business.

"Be prepared to shop tomorrow afternoon at five sharp."

"Tiffany to the rescue," I whispered, both relieved and irritated.

She moved her purse strap onto her shoulder, then dumped my dozen beautiful, deep-red roses into the trash can.

She strolled to the door, her heels at least three inches high, and her ankles didn't even wobble.

"Sis, congrats on your divorce."

I watched her prance to her car on a mission, leaving me alone and divorced, but with a plan.

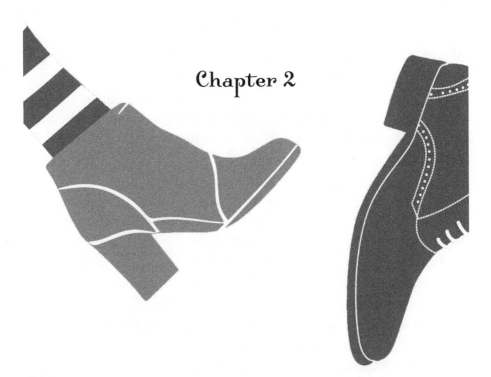

Chapter 2

B y the time the sliver of the waning moon had risen in the sky, the swing on our . . . no, *my* front porch had beckoned me to lounge on its cushions hidden behind orange flowering bushes and a miniature palm tree.

I took the swing up on its offer, bringing my notebook and binders with me. Not long after sitting down, the sway of the gentle rocking and the soft creak of the iron rods underneath settled me, lulling me to a level of relaxation I hadn't felt in a while.

Across the road stood a cream-colored house with purple shutters. Each house on this street appeared the same except the color of the shutters— taupe, green, or blue. Since I didn't know most of my neighbors, this being the fast-growing town of Murrieta, California, and all, I couldn't help but wonder if the people living across the street would even know a divorced woman sat staring at their house, wondering if a happy, successful couple lived there. Couples who liked each other and believed in each other, and wanted to be in one another's company.

Divorcing someone seemed so commonplace and normal to me.

Almost like an adult admitting they have a pimple even though they grew up believing their mom's promise that acne would end after puberty.

But to me, being divorced weighed much more seriously than a stupid oozing red pimple. I'd thought about it for months before I contacted a lawyer. I wondered what it would be like to run into a grocery store without being timed. Or to talk to another male under the age of sixty without Damion calling me a "slut" or "unfaithful."

In those years of our marriage, I dreamed about being able to make my own decisions, like what milk to buy or what to spend my extra five dollars on without getting permission from Mr. Bank.

I'd never actually thought I'd call a divorce lawyer and say, "Get me out of my marriage." After all, I'd made a vow before God and my sister.

Then one night, my friends raved about a romantic getaway they were going on with their spouses. As they enthusiastically rambled on and on, all I could think about was the possibility of a romantic *anything* with Damion was about as likely as the sky opening up and raining gold bars.

Late that night over a year ago, after my friends left, Damion stumbled onto the backyard patio, finding me sitting on the glider in the dark. He brought the smell of beer and his sneering attitude. "What's your problem?"

A rainfall of tears fell for his answer. My period had just started. At the time, I was crushed, again, because there was no child on the way.

"You don't need to make yourself even less attractive," he snapped.

Wiping at my tears, I asked, "What do you mean?"

"You know." He stood in front of the glider like a military statue in the shadows. "You're fat."

Those words hit me straight in my chest with a thud. I gasped. I blinked into the darkness to make out my husband's features. As though seeing his expression would give me a clue as to why the man who had promised to be with me forever through thick and thin, sickness and health, who was going to be my children's daddy—or so I had thought—would say something that awful.

I continued to blink up at him.

"You probably put on all that weight so I wouldn't want to have sex with you," he added for effect. "And by the way, we're *never* having a baby, so you might as well get over that."

And I was done.

Somehow, I found the courage to stand, and brush past him to get inside, snatch the car keys, and flee to my sister's. Twenty minutes later, I stood in front of Tiffany's apartment door, tears pouring and anger pounding.

"Get me out!" were the only words I needed to say for the end of our marriage to become real.

All of that brought me to this moment, staring at my neighbors' houses, thinking about their lives, wondering if they received a better roll of the dice.

That didn't do me any good. I picked up one of my coaching manuals, forcing myself to focus. The answers were in them. Ignoring the cold void I suddenly felt, I flipped open my coaching institute binder and read the subtitle, "*Taking Out the Complexity: The Science to Ultimately Fulfilling Relationships.*"

A ripple of calmness flowed through me. A road map to relationships and love and babies. If my mom had known this stuff, things would've been different for Tiff and me.

The evening brought in a misty marine layer and an occasional dog bark. I snuggled into the swing cushion, reviewing the material, which delved into the power of vision and clarity. When a person knew what they wanted, that knowledge gave them the ability to make it real. I closed my eyes for the hundredth time and asked the all-important question: What did I want?

A man. Clean-shaven. In a polo shirt. Corporate. Entrepreneurs were too up and down, too much risk. They always had to be achieving the next thing, which didn't include a family or much time for a relationship. They focused on the big picture of business, not the day-to-day things.

The man I loved would be stable, have a good corporate job to balance out mine, and . . . love Disneyland. At least what it stood for, not any of the shady business deals that hit the news sometimes. My mouth curved into a smile. Disneyland. The ultimate family vacation. The ultimate family.

"Hello." A male voice broke into my reverie.

My eyes snapped open to find a tall, attractive man standing in front of me on my porch. His trimmed beard outlined a pronounced jawline. A dusty-gray polo shirt fit snugly across his broad chest. A smile danced at the corner of his mouth.

"Sorry," he said, his gaze still on mine. "I didn't mean to startle you."

I glanced at my relationship book, then back to his slightly irreverent, cocky, free-spirited nature. He had the chutzpah to walk up and say hello to a stranger like it was a normal thing to do. In California, that was not so normal.

"I'm Reynesh Bayaan Babu." He extended his hand for me to shake.

"I'm not interested," I shot out so he'd know I wasn't up for whatever he was selling.

He dropped his hand. "My nephews and I are your new neighbors."

"New neighbors?" I glanced across the street. He pointed to the house directly on the other side of the road.

"I didn't even know the house was for sale."

"We bought it privately."

"Ah. Well, welcome to the neighborhood." I bit down on my lip. Popping up in someone's yard out of nowhere was a bit creepy. I tried to repeat his name, but the unfamiliar syllables became tangled in my mouth. "R-r-ra—"

He chuckled. "Call me Ray for short. Most Americans do."

That was curious. "I'm Zoey."

"Cute name."

I couldn't hold back a smile. "Thanks. So, where are you from?"

"America. Born and bred, but my grandparents are from New Delhi, India. My nephews are straight from Bangalore. I have visited enough that I feel like I'm partly from there too."

I stared at this strange man who had just showed up on my doorstep, part American, part Indian. He appeared to be close to my age, in his late twenties. He had two rings on his right hand, both thick gold bands with stunning deep-colored jewels embedded in them.

"I'm guessing you weren't 'born and bred' around here," I said.

He smiled a little. "Why?"

"Californians don't just walk up to the front porch and introduce themselves."

He laughed. "Sorry."

I eyed his smile and relaxed my shoulder against the swing. He was cute. "Where were you before this?"

"Arizona. Just left. Came straight to California."

That made sense, I guess. People must be friendlier in Arizona. "Good choice to come to the land of beaches and Disneyland."

He gave a shrug. "I don't like Disneyland."

"How could someone not like Disneyland?" A frown edge onto my face. "It's the place of dreams. When I was little, I'd watch those magical commercials hoping that someday . . ." My voice broke. "Someday I could go."

The new neighbor leaned back, taking me in. "It pushes dangerous ideology."

He had to be kidding. A place where a kid could be a kid was dangerous? A place where families could have fun was dangerous?

"How?"

"By focusing on commercialism, pumping the romantic ideal of someone saving you because you are pretty or have a good voice, or whatever, instead of saving yourself."

My smile fled. "You're trying to destroy the dream. It's about being happy and celebrating the innocence of childhood."

Ray shook his head slightly. "Their TV shows undermine parents by portraying them as mindless fools." His forehead crinkled as he spoke. Somehow that nuance created an emphasis on his words.

I wasn't going to let his insistence ruffle me, though. This was Disneyland we were talking about. "It's the happiest place on earth."

His eyes flickered.

"It's the American icon for happy family vacations. The very symbol that gives hope to children who are in miserable homes. Maybe *you* don't need a symbol of the happy American family, but a lot of kids do."

"Okay, then . . ."

"Did you not go to Disneyland when you were little?" I asked sharply.

He shook his head. "When in the States we are to focus on surviving and there isn't a Disneyland in India, but it isn't because Indians don't like Disneyland. Of course, many would like to have one there."

I stared at him in utter surprise. "Why isn't there one in India, then, if many parents would like it? Disney isn't against making money, that's for sure."

He sighed heavily. "The area where I am from, it has scorching weather and gets extremely wet in the monsoon season."

"Monsoon, huh? So, not good for a roller coaster?"

His eyes flashed irritation. "Neither is poverty."

Heat prickled my neck, from shame at my ignorance. "Oh, that's true."

"Disney doesn't even pay the bills."

"What?" I asked.

"They work with other companies who step up and pay the expenses of building a park."

"You've got to be kidding."

"Right?" Ray agreed. "So far, no company from India has stepped up to pay."

I shook my head. The crickets in my backyard pond chirped. "Sounds risky." I wouldn't take that kind of chance. It was scary enough to put a few thousand into my coaching certification.

He shifted his weight. "Yes, exactly. Most people in India live day to day. They couldn't handle the entrance fee, food, souvenirs, transportation, and hotel."

"That's not so different from here," I admitted. "Many families in America save up for years to go. I can see how it'd be much harder for families there."

"Yep, capitalism at its best."

He had a lot of good points, but not good enough to make me give up on my Disneyland Dad dream. Oddly, even if he was wrong about the dangers of Disneyland, I liked his passion and his kind face.

"You feel really strongly about this."

He chuckled. "I guess I do."

"Do you get this passionate about everything?"

His smile grew. "Maybe. I'm definitely excited about my new app."

I straightened. "App?" Tech guy. Entrepreneur. Risk-taker. I piled my books and notebook into my arms. "What kind of app?" I asked, unable to resist.

"Dating. Relationships."

Arms piled high with books, I stared at him. I didn't need some smart, charming tech guy stealing the clients I didn't have yet.

He must have misinterpreted my stare because he flipped out a card. "Maybe you'd be interested in our services."

Ah-ha! I knew he'd eventually try to sell me something. My books threatened to fall out of my arms.

"I seriously doubt I'd be interested."

"Why's that? Married?"

"No," I snapped. "Not anymore."

Surprise widened his eyes for a split second, then he gave me an easy grin. "Well then, maybe my app is the perfect thing for you."

I lifted my chin. "I *happen* to be a *relationship* coach."

He considered me for a few long seconds. Each second made me more uncomfortable and fidgety.

"Really?" he finally said.

Was that mockery? "Yes, really." I glared at him over the top of the books. "Maybe *my* coaching would benefit *you*."

A smirk crossed his face, which was flat-out annoying.

"Why is that?" he asked.

I shifted my binders in my arms to be more secure. "Because you don't know what relationships are *really* about. It's not data points and software."

He smiled like he enjoyed my efforts pointing out his flaws.

"You can't program love," I countered.

Instead of getting angry or seeing my point, he broke out into a laughing fit. When he finally settled down, he said, "If I could program a healthy romantic relationship, I'd be all for it. Why not?"

My jaw fell. "Why not?"

"Yes, why not?"

"Because . . . I mean . . . obviously because . . ." I sputtered. Love wasn't cold and programmable the way he was suggesting. It was . . . it was . . .

Okay, fine. I didn't know what love was. But I knew what it wasn't. It wasn't someone abandoning their family. It wasn't constant disapproval. It wasn't sitting in a room with family members feeling all alone. And it wasn't something you could program.

"You have to know the dynamic of relationships, the behaviors that forge unbreakable bonds. You can't just hand that over to a computer—a machine—to control your life. A machine only knows what someone tells it to know."

The idea of giving a computer that much power over your life was unsettling, to say the least.

He let me ramble into silence before saying, "Bad relationships cause so much pain and suffering. If we could program happiness, why not?"

"That's crazy talk."

He shifted his weight. "So, you believe you have the answer?"

I patted the binders still in my arms. "I do have the answer."

"Good to hear."

I lifted my chin. "I base my coaching on the truth, and gaining control over your *own* life. Love is a science."

"That's ambitious to bite off. I don't do anything as complicated as teaching about love. I just developed a matchmaking app to help people find their destined partners."

"Destined?" I echoed. Worse and worse. "First, you want people to give up control to a computer. Now they're supposed to choose to give it up to the *stars,* too?"

Ray shrugged as if this wasn't insane. "It's not a choice. It just is. All my app does is recognize and apply the wisdom."

I glared at him and his ridiculous, extreme, slightly terrifying beliefs.

Give up control? I'd been doing that my whole life. Now I was committed to doing the exact opposite. And Ray was . . . he was . . .

I frowned at his handsome face.

He was *nuts.*

The sound of a thunderous car engine driving up the street broke my glare. A Civic rumbled into my driveway.

Damion. My now X.

He climbed out of the car. I clenched my hands around my binder. What was he doing here? And his red roses. I had coasted through my whole marriage without flowers, and now he had the gumption to give them to me in effort to get me back. That man was ballsy.

I turned to my new neighbor. "Welcome to the neighborhood, Ray. If you'll excuse me, it seems like I need to talk to my X."

His attention slid to the roses in Damion's arms. "Your X, huh?" he murmured and took a few steps backward. "Nice to meet you. Just wanted you to know if you ever need a cup of sugar or anything, I'm across the street."

My gaze was pinned on Damion's red roses. Another one of those "small details" he'd said he couldn't be bothered with when we were actually married. It was kind of like when I asked for him to fix the few dry grass patches or help me clean the house. He just seemed to be unable to do it.

He marched up the steps.

"What do you want?" I snapped, trying to sound tough and in charge. But at that exact moment, the frogs in my backyard croaked out a loud amphibian concert, so I had competition to be heard.

Ray stood at the sidewalk in front of the house, watching.

Damion strutted way too close to me. His cologne was strong, woody.

I stumbled back and cranked my head up to see his face. He showed none of the awkward telltale signs of nervousness. Instead, he wore a grin that emphasized his dimples. His eyes shone the light green I had once so loved staring into when we were together.

Of course, he'd found the gel and slicked back his dirty-blond hair, which he'd never done in our whole marriage. Despite my bitterness, I could acknowledge the gel was a nice touch.

"Whatcha doing?" His voice sounded breezy and if I wasn't mistaken, flirty.

I pressed my lips together. When in doubt with Damion, say nothing—my new strategy. It was the only way I could wrestle control back with this guy who'd always out talked me, outshone me, and outmaneuvered me. He was also my past. Not to mention, two dozen flowers in one day was overkill. Manipulative.

He waited for me to answer. Not talking wasn't getting him to go away.

I glared. "Why are you here?"

He extended the flowers. "For our second year. I was a jerk during it."

"That's the truth." I juggled the books in my hand and took the flowers. *Small details.*

"You need to move on," I said. Just like I'd been saying to myself for the past seven months as I studied for my coaching practice and took the steps toward divorce.

The flowers bloomed freely in unencumbered splendor, and his green eyes popped over them.

"Take them." I pushed the roses back to him.

"Zoey, I just want to talk—"

"Well, I don't."

Out of the corner of my eye, I saw the neighbor move closer to me.

My X shook his head. "No, they're for you. They're my apology. Let's leave it at that."

"Are you all right?" Ray called to me.

I inhaled deeply and said loudly, "My X was just leaving."

Damion eyed Ray. "Who's that? Did you already find someone new?"

I bristled at that, not liking the implication. "No. A neighbor. Saying hi."

Ray moved onto the grass, coming closer. "Zoey, are you sure you're okay?"

Damion put his hands up in the surrender position. "I'm going. I don't want any trouble."

He stepped back, keeping his gaze on my new neighbor.

Armed with flowers, I headed inside, trying not to think about what was happening with that Ray Destiny Guy and my X.

The slight hint of rose fragrance washed over me as I strolled through my home, through the open sliding door, out into the backyard, and over to the trash can. From the moment I opened the lid, the scent of rot floated up, engulfing me. Tiny fragments of the first bouquet of red roses and their leaves had broken off and littered the trash, kind of like Damion's and my love.

I dropped the newest flowers in.

On my way back into the house, I thought I saw a whisk of a tip of a cat's tail. I examined my fishpond. What would a cat be doing back here? Drinking from my yucky pond with murky water would not be a good idea.

Voices floated back to me.

Uh-oh. Were Ray and Damion still talking about *me*?

I hurried to the front porch to find Ray and Tiffany in a conversation.

"The chamber can be a joke," Tiffany was saying to him, confidence oozing off her. "You have to be careful who you align with."

"What are you doing back here?" I asked.

"Hey." She gave me a hug, balancing a pan of brownies.

My body stood stiff as her arms encircled me.

"You didn't think that we wouldn't celebrate such a big day? We have to mark your first day of freedom." She handed me the brownies. "I know how much you love brownies and . . ." She waved a paper in her hand. "A gift certificate for high-heeled shoes!"

Flowers, brownies, high heels . . . and all I wanted was to follow my path to a nice husband and children.

She continued to wave the certificate.

Only Tiffany would think of celebrating an end of a marriage with shoes. I took the paper from her and studied it. High heels and I had a long history of not working out. Brownies and I had a better history. I used to bake them all the time whenever Mom would pass out drunk.

"Thanks. You might have to help me with this one." I held up the certificate. She winked at me. "Tomorrow."

I'd already forgotten our plan to go shopping to help "reclaim my life." She clearly hadn't. It was time to change the subject.

"So, do you two know each other?"

I looked back and forth between her and the neighbor to see if I could spot a spark. It was about time for Tiffany to have a relationship. But so far, she didn't even have a hint of anything.

"Yeah, through networking," Tiffany said.

Of course. She knew everyone. Seemed like Ray might too. Wonderful.

"Tiff, I appreciate you coming over and for the gift, but . . ."

My mind scrabbled on how to get out of the shopping adventure.

"No problem. With the news that it's 'official,' I figured you'd be lost the first night."

"I can figure out how to handle it."

"Don't worry," she assured me. "I crossed everything off my calendar tonight, even game night."

Game night? Tiffany played games? Not since I'd known her.

"Ah," I said, a little confused. "Well, I'm sure I'll be fine, so you can go play—"

She shook her head. "Nope. I won't do that to you."

Man, she was never going to leave, was she? Not if I was alone. I glanced at Ray. He seemed to be watching me with compassion. Maybe he understood what it was like to have an overbearing sibling.

"Ray's here with me."

His eyes widened. I gave him a pleading expression as I started sweating.

Tiffany's jaw dropped. "What?"

Ray gave me a slight nod.

I stepped over to him, praying he'd go along with me. I hooked my arm through his. "We're on a date."

Tiffany flipped her gaze to Ray, who gave her a "What can you do?" face.

"Yep, a hot date," he added.

My fingers twitched, feeling as awkward as a teenager. "We're really just getting to know each other, but I had just said that I would spend the evening with him."

Ray bobbed his head in agreement. "Lots of interesting conversation about science and love and apps."

Tiffany peered between us, then flipped her keys in her hand, hesitating. "Well, okay. You two have a good evening. Sounds fun."

After her car rounded the corner, Ray asked, "Does science recommend making up fake boyfriends to get rid of unwanted guests?"

"Maybe it was destiny," I retorted. "You were standing there when she showed up. Like magic."

"That's destiny?"

"Apparently." I focused on the pan of brownies still in my hands. So did Ray. I thought of my new diet. My commitment to the new me.

"Like brownies?" I asked.

"Absolutely."

"Then they're yours. A thank you for being my pretend boyfriend. And . . ." I paused. "An apology. I probably shouldn't have roped you in that way." Discomfort made my face grow warmer. "Count them as a sorry for putting you in that position."

Ray lifted a corner of the plastic wrap and enthusiastically tossed a chunk of brownie in his mouth. "I'll be glad to be your destiny date anytime."

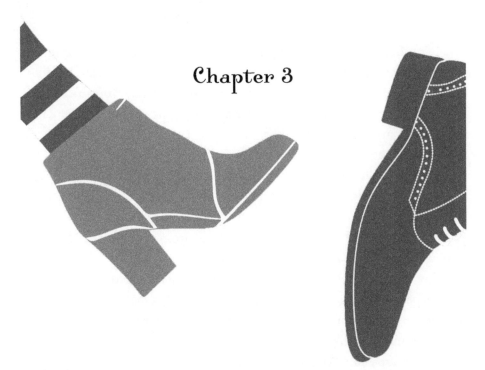

Chapter 3

The early yellow rays of light teased me awake. I blinked to orient myself. By reflex, I dug deeper into my blankets for comfort as the emptiness of the house surrounded me.

Maybe a hot steamy bath would do the trick of waking me up to claim my new life and help me not feel so alone. Today, I needed to find the courage to plow further into my relationship course material.

As I wrestled with myself to climb out of bed, the neighbor's attractive face flashed in my mind, the way he tightened his jaw and his theories about destiny. I kicked at my bedsheets. I made things happen by going by the books and science, not the stars miles away.

Once out of bed, I stumbled downstairs to find coffee, took a hot bath, and did my makeup and hair, noticing how my bangs needed trimming. The whole time, Mr. Stars was on my mind.

To distract myself, I called my friend Nicol.

"How are you?" she asked.

Watching out my front window, I spotted Mr. Stars standing on his porch, staring into the sunlit day. "Well, the divorce is final, so . . . Hanging in there."

I continued to stare at him, probably because I was still feeling intimidated by my neighbor's business. I was *not* responding to his broad shoulders, deep brown eyes, and a dimpled smile that could steal any woman's heart.

"What are you thinking?" Nicol asked, bringing me back to the call.

"About my hot new neighbor."

"Zoey!" she snapped.

Ray stirred and headed for the mailbox, taking long, confident strides.

Nicol's voice infiltrated my ear. "Give yourself at least two years. Zoey, you need to—"

"Have babies," I butted in, swinging away from the window. "I have an expiration date, you know."

Ray secured several packages in his arms in addition to what might be newspapers and magazines. Destiny magazines? Maybe he read the horoscope? He slipped into his house and closed the door to his world of stars and apps and most likely clients.

"What are you talking about?" Nicol asked.

Moving from the window, I switched to straightening pillows just like I'd been doing for Damion for years. "I want to have four kids." I picked up dirty plates, longing for the busyness that came with family. "I need to get going if that's ever going to happen."

"That's crazy . . ." Nicol spilled forth a lecture about women's empowerment and not being just a baby machine.

Babies. I'd kiss them and hug them. Oh, I'd give them so much love, and they would love me back. That would be magical. All I had to do was keep my eyes on what I wanted and not on other people's opinions, and soon, that would be my life.

"Zoey, you really need to—"

Nicol went on and on telling me what to do. Letting her lose steam, I wandered to my desk. The coaching manual said that to attract Mr. Right, I needed to close all the open-ended energy loops of messes and incompletes in my life. If the science said that more-organized people had healthier relationships, then I was going to be organized somehow.

I snatched the papers on top of my desk. My divorce papers that I'd printed off from my lawyer's email. My hand trembled slightly. It felt so heavy.

"Sorry, Nicol, gotta go," I whispered, then clicked off the phone.

I set the papers back on my desk and escaped to the kitchen. The quiet of the house hovered over me. I shivered. No one to demand things of me, but no one to need me.

For anything.

At all.

My breath came loud in the silent space. My knees felt weak. I flung open the fridge and stared into the fluorescent void—nothing new magically appeared. Not wanting to see the world today, I settled for a PB&J. I ate while watching a bird chirping outside my window and then spent the day doing my coaching coursework—kind of. There was some time spent wondering what the neighbor, my competition, was up to.

In the late afternoon, a gentle breeze picked up. The wind created a hypnotic dance spinning the leaves. A rumble of an engine sounded from out front. A florist's truck. Again. Third time in less than twenty-four hours.

Why was Damion doing this?

The roses were white—my favorite after red. I took them in my hand, thinking about the lonely, empty day and my commitment to have my hours filled with children.

I needed to stay away from that man even though I secretly missed him.

Just as I thought that, my sister screeched up in her navy-blue Mercedes with her uncanny timing. She burst out of her car in deep-red high heels. Today she wore snazzy leopard-print dress pants and a droopy black ruffled shirt.

The delivery guy flushed, a reaction Tiff often caused in men. He stopped and watched her plow over to me and snatch the roses from me. "I'll take those," she said.

"They are mine," I mumbled. "You can't just take—"

She flipped on me. The flowers in her hand were weapons. "Get in the car."

"Tiffany—"

She headed toward my trash cans at the side of the house.

"Those are my flowers."

She stopped and turned to face me. "Do you honestly want to go back to him after everything?"

My head dropped. "No."

"Okay, then." She was determined to throw my flowers away.

I watched her glumly, wishing she wasn't always so right about everything, including my need for a makeover. I glanced at my stained green T-shirt and jeans. Definitely needed a new wardrobe to send the message to the universe that I was serious. This shopping trip was important for finding Mr. Right. I slipped into her car, promising myself not to take orders from Tiffany . . . after this.

A wave of vanilla car scent hit me, causing my belly to turn. A few minutes later, Tiffany slipped into the driver's seat. Hands on the keys, she asked, "Doesn't that feel better?"

"If you say so," I grumbled.

She tapped her fake nails against the zebra steering wheel cover as we barreled down the road. "What were those flowers about, anyway? Does he think he has a chance of winning you back?"

"No idea. I don't have control of Damion."

If I had that kind of power, I'd have three kids by now and would be pregnant with the fourth, but I refrained from mentioning that.

"No pink and no ruffles," I warned Tiffany.

She glowed with the thrill of finally being able to remake me into the person I needed to be.

———

Rich chemical smells of floral and citrus competed against each other. The question at hand involved the relative merits of "naughty nude" versus "to die for pink" on my cheekbones. Both names were ridiculous and had no professional or romantic connotation.

A short lady caked with makeup and a sweet myrrh scent plopped me on a styling chair and lunged into her critique. My natural eyebrows were offensive. If they weren't plucked and penciled like a clown, they would throw off the balance of my whole face.

Before I could refuse, she applied hot wax to my brows only to rip it off with a sharp pain. My eyes teared from the brow picking as I learned I had a T-zone face. That meant my skin couldn't make up its mind which problem to have, oily or dry, so it took both. More plucking, pulling, brushing, and applying goop—it all happened in a haze. Soon, I found myself staring into the mirror at a stranger who was supposed to be me, only 2.0.

More pale and frankly, more ghostly, and not myself at all.

As the clerk ran up the total of all this ghost-making makeup, I glanced behind her into the mirror and cringed, hating what I saw. But this was the point, right? This *look* was apparently the *look* needed to attract clients and eventually, the Perfect Guy, not whether I liked it or not.

"That will be $496.23," the clerk said.

"For makeup?" My voice cracked.

Tiffany laughed. "It ain't cheap."

My fingers clutched my credit card. I pressed my lips together, staring at the goop, and took a deep breath, handing over the card. If being a ghost was what I had to do, then that's what I'd do.

After paying way too much at the makeup store, Tiffany grabbed my hand to yank me to do more.

"We're not done yet!" She rushed straight into a packed store filled with bras and underwear.

"I'm fine. Really. I don't need—"

The clerk approached us. "Can I help you, ladies?"

"Yes," Tiffany said. "My sister here needs a fitting. She has been hanging low for too long."

My jaw dropped, but that didn't stop the tape measure from coming out and my card getting dinged again for quite a lot. Then after that, off to find dreadfully high ankle-breaker heels to go with the power suits we purchased next. The gift certificate at least covered the heels, but unfortunately not the suits.

When all was said and done, I was thousands of dollars poorer, but I had plucked eyebrows, makeup to smooth out everything wrong on my skin, a bra and shoes to lift, and outfits that pinched.

Yep, my sister was happy.

————

The parking lot had emptied by the time we crawled into my sister's sports car. My head pounded, my feet throbbed, and my wallet bled, but I had done what I needed to do.

I leaned back in the passenger seat and lay against the headrest. I closed my eyes as the energized shopping bunny rambled on about mixing and matching the various outfits.

Did destiny people have to go to so much work to find love? I smiled to myself. Of course they did. That was what Ray's app was about. Cutting down on finding-the-person time. He was literally creating a spouse-shopping company.

Hmm. Did have some appeal. Instead of going to the mall and all the torture of being shaped into an ideal, a person just went online, punched in information, and voila! They hooked in with their soulmate.

Tiffany's voice pitched high, drawing my attention. "Who's on your porch?"

I glanced out my window to see a dark shadow sitting outside my front door. I leaned in closer. "No clue."

The yellow fluorescent porch light flashed on. I sucked in my breath, not daring to breathe until my eyes adjusted. Finally, I could make out the person's features—the neighbor, Ray. On closer examination, it seemed like he held something in his hand. Wha-a-t . . . White flowers? That was weird.

Nothing was making sense tonight. Nothing.

"You two are actually dating? I thought you were pretending just to get rid of me last night."

Avoiding her eyes, I whispered, "We were." I swallowed a lump. "Sorry."

She shook her head like that was a small irritation. "I thought so." She wrestled with climbing out of the car. "Do you have a pheromone suddenly attracting all these men?"

I joined her side.

"He's your friend," I whispered back.

Her high heels clicked in a fast staccato as she pranced toward my front door . . . until her phone rang. She glanced at the screen, sighed, then stopped to answer as I charged ahead.

"Ray," I called out. Whatever he wanted, it would probably be best to handle it before my sister added her two cents.

He shuffled his feet. The water in the rose vase threatened to spill.

"What are you doing here?" I asked.

His dimples of charm shot into full display. "You look great."

My gut clenched harder than when Tiffany made me slip into the red skirt. "Um, thanks."

He glanced at the roses in his hands and then handed them to me. "Popular girl."

The roses had a faint scent.

"It was your X."

"I know." I didn't glance up at Destiny Man. "I don't know why—"

"He left these on your front porch," Ray interrupted. "After he was gone, I saw cats snooping over here, and I didn't want them to ruin the flowers."

At least he was giving me a choice, unlike my sister.

"Thanks."

He shoved his hands into his front pockets. "I'm glad to do it."

"You don't need to watch out for me."

He shrugged. "Okay then, I won't. You're on your own."

I smiled a little, hearing the words I'd been saying to myself come out of his mouth. He sounded friendlier than I did in my own head.

"But . . ." His expression came across as sheepish.

I lifted a brow.

"Maybe you could keep an eye on my house when we're out? I don't know anyone here yet, and it would be a big help."

That might be the first time someone asked for *my* help. "Well, sure," I said enthusiastically. "Absolutely. Happy to."

"And if you want me to return the favor?" Our eyes met. "It's a fair trade. We're neighbors. We both have something to offer here."

I hesitated, glanced back at Tiff still on the phone, then grinned and thrust out my hand. "Deal."

His hard, broad hand closed around mine with a gentle, firm grip. "Deal."

My first partnership in my new life. With my new neighbor . . . and my competition.

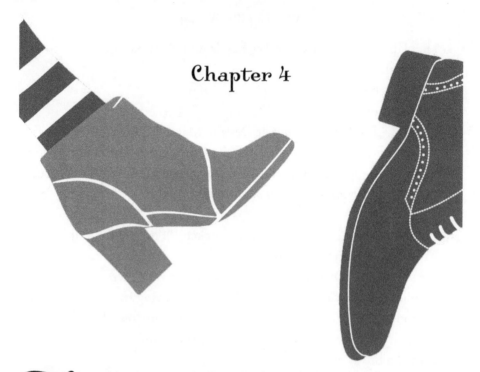

Chapter 4

The golden moon sat high in the dark sky by the time my sister and I stumbled into my house after saying goodbye to Ray. Before I even had a chance to digest all that happened with my X and the overly helpful new neighbor, my sister said, "Reynesh seems interested in you."

I stopped short. I laughed and didn't like its light, high pitch. "Not a chance. It was a joke, Tiff. A joke about us dating. Besides, no woman could survive *two* entrepreneurs. One was enough for me."

She raised a skeptical eyebrow. "Uh-huh. Then explain what *that*," she gestured to the front door, "was all about."

I studied the door to buy some time. Confusing. Why would I need to buy time to tell my sister a simple truth? "We were just being neighborly."

"Ha. He was protecting you."

A shudder shot through me. I did *not* want protection. It was time for me to stand on my own. "How did you get *that*?"

She flipped on the kitchen light. "He rushed over to check out who was lurking around the house while you were gone."

"Good neighbor action."

I hurried into the kitchen and grabbed the card inside the roses before my sister nabbed it. Even though I was over Damion, I did want to see what he had to say before Tiffany ripped up the card and refused to tell me.

Third year. One of my favorites.

Favorite year? That was the beginning of the end.

My sister's footsteps clicked on the wood floor, and the front door closed. Was she leaving? Before I took the time to figure out whether my sister was staying or going, I hid the flowers in my bachelor kitchen.

Noises came from outside. I hurried to the front of the house and opened the door.

There stood Tiffany, with Ray and Damion. My X peered around Ray, his green eyes first widening—probably because of my makeover—then pleading with me.

"Um, I came here to talk."

Tiffany puffed up her chest, but standing four inches shorter than the men, it had the effect of a Chihuahua going after an elephant. "She's no longer your wife."

Damion shoved his hands deep into his pants pockets as if trying to act patient. "Zoey, can I please talk to you?"

Sighing and wishing my headache would go away, I said, "Fine." It sounded angrier than intended. It was time for Damion to actually hear me. "I'm going to talk to Damion *alone*." I spoke with an edge to my voice, which I hope sounded commanding. I shooed Tiff and Ray back toward the house with a gesture. I don't think I had ever taken control like this with Damion around.

Tiffany shifted her weight. "Reynesh, come inside with me." She grabbed the neighbor's arm and yanked him to her.

He looked back at me, hesitating.

I nodded for him to go into my house. It would do my sister good to have someone with her as she worried.

The two slipped inside. The door clicked shut behind them. Several dogs in the neighborhood howled to the moon with a sorrowful high-pitched tone. Despite the creepy mood, I yawned.

My X stared at me, his eyes still green as jade. "That look doesn't work on you. What are you doing?"

I flushed as he voiced what I secretly felt. I wasn't going to defend my new life decisions. I wasn't. I was moving on to Disneyland Dad and children. Knowing Tiffany and Ray were most likely watching us, I squared my shoulders. "What are you doing here?"

For once in our relationship, he said nothing. He stood there with a stoic expression.

"Damion, I'm not coming back."

Even though it would be easier to pay the bills, get the yard fixed, and in another thousand other ways. Even though it was hard to stand on my own.

"Can't we do lunch?"

"The divorce papers said it all."

See, Tiffany, I thought. *Immune.*

The crisp, clean air trailed behind me as I strode into the house, flinging the cheap metal door open wide. It barely missed Tiffany and Ray. They had apparently huddled close by, and were lucky it didn't hit them.

Both of them watched me, waiting to hear what I had to say.

"Unbelievable." Tiffany brushed past. "Is he still here?"

"No," I blurted. "He wanted to get back together."

She shook her head. "I told you. After the way he treated you—" she started in.

"Please stop." I looked over at Ray, embarrassed. "Sorry you were in the middle of this."

"I can tell this is hard for you."

He could say that again. Today had been another hard day on top of the one before. This divorce thing was like a roller coaster of emotions, and not all of them were good.

"Do you need us to go?" he asked.

I blinked at him. "Yes."

"I'm not leaving her here alone. That man," Tiffany gestured her thumb toward the door, "might come back."

"I doubt that," I said, growing tired of my sister's paranoia. And her fear that I'd somehow crumple up like a piece of paper.

A frown line appeared on Ray. "Zoey, if you like, I'll stay for a few minutes to make sure he doesn't return."

"No. I don't need that."

"We could sit on your porch swing and drink a cup of hot chocolate."

What could I say?

Ray's eyes held mine again for another beat, then he reached for the door. "I'll head home. You look like you've had a long day."

My fingers swept along my unruly bangs. "I do?"

"I can see it in your eyes."

And that, right there, was so different from what I'd been getting from Tiffany all evening, from Damion for the last three years, and from everyone in my life for a very long time. Years, maybe? Someone finally *saw* me.

I opened my mouth to say "Thanks," and instead, said, "Actually, hot chocolate would be nice."

That surprised me. Maybe I agreed to the drink because there was something calming about having him around. Something settling. Right now, I'd take "calm" any way I could get it.

This arrangement must have worked for my sister, too. It didn't take much convincing before she was uttering her goodbyes and telling me she'd call tomorrow.

Ray slipped out onto the front porch.

As I walked into the kitchen, I took a moment to breathe, then turned on the stove to wait for the kettle to heat up. Today had been a crazy day, and I might have a couple more of those in the near future. Hopefully, whatever was between me and Damion was completely over, and he would quit trying. From the anger in his eyes, I felt confident I would receive no more roses. He liked winning. He'd blame me, of course, and maybe Ray, and I was okay with that.

Yes, I was creating a new life for myself, but so far, this wasn't turning out anything like I had intended. At least I had chocolate. And Ray.

The kettle whistled, and I poured water into the mugs, watching the chocolate powder dissolving. It would take one quick cup of chocolate to ease my woes, then a cordial goodbye to Ray before slipping into my empty bed. Tomorrow I'd begin again.

I carried the steaming mugs of chocolate out to the porch.

Ray had left me plenty of space to sit on the swing. A genuinely nice guy. "You didn't have to stay," I said.

Taking the mug, he said, "I am here."

Several cars drove past my house as we sat in comfortable silence, which I knew wouldn't last. Eventually, more likely soon, Ray would ask about my failed marriage, and the comfort would immediately dissolve.

I wanted to learn more about this man, my competition and my neighbor. "So, you grew up in America. Did your parents move here as kids, or when they were adults? What part of India did they come from?"

"New Delhi. My parents married young. Came here on work visas, since my uncle ran a cleaning business. My father got involved in astrology on the side. He did birth charts and astrology consultations." He smiled. "I used to love learning about that from him."

I gave him a confused look.

"He passed away a while ago."

"Sorry to hear that."

He slapped his hand on his leg. "Well, enough of that. Back to your question. It was a struggle for them, leaving everyone they knew except my uncle and dealing with how much more expensive it is in the States. But their biggest struggle was that India is so much more alive than America."

My brows narrowed. "What are you talking about?"

"India has an energy and richness about it. Outsiders see it as chaos, but they don't understand what they are witnessing. My mom especially missed the rhythm of the place when they were confronted with straight highways and lanes."

"What?"

"The travelers there—the rickshaws, motorcycles, tourist buses, cows, and camels—all go in the direction they want, for the most part, except on the super-big highways."

I frowned, picturing what it'd be like without a set order for traffic to follow. Chaotic. Out of control.

"Cows and camels?" I confirmed.

He nodded.

"But—"

"They like to eat the trash on the roads."

I pulled a face. "Sounds unsafe."

"It's thrilling."

I shook my head. "Reckless."

"Safer and more vibrant than here."

I seriously doubted that.

"The States is definitely home, too," Ray went on, "but I try to go to Delhi every few years on summer vacation if I can swing it. Both countries are a part of me, but India is better. Family is a bigger deal there. I respect that more."

I took a sip of hot chocolate. "You seem to be close to your family."

"Talk to them back in India twice a day." A faint edge tinged his voice.

"Wow, every day? Why would you do that?"

He gave me a weary smile. "To see how I can help them out."

I stared, unable to imagine what that kind of connection would be like. Yes, Tiffany and I talked often, but most of the time, it wasn't twice a day until lately, which was getting a little much.

"They have more culture there. There's always a festival going on."

I shifted on the swing, settling in. "Sounds busy."

"Sometimes, yes," he agreed, the faint edge gone, overtaken by the affection every time he mentioned India. "Efficiency isn't the only thing that matters."

"What matters?"

His face relaxed. "Being part of the whole. Being part of something more than your own desires. Being individualistic all the time can be sterile . . ." Slowly, he smiled. "And it lacks spice that brings vitality. It's a different world. One I'd like to bring a bit of to America."

I pressed my lips together. This guy's philosophy would never work for me. "Wanting to create chaos . . . not a good idea. Science and data are a more solid reference point."

"All wisdom lies in the stars." He pointed up to the sky. "And there's wisdom and beauty in chaos."

My whole life was about building control. "Is *that* what you are trying to bring to Murrieta?"

He appraised me. "You afraid I'll be too much competition for you?"

"I don't think we're in a competition," I said rather stiffly, seeing as that was precisely what I thought. "After all, yours is just an app, and I'm an *in-person* relationship coach."

He bristled. We both sat up on the swing, staring at each other. "Just an app? Do you know how much work went into that 'just an app'?"

"About as much work as went into studying to be a relationship coach," I said, bristling back.

"How long?"

"How long what?" I replied, equally sharp.

"How long have you been studying? How many clients do you have? How many people have you helped?"

I opened my mouth to answer, but the barrage of questions froze my reply. They were good questions. I didn't have good answers.

Still, the best defense was a good offense. "How long has your app been around?" I countered, yanking my feet out from underneath me and sitting up straight. The hot chocolate was cold in my cupped hands. "How many people have downloaded it? How many successful relationships have you helped people find?"

I pressed my lips together, not wanting to hear an answer to all those questions, and having a sinking worry that he might have good ones. I was getting the feeling this business game was too much for me.

"I've been developing the app and testing it for over three years." All of a sudden, Ray's face appeared very set, focused, and determined. "I've devoted my life to it. You'd be amazed at all the moving parts. We've beta tested over a thousand users and have the data to claim twenty-five happy marriages."

I swallowed a lump in my throat. Yep, that was a good answer.

"We're officially launching at the end of the month."

He was almost there. Unlike me. I took a sip of cold chocolate. "Well, I wish you luck with your app. It sounds impressive."

He studied the sky. "Thanks."

A quiet fell between us. The evening had grown chillier. "Well," I said, standing up. "Goodnight."

He put down his mug on the porch, then sprang to his feet. "Night."

He bolted off my property. I watched Mr. Wrong cross the street, taking all his answers and crazy beliefs into his bright, noisy home. I slipped into my silent one.

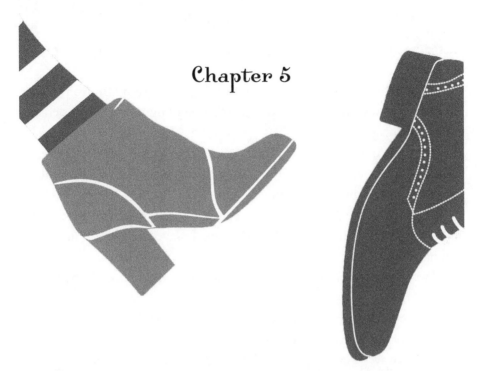

Chapter 5

A loud, sickening wail filled the room. I sat up in my bed, alert as my eyes struggled to adjust to the dim morning light. Was someone or something being killed? Another wail pierced through the stillness close to the house.

The gray morning made it hard to see as I stumbled around, fumbling for my lime-green threadbare bathrobe and thrashed mouse slippers as the wails continued. I slid them on, and I hurried down the stairs.

The wailing continued and maybe a growl. To arm myself, I grabbed a plastic water bottle sitting on the end table. In the worst case, I could hit whatever was causing so much suffering. I opened the front door.

My slippers flip-flopped against the soles of my feet as I scurried to the noise along the side of my garage. The moment I rounded the house, I saw two cats hissing, wailing, and backs arched.

One was plumper, bigger by at least twice the size, with a silky, shiny black coat. The other—the runt—small, orange, with bloody wounds scattered across his torso. Plus, dirt dulled his coat. Despite his condition, his size, and clearly his lack of ability to dominate, he hissed an angry warning. The poor thing looked like he'd been beaten up by life.

No way he had any chance at all, but that didn't stop him from trying. He swiped at the other cat, claws out. His unwillingness to admit defeat, I found downright impressive.

The cats circled each other. Both spines fully arched, and both moving back and forth, eyes locked on the other, constantly hissing and wailing. The rumble was about to begin.

Thinking twice about throwing a water bottle into the middle of a fight, not trusting my famously poor aim, I waved the bottle in the air, yelling, "Go."

The cats' backs arched even more, ready to attack whoever they determined a threat.

I stepped toward them frantically, trying to figure out how I could save the scruffy orange half-starved cat.

"Step away! They'll attack you," I heard a male voice warn.

Taking my eyes off the warring cats, I caught a glimpse of Ray in an elaborate colorful bathrobe, hair disheveled. He brushed past me with a broom in his hand.

I stomped my foot at the catfight, hoping to spook and separate them before Mr. Stars joined the rescue mission.

The cats hissed and arched more. The black cat swept his paw at the face of the little orange creature. Fortunately, this time he missed the connection.

The orange cat growled deeper, not intimidated or at least refusing to stop fighting for himself.

"Back up," Ray demanded as he thrust the end of the broomstick between the two cats.

The cats scurried away in different directions.

Triumphantly, Mr. Stars gave me a pleased smile. "I guess today wasn't your day."

My fuzzy lime bathrobe was still wrapped tight around me as I stood in my messy bathroom. "Today wasn't my day?" That was what Mr. Stars said.

I wandered out of the bathroom. "Wasn't my day for what?" I asked my empty house. Though listening, the house didn't respond. I picked up my coaching binder and pen off my bed.

By the time I made it downstairs to the couch, I tried one more time. "What did he mean by that? Granted, bringing a water bottle to the fight might not have been the brightest idea, and I didn't manage to stop the feline altercation."

Still no answer.

Sitting down on my couch, I tugged my robe tighter around my shoulders and prepared to study for my upcoming coaching test. The words blurred. The man had worn a coffee-colored paisley bathrobe made of silk. Or was it satin? I didn't know my textiles. Tiffany would know. Whatever it was, that bathrobe stuck in my mind, and his horrible comment.

When I wasn't thinking about him while staring at the blurry words, the orange cat occupied my mind. The poor thing was picked on and starving . . . I flopped my binder beside me on the couch. The cat needed food.

I hustled around my kitchen and gathered the supplies to leave a bowl of milk out for him. When I set the bowl by my sliding glass door, I waited to see if the cat would come.

The morning stretched out, casting a yellowish tint on my baby palm trees, on the tiny red flowers, and also on my disappearing green/brown grass.

Apparently, the wild brown bunnies loved to attack my lawn at night, acting like my grass was an all-they-could-eat buffet. The result was lots of dirt spots that had once been my lawn.

Mr. Stars didn't have a lawn like that. His lawn was luscious like that bathrobe. What kind of guy had such an elaborate bathrobe in coffee-brown with a turned-down collar and elegant golden and cerulean blue swirls?

Focus, I reminded myself. I needed to claim my life, not think about the neighbor who wore a kimono, or about my buffet lawn, or the helpless cat making his way in this harsh world.

My cell rang. Sis.

"Hi." I walked back into the house. She didn't think I could rebuild my life without her. That was why she was calling. I'd show her. "Just about to eat spinach and an egg for protein."

Tiff laughed. "Have you seen inside your fridge?"

She had a point. "I meant I'm going on a power walk and networking."

According to the Rules-Based Relationship Coaching binder, networking was the best way to build a practice, and I didn't have time to dillydally. My bank account didn't want me to waste my time, especially not after that shopping spree.

"Oh, which group?" asked my smart-aleck sister.

This was going to surprise her. I had already googled networking groups in Murrieta. "Networking Professionals Incorporation."

She grunted, which she always did when preparing to rip my attention to shreds. I had forgotten my sister was impossible to please.

To prevent the criticism, I blurted out, "I'm just going out the door. Call you later."

Leaving my phone on the kitchen table so as not to hear her calling me back, I hurried upstairs to find my lifeless, worn-out, decades-old jogging shorts that bagged around my hips. My legs poked out underneath, blaringly white, and my shirt hung on me like a tent.

Actually, I looked like a zombie wearing a tent in a horror flick, but if a poor helpless cat could put up a good fight, I could too. I stuck my earplugs in my ears, determined to get the business and the man no matter what I looked like jogging.

I hustled downstairs and out the front door. The light spilled on me, bright, almost glaring. After gliding on my sunglasses, I took a few steps down my porch then launched into a light jog.

Before I made it eight hundred feet up the slight hill, a sharp pain jabbed into my side. Sweat dripped from my hairline. My breath sounded ragged. What an absolutely horrible activity.

As I kept going, the jabbing pain intensified. I stumbled to a stop, panting, and crumpled over in pain. Sweat trickled down my back as the steep hill waited. I looked up at the pending climb to see a preppy jogger headed my way at a brisk, confident clip.

I lifted my water bottle to my lips, pretending I'd paused for a drink, even though I panted so hard, I couldn't drink anything without choking. My focus stayed on that happy jogger, who seemed familiar.

Before I could tighten the cap on my water bottle, Ray stopped right in front of me rather than jogging on by.

He gave me a bright, sexy smile. He wore shiny silver shorts and a black T-shirt showing off strong arms and a defined chest. "Morning."

"Morning," I muttered in my tent-clothes zombie look. "You're up bright and early."

He jogged in place. "I love the early mornings here." His voice didn't even sound breathy.

Behind him, purple-hued mountains were capped by creamy clouds floating over their peaks. It was pretty and I hadn't even noticed . . . too consumed with my impending heart attack.

"Have a good run?" he asked.

"Yes, yes." I bent my right knee, pulling my foot to my backside. This caused me to wobble like a camel wearing high heels. I let go of my foot. It might be best if I kept both feet on the ground.

"Just cooling down." I forced a chipper smile as sweat trickled down my temples.

He glanced at his watch. "I only jogged five miles, since I need to dash to the chamber of commerce meeting."

Five miles? He hadn't even broken a sweat.

"You going?" he asked.

A chamber of commerce meeting? If my competition was going, I guessed I'd better be there. "Of course." I wiped a loose strand of hair off my sweaty forehead. "Where is it again?"

"The Olde Irish Pub."

"Oh, yeah, right," I said brightly, like I'd known about the meeting all along.

Ray jogged in place faster, then glanced at his watch. "I'll see you there." He waved goodbye and sprinted for his house like it was nothing.

Show-off.

Chapter 6

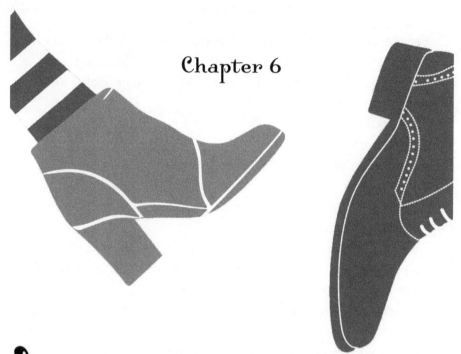

I couldn't stop watching him run. His shoes barely touched the ground as he glided to his house. The man, despite all his obvious flaws, was cute. My lips went dry as I stared after the next-cover-of-GQ.

He made it into his house, snapping me out of the trance. The sun grew hotter. I staggered back home to learn the small orange cat had found the milk. I was glad and put out the last of the milk I had for her.

It took me awhile to shower and try for perfect hair. No go. Squeezing into my new tight-fitting business pants and shirt that Ray liked and Damion didn't wasn't any easier than it had been last night.

The clock counted down. Thirty minutes to get there. I snatched my phone and called "The Connected One" back.

Tiffany picked up on the second ring.

"Where's the Olde Irish Pub?"

"That's a great place for you to go. It's filled with—"

"Tiff," I said, applying eyeliner, "where? I don't have time—"

"I'll be there in ten."

"Thanks," I whispered.

Twelve minutes later, the beeps of my sister's car switched me into go mode. I hurried to her in pants that jabbed my sides, a perky bra that pinched my rib cage, and flats that kept slipping off my feet.

"Where're your heels?" Tiffany asked when I opened the door.

Getting into the passenger side, I muttered, "I didn't dare do high heels." Then I glanced over at her. "Wow. You look great."

Clothes seemed to fit her perfectly. A lot like clothes did for Ray. I glanced at the wrinkles already in my shirt. I certainly wasn't in *that* club. Yet.

"I slept well," Tiffany said as she pulled the car out of the driveway. "All that shopping wore me out."

"Sleeping in a bed alone doesn't bother you?"

She gave me a raised brow. "Why would it?"

"Never mind." No point in making this car ride about me. "You know," I said thoughtfully, "if shopping makes you so happy, maybe you should help more people do that."

She laughed. "Too busy." She pressed on the gas, compelling us back into our seats . . . my hint that I was making her late.

A smidgen of remorse moved through me. "Thanks for the ride."

"You sounded anxious."

And I had tried to sound so casual.

"I'm willing to help you get on your feet."

She talked like she was doing me such a favor.

"I appreciate that, but—"

"Because you'll never get there on your own."

My mouth snapped shut. "I just need some practice—"

She cut me off like I wasn't even speaking. "You need business cards. Have you ordered them yet?"

I swallowed. "I was going to do that this morning, but then the chamber meeting came up—"

"I have a guy. I'll give you his number. Call him, mention my name, and you'll get a discount. And Zoey . . ." She glanced over as we raced toward the east side of town. "Take me with you."

I was trying so hard to make myself independent, and Tiffany seemed to be working really hard not to let that happen. She had picked up a nasty habit of being a helicopter sister-mom when we were young. I had liked feeling taken care of when I was younger, but now it had to stop. Somehow.

"Why?" I asked irritably.

"How you present yourself on the card is important. I'll make sure you get it right."

Take over, I thought. Well, that decided it. I'd find my own business card person and make my own mistakes. I couldn't be in my sister's shadow forever, no matter how willing she was to help me out.

But for now, I had to stop thinking about my turning tummy and remember to smile at this business thing. I wiped my clammy palms on my suit pants.

My heart did a jitter dance as I thought about going into a room of super-duper professionals on top of their game in this world I knew nothing about. People like Ray and Tiffany would be in their space where everything came so naturally to them.

I took a deep breath, struggling for a way to handle this and get a grip on my nerves. The truth was, all I had to do was mirror the person speaking. When they leaned forward, I'd do the same. I leaned forward in my seat to practice. The manual claimed mirroring the person creates a connection. Yeah, I could do that. What else?

Last month's training came to me. Match their speed of speech. If they talk fast, talk fast. If they speak slowly, slow down even if it feels unnatural. A little harder to talk slowly with nerves, but I could do it if I stayed away from the coffee and the matcha tea. Next thing I needed to figure out was what to say.

I drummed my fingers on my lap. "Tiffany? When recruiting clients, what are you supposed to focus on?"

She swiped a loose bang behind her ear. "The value you bring them. Sell the island."

"An island?"

"Yeah, the destination of what they want, the problem you solve, not the process."

People always used to come up to me in high school or the grocery store or clothing store and tell me their troubles. They probably still would now if I actually got my act together and visited the store. Of course I could do this. In fact, I had been helping and talking to people about their struggles for years. Now I just had to make sure I did it the right way.

We entered the dark, stale-smelling Irish pub. My legs shook hard. The pub had transformed into an early morning breakfast networking meeting room filled with people in uptight business suits complete with sharp angles, starchy fabric, and closed-toed shoes.

More than thirty of those people milled around the tall wooden four-person tables, buzzing, shaking hands, and chatting as more super-professional people streamed in through the front doors. We weren't late.

I searched the room to see if Ray had made it. No sign of Mr. Stars, which didn't matter. Actually, it was better if he didn't show up. Only one relationship expert at a time, please. Yes, he could possibly steal my new clients, but other than that, I shouldn't be thinking about him.

Cologne and perfume wafted in the air around me, making my head spin. I lifted my chin, preparing myself to talk to these people as my sister checked us in at a registration table in front of the bar. Everyone was already in conversation, making me the odd person out and wishing I had the keys to the car.

My sister's bubbly laugh carried across the room, letting me know I was on my own. I pulled my purse strap up my shoulder as a man a few years older than me with curly blond hair approached.

"New here?" He extended a hand.

I shook and tried to let go, but he held on to it in a tight grip as smiling eyes locked on mine.

Prickles shot through me.

"Welcome to the chamber." He let go of my sore fingers.

"Thanks." I rubbed my hands together.

He wiggled his eyebrows. "Is this your first time?"

"Ah? Yep." Might as well own it. "I'm a newbie."

He reached out and put his hand on my shoulder. The warmth of this man's touch seeped into me.

"If you have any questions, ask. If you want to meet any particular person or someone in a particular industry, just let me know."

My face grew hot as I realized I had no idea who I wanted or needed to meet.

Mr. Welcomer leaned in again. "I see you decided to stand out today. Clever."

"How?"

He gestured at my feet. "No heels." His lips tugged up into a smile.

I glanced around at the other women in their heels—high ones—then at my flats. I guess Tiff had been right. High heels were a must.

"So," Mr. Welcomer said, "my name is Nick, and I'll be your guide through this chamber of commerce maze. Tell me, what do you like to do in your spare time?"

This cute, connected guy wanted to get to know me despite my lack of heels. That was a good sign.

"Well . . ." I scanned the room for my MIA sister. "Um, I like going to Disneyland."

He gestured for a high five. "Give me five for that one."

I smacked his hand with enthusiasm.

His eyes focused on nothing in particular, but they sparkled. "I just took my nieces and nephews there the other weekend."

"Oh, wow," I said, genuinely surprised.

"It was so fun running with them from ride to ride."

This was the kind of man I was searching for, not someone like Ray, who thought Disneyland was a sneaky way to destroy families with a cute mouse and lots of princesses.

Feeling a tad brave, I plunged in and asked, "What about your own kids?"

He shook his head. "None of those. No wife either. Yet. You?"

I shook my head. "Nope. None of those yet either."

He leaned closer to me and smiled.

With my heart picking up speed from his flirtatious nature, I moved the conversation away from our unmarried status. Too much, too soon would be bad. "What was their favorite ride?"

He leaned back to give that thought, tapping his index finger against his lips. "I think I'd have to say Splash Mountain."

I was finding it hard to breathe. "I love that ride. It's so intense climbing up the mountain as the crisp, cool air cocoons you right before you plummet into the darkness." I lifted my hand and plunged it downward to reenact the ride.

He laughed. "My nephews and nieces clung to me so tight, I still have bruises."

"That's the best part. Roller coasters force people to let go of any pretense. No matter what, when the roller coaster free falls down the track, you scream."

"If I had kids," he said, "I'd take them there every weekend."

"You would?"

"Absolutely."

"How many kids do you want?"

"Three or four."

A flush crept into my cheeks.

He chuckled lightly as he watched my reaction. "Want to meet some of the heavy hitters in the chamber of commerce?"

Before I knew it, he strolled me around from one table to the next. Everyone thanked him for his help with this or that charity event, then he'd introduce me as the newest member, and said I was fun to talk to.

In between meeting people, he whispered to me, "We singles need to stick together." He patted my hand.

Electricity hummed through me. I liked the idea of sticking together. But before I could say anything, Tiffany strolled up to us. "I see you've met Nick."

He moved away from me.

I nibbled on my lower lip. "He's giving me the lay of the land."

Her right eyebrow rose a little, letting me know this didn't settle well with her.

"Tiffany." A large former-football type barreled toward her. "Give me a hug."

She threw her arms around him. "John, are you ready to do more business?"

He grinned. "I'll be in this afternoon, if that works."

My sister patted his forearm. "I always have time for you."

Yep. She was a master at networking.

"Well, it's great to see you." Tiffany gave him a brilliant smile.

The man flushed several shades of pinks and reds.

After he left, she grabbed my shoulder and ushered me to a table. "Stay away from Nick. He's *that* guy."

What did she mean by *that* guy? Did she mean he was *that* guy I might actually like?

"Let's sit here."

I stumbled on my flat shoes.

Taking me in, Tiffany said, "You don't need to be so nervous."

Easy for Miss Extrovert to say.

"I'll be back in a bit. I'm going to lock me up some business."

She rushed off, leaving me at an empty table guarding our purses. Nervous, I glanced around for Disneyland Dad. A pleasant-looking baby boomer with short grayish hair smiled at me. She was alone.

I stepped over to her and extended my hand. "I'm Zoey."

She leaned away from it. "I don't shake hands."

My hand tumbled to my side as I realized all those magic words I had practiced in the car had disappeared.

The gray-haired spoke like she was bored, "What do you do?"

Time for me to own it. "A relationship coach."

"Really?"

"Yeah. Good relationships are a science."

She tilted her chin up, unimpressed.

"Maybe not simple," I thought of my recent failed marriage, "but doable *if* you learn the science."

Coldness flashed in her eyes. "Nice meeting you." She turned her back on me and left.

As I struggled to recover from that, I heard a deep male laugh and a comment aimed at me. "Someone is not a fan of science."

My body seized. I recognized the voice. Slowly, I circled around to find the teasing smile of Ray.

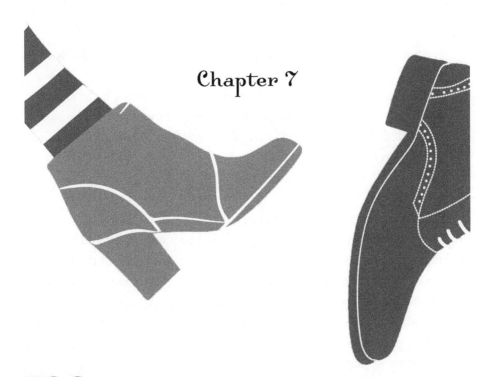

Chapter 7

my friendly neighbor wore a sky-blue polo shirt and a mischievous grin.

"Um, hi." I tugged on my shirt, wishing I had worn those silly heels and he hadn't already seen me in that clunky lime-green bathrobe and tent workout clothes.

"You'll learn who to bestow your words of wisdom on and who not to." His head jerked toward the lady who just left.

I forced a laugh. "Yeah, if it's my destiny."

A micro-movement flashed on his face, recognizing my callback from yesterday. "Yes, that's true."

A man's voice came over the sound system. "We're about to get started, people. Grab breakfast, if you haven't already."

Ray took a step toward me.

The man made me nervous. He was too put together and very calm about everything.

Unsettled by my reaction to him, I asked quickly, "Where's the food?"

He pointed at a line of people gathering at a long table in the back of the room.

"Oh, yeah." I forced a laugh. "To be honest, I'm not too experienced at this sort of thing. Not quite sure what's going on or what to do."

He smiled. "Well, now you know about the food. How about business cards? Can I get yours?" he asked.

Card? Card? Oh, my business card. The one I was scheduled to make today.

I cleared my throat. "I, uh, forgot them."

He seemed unconcerned. "Don't worry. I can get it later. I would like some on hand to be able to refer people if your approach is a better fit than mine."

I narrowed my eyes. I wasn't sure what game he was playing. "Why would you pass out my cards? I'm your competition."

He pulled his head back in surprise. "We're not competition. The job of helping people form a healthy, loving relationship is a global one. It's a noble destiny we have."

Noble. Wow, I'd never thought of it that way. I was just trying to pay the mortgage and reinvent my life.

"I want one of your cards too," I said impulsively. "Maybe I can, you know, help you too."

He snapped one over to me. "My last one."

"I'm honored." It was black with gold and had a picture of his attractive face smiling. *Discover Your Destiny* was scrolled on the back. He certainly set a high bar.

"Yours looks nice."

Before I could dig myself deeper into realizing how subpar I was, I asked, "What destiny are people supposed to discover?"

Ray smiled. "The person they're destined to be with."

I nearly choked. "So, a person finding their soulmate."

Ray tossed that around. "Something like that."

"Does that mean you believe in true love? That it's possible in this modern world?"

"Sure. You?"

He had seen me and Damion the past few days. It didn't bode well for love. "No." I darted a glance at his sincere, attractive face. "Maybe."

Sure, Ray might be my competition, but I suddenly felt I could be honest with him. More than that. I wanted to be.

"Honestly," I said with a sigh. "I'm trying to believe in love after . . . after . . ." Our eyes connected. "After, you know."

He took in my reference and seemed to reflect on it for a long drawn-out silence. "You know, I'm great at saying no to jerks. Let me know if you need help."

He had seen Damion for a whole whopping three minutes, and he knew who Damion was. It had taken me three years to get that clear. I laughed. "Thanks. I'll let you know. We'll need a code."

"Blink twice, real slow," he suggested.

I laughed again, liking the lightness of our conversation after all the anxiety I'd been feeling. I practiced blinking at him real slow.

He chuckled.

A rush of heat moved through me.

Nick caught my eye across the room, and I immediately turned away, not knowing how to handle all this attention.

I slid Ray's card deep into my purse. "So, what about your business and that destiny stuff?" I asked to get us back to the professional realm. "How does that work? Do you really believe it?"

His eyes twinkled. "My work is science too. We use the science of the stars to help people discover their sufferings. Once you know a person's sufferings, you know who they'll be compatible with."

"Explain?" I asked, confused.

"People with similar sufferings do better together because they understand each other's pain."

I blinked at him. "And that's science?"

"Astrology."

"Hmm. That's kind of out there."

Instead of being offended, he winked at me. "Just so you know, Indian astrology, Vedic, is very different than what's practiced here in the West."

A cord of heat flowed down my belly. This just got out of my depth.

"We're a modern matchmaking service. We're bringing the wisdom our ancestors have known for thousands of years to the United States."

I cleared my throat. "I don't know how to break it to you, but I don't think that's going to fly. Americans don't like wisdom and ancestors. We like burgers and fries."

He shrugged. "We'll see."

"You're certainly confident."

"That's in the stars." Amusement played in his face. "My sun sign is Sagittarius, which means I have traditional values, but my rising sign is Leo, thus the confidence."

"The stars determine that, huh?" I crossed my arms over my chest. I was going to have to work on how to talk about relationships if I had to compete with this confident man, and I did have to compete with him.

He tilted his head back, amusement playing at the corners of his lips. "We should do coffee sometime and see how we can help each other."

Get together? Explore? That didn't sound good. I needed to get together with Disneyland Dad because he might at least be a future love interest. Ray was a distraction from work and finding love.

"Um . . ." I took a step backward, hitting a younger man who was passing by. "Sorry."

The passerby nodded and kept on his way.

"I—I, um, better grab breakfast."

I dashed up to the growing line with the lingering thought that kissing someone who looked at me the way Ray did would be a much different experience than it had been with Damion.

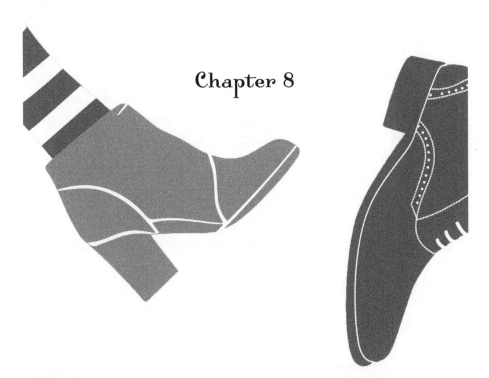

Chapter 8

The noise of the restaurant increased to a booming volume. I shuffled carefully back to the table and my sister. Even though flats were out, my shaking knees were grateful not to maneuver in heels. Something about that whole conversation with Ray had clearly unsettled me.

When I made it back to my chair, I stared at the cold eggs, soggy hash browns, and wilted melons. Not something I'd want to choke down. I pushed it away. The condition of the food did nothing to curb the increasing uneasy jitters.

Tiffany smiled over at me, but didn't say anything as she continued spinning her business magic with the person sitting on the other side of her. Tiny mercies, since it gave me time to re-center myself. I scanned around the room. The conversations had shifted into overdrive with people buzzing in an ever-increasing thunder.

In the midst of color and hype, Ray's bright face stood out in the crowd two tables behind me. Our eyes met. I gave a half smile before glancing away to spot Disneyland Dad, who smiled from a table off to the side. I gave him a nod as the meeting started with a welcome.

After the news, the president snatched back the mic like she owned it. "Time for introductions," she declared with way too much enthusiasm. "The mic is going to travel around the room. You have one minute to introduce yourself and your business. We need to keep it going because we have a lot of people here."

I tapped Tiffany on the shoulder. "What did she just say? That doesn't mean that I—"

The other people at the table glanced at me with scowls.

Tiffany leaned closer. "Introduce yourself and your company."

"What?"

She put her finger to her lips and pointed to the first person to take the mic. "Watch."

My heart pounded like a rock band in my inner ear. She had to be kidding. But she wasn't. The mic traveled from one person to the next. Each person offered their name and some spiel about their company. No matter how much I willed the mic to slow its travels, it kept coming, making its way around the tables with tremendous speed until it arrived at Nick. He talked about his involvement with the local baseball charity game.

"Come out and get on the team. It's for a good cause and is a great way to build a connection with your son or daughter who can join with you."

He used his time to promote making the community better. And he mentioned kids!

Someone catcalled him. "Go, Nick. Way to enlist us."

Another person yelled out, "Our family guy who doesn't even have a family."

He smiled, revealing his slightly crooked front tooth. "Just a matter of time, Walters. Searching for the right woman." His eyes flickered over to me. "And if she's up for it, we're going to field an entire Little League team."

The group laughed.

I liked the idea of a Little League team. Well, at least part of one.

"Oh, yeah," Nick continued. "I'm also *the* social media guy. So, if you need to be found on the Internet, I'm your guy."

Well, there it was. He was my answer to securing clients.

The mic had migrated to three people away. I couldn't hear the current speaker over the noise of my panic, but after taking a deep breath, I reminded myself to establish my value and sell love.

The mic moved two people away.

What on earth was I going to say about love? That there were rules to happiness. Scientists had proven a way to making relationships work.

The mic headed to me faster than a yellow light snaps to red. I stayed frozen in position for several breaths, a cold mic thrust into my sweaty hand.

Tiffany signaled me to stand.

My knees shook as I rose and took a breath. The room full of eyes shifted onto me. My hand quivered as I pulled the microphone closer to my mouth. Nick's eyes caught mine. He winked, and I could feel myself flushing.

"I'm Zoey Woodland." I shifted on my feet so he wouldn't be in my direct line of sight. He made it hard to think.

"Tell them what you do," Tiffany whispered.

I focused on the table over to the right. "I'm a relationship coach."

Tiffany whispered, "Say the name of your company."

My throat closed as I heard banging dishes in the kitchen. My knees bent of their own accord, depositing me back into my seat. Back into the shadows. Back to the old way. No! I was sick and tired of being that person. I forced my knees straight again.

"I believe in science. There's a science to love, and there are rules that, if followed, will help you not only find love, but keep it alive."

There, I said it. Mission accomplished even without a company name. The fact that my approach was scientific was *the* point.

Tiffany stood next to me and laughed. "That was my baby sister."

People clapped, and I sank deeper into my seat, feeling both relieved and annoyed as Tiffany took the mic from my hand.

"Zoey actually loves helping people improve their romantic lives," she told the crowd. "She's becoming an expert on the science of love." She wiggled her shoulders up and down. "If you want that in your life, I'd seek her out after the meeting."

She redid what I had already done, like always. I hadn't been that bad. That was it. Next time, I was doing this by myself. Time for me to win or lose on my own.

Fortunately, the rest of the time passed fast, and soon the president ended the meeting. Before I could grab my purse, people gathered in groups, networking again.

Taking deep breaths and searching the room, I spotted Nick, Mr. Social Media, at the far end of the place. For the first time in my life, social media sounded good, and like an answer I needed.

I pulled my purse strap up over my shoulder. I had a plan and someone to talk to—someone cute, who wanted kids, and loved Disneyland.

A woman with short hair and wearing a polka-dot shirt held her hand out to me.

I took it, not sure whether to grasp tightly or softly. "Hello."

"I'm Philippa," she announced. "Mortgages."

She had a firm grip. I tightened mine.

"Ah, wonderful. And I'm—"

"Tiffany's sister." She flashed me a smile, gripping even more tightly. "She's sure a treasure, isn't she?"

She released my hand, which now throbbed. "I think we could really help each other."

"You do?" *How do relationship coaches and mortgages brokers work together?* "I mean yes, so do I."

"You should see some of the couples I work with." She grimaced. "They can barely sign the paperwork without arguing. And some of them are on the fast track to divorce. You could really help them."

"Oh, I don't do marriage therapy—"

"You should come to the Riverside County Women Entrepreneurs meeting. Next Wednesday."

Another meeting? What? Did people go to networking events all day long? When did they actually work?

Philippa talked on. "We don't have a relationship coach yet, and you would probably do well there."

Nervous excitement shot through me. An opportunity to do exactly what I needed to be doing—selling myself. And it happened all on my own without Tiffany's involvement. Well, almost without her involvement.

I flashed a bright smile. "That sounds great."

It sounded awful, actually. But if I wanted to be in this world, I had to play the game. Put on the tight clothes and the fancy face, act interested in things I disliked, go to networking meetings, and "sell myself." I ignored the knot of despair in my gut. "So, tell me, how's the housing market right now?" I asked. "Rates good?"

Philippa discussed mortgage interest rates with great enthusiasm for a very long time. I nodded and listened, absorbing nothing except the way this woman loved what she did, and that the market was apparently good.

Tiffany nestled in a far dark corner, intently talking to a lady decked out in a flowing turquoise-blue blouse, four-inch-high heels, and a turquoise rock necklace. A supermodel.

Nick, too, was in a deep conversation doing his thing. He stood there with a carefree smile, making this appear second nature.

The mortgage lady handed me her card.

She leaned toward me, covering the side of her mouth. "I'll let you know who the single ones are so you know who might be interested in your work." She pointed out three ladies who might be good to talk to, and then Ray.

"He has interesting ideas about romance and the stars, so you might want to steer clear of him. But Nick over there . . ." She pointed to him as he handed his card to someone. "He's cute and single and will do almost anything for you if you give him blueberries."

"Blueberries, huh?" I asked. We simultaneously ogled Nick for a second.

She swiveled her gaze back to me. "Well, enough lollygagging. I need to get back to work."

She waved goodbye, leaving me standing there wondering what to do, and about the blueberry tip. That seemed weird since blueberries were so common, but if it did the trick, who was I to complain? I fussed with my purse to appear busy, and thought about finding a chair to wait this out until Tiffany wound down.

"I liked what you said about how *controllable* everything is," said a voice behind me.

I turned to find Nick.

"You did?" I said in surprise, pretty sure I hadn't said anything about control.

"Yes." He drew up in front of me. "And how you said there's a science to it."

It was nice that he appreciated what I was up to. I blurted, "Knowing the right formula is important."

He nodded as though he agreed.

Shocker! I certainly wasn't used to being agreed with. I tipped my chin up a little. Mom, Tiffany, and Damion all knew I needed help. Well, so did this guy . . . but he was different somehow. Maybe it was the fact he actually liked kids.

"If the rules work, everyone should know about them. How's your social media footprint?"

My smile froze. "I, uh . . . what footprint?"

He laughed like I'd made a joke. I joined in, wondering what we were laughing at and hoping he wouldn't figure out how utterly clueless I was. The excited little flutter changed into nervousness that I'd be found out and could never make it in business or life.

I melted into his confidence. "And I'm here to learn."

His approving gaze held mine. "A perfect team. I'll lead . . ."

"And I'll listen."

The flutter in my belly turned to a shiver of . . . excitement?

He gestured with his head. "The first thing is to get you to the top of the Murrieta relationship coaching search engine results."

I nodded in agreement, so happy someone was going to make sense of all this.

"It's a good thing you ran into me."

I gave him a weak smile, grateful I had found him too. There was no way I could do this on my own.

His questioning went on like this. Me panicking, and him telling me he'd get me out of this hole I was in.

He stepped closer. "Don't worry, I can help you out."

He gestured with his head. "Come here. I'll show you." He strolled over to one of the tabletops and set down his iPad.

I followed, ready to get my life fixed. We stood side by side. The noise had faded in the restaurant, making it feel more intimate. He towered over me, even when he bent at the waist and pointed to his computer screen.

"See, here?"

I dragged my gaze off his broad shoulders. "What?"

"You only have one person to compete with."

I followed the point of his finger.

Reynesh. Of course. Seeing his name on page after page of search results was like a splash of cold water. "Oh," I said dully. "He's everywhere."

Nick shifted. Our shoulders brushed, and the musky scent of cologne washed over me. It was a lot like Damion's, which made my nasal cavities contract.

"Don't worry," Nick said. "It's doable, but it's going to take work because Ray is doing things right."

"Of course he is," I muttered.

"He's got sixty-five rave reviews totaling a 4.2 approval rating."

"I see that."

Nick tipped his head to the side. "Want to beat him?"

I straightened. "Yes!"

He grinned. "I'm your ticket. Do what I say, and we'll win."

There it was again, that shiver of excitement. We. Win. He seemed to be happy to help.

"It's only four hundred dollars to get started."

He talked like it was no big deal to beat Ray and to turn me into a functioning businessperson. That was what I wanted to hear, and I hoped he could. But paying for anything was a lot, especially after all those clothes I bought last night. Maybe I could return some.

"For starters, I'll set up your social presence on search engines. Your job is to collect as many testimonials as possible."

I bit down on my lip. I needed to prove to Tiffany, to Damion, to Ray, and to myself that I could do this. And Nick had the answers.

"Okay, let's do it."

He turned off his iPad. "Great. Give me your phone number and your credit card. We'll get you rocking."

I gave him all the info.

"See you soon." He winked and strolled out.

A tremble shot through me as I watched him. Just as he moved out the front door, Tiffany waved me over across the room. Ugh. Lecture time for being with Nick.

I hurried over to her, but instead of giving me a lecture, she gestured to a new acquaintance. "Zoey, this is Tami."

I nodded at her, and she did the same.

"She's new in town, and she'd be perfect for you to work with."

A client!

"I was just telling her what you do," Tiffany continued, "and Tami would love to make a romantic connection."

Both she and Tiff stared at me, waiting.

My turn. "Don't blame you," I said softly, clearly not good at this conversation stuff.

She gave a soft laugh.

"She's short on money," my sister explained.

My smile froze.

"But she was a massage therapist back in Idaho Falls," Tiffany went on. "I'm sure you two could figure out a trade."

"Sure . . ." I sounded too anxious.

Tami and I exchanged info as Tiff's phone buzzed and buzzed.

She glanced at her phone and gasped. "Attention, everyone!" she yelled. The room grew quiet. "I just got word that the keynote speaker's plane was delayed for tomorrow's function. He won't make it here on time."

The room exploded in upset.

Tiffany leaned closer to me. "He was a noted speaker for the Entrepreneur Business Association."

"Oh," I whispered. I shifted my weight, glad again I wasn't on heels.

"If we cancel our big event, the town and local businesses are not going to be happy." Her gaze narrowed, skipping over the crowd, already working on a recovery plan. She was never knocked sideways for long.

I crossed my arms and waited to see how she fixed things because she always did. Even my things. Even the things I didn't think were broken or needed to be fixed, like my desire to marry and have a family.

"So, who are you going to get instead, Tiffany?" someone shouted.

The demand was echoed by a chorus of similar questions, all wanting Tiffany to find another top-notch speaker out of thin air.

She winced.

I experienced a strange moment—part satisfaction because I wasn't used to seeing her blindsided, and part rooting for her to pull it off. Since I'd been nine, she'd been my protector and my point guard, always two steps ahead of me, clearing the way and leaving me behind.

From out of the bickering crowd of irritated professionals, Ray appeared next to us. "Hey, Tiffany?" he asked quietly.

I stepped between him and Tiffany, all protective bear for the moment. "Can't you see she's trying to figure it out? Give her a minute and—"

His dark eyes caught mine. "I was going to say maybe I could help."

I frowned. "How can you help find a top-notch speaker in under twenty-four hours?" I drew Tiffany away, almost enjoying my role as protector.

As usual, though, she didn't need my protection. At Ray's words, her face brightened. "You do presentations?" she asked.

He gave a careless shrug. "Sure. I spoke on the Small Business Riverside circuit last summer."

I frowned at his shameless self-promotion and his nice shoulders.

"You don't charge a thousand dollars, do you?" I grumbled.

Tiffany glanced between us. "I could actually use two speakers. Two, actually."

Ray and I stared at each other. I took a step back, "No, I don't think so—"

"It's perfect," Tiffany said as she reached for one arm and tugged us back together. "Garret was going to talk about creating healthy relationships, which totally relates to the work you both do. You could present together."

I shook my head adamantly. "I've never even talked about my work before today, let alone a presentation—"

"Sure, I've got no problem doing it," Ray piped up. His eyes locked on mine. "But if you don't feel up to it . . ."

I straightened my shoulders, not wanting to be outshone by my competitor, especially not by Destiny Man.

"Oh, I'm in. I can't wait," I said. But then I couldn't help myself from adding, "I want everyone to understand how science is a better guide to finding real happiness."

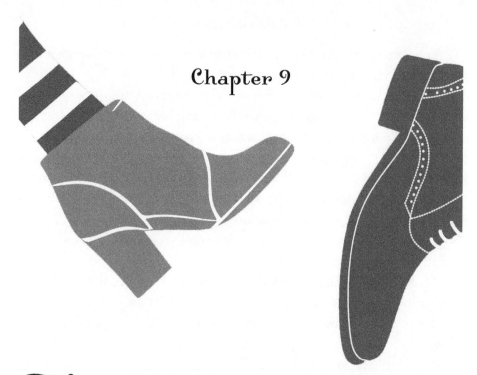

Chapter 9

Tires squealed as Tiffany gunned the car out of the parking lot. The blaring sunlight sent me scrambling for my sunglasses. My sister was a bit of a lead foot, but that didn't stop her from running her mouth.

"You need to work on your networking skills."

And she was off . . . I should have appreciated it, but I had hit overload. The meeting had been intense, and now I was booked as a keynote speaker.

I gave her a withering expression. "Well, I got a client and a speaking gig. That's pretty good, if you ask me."

Tiffany replied with a loud throat clearing. "You mean, *I* got you a client and a speaking gig."

My eyes narrowed as my confidence lessened.

"You were unbelievably uncomfortable, Zoey. You need to learn how to walk in dress shoes. I saw you stumble, and you're wearing flats."

"But it was my first—"

"And you have to prepare to speak at meetings to ensure your voice isn't shaking. Especially since you're presenting in front of the whole town."

I shifted in my seat. "How am I supposed to stop that?"

"And not having business cards . . ." She shook her head at the rookie mistake.

A spark of anger lit my chest. "I did the best I could. I didn't even know I was going until an hour before the meeting."

Tiffany gave me a scolding expression. "That's a problem."

I stared at her. "What's that supposed to mean?"

She glanced at me through the moving morning shadows as we zipped past telephone poles and neighborhoods. Inside the houses lived people—families—sharing family moments. And I was stuck in a car being picked apart by my sister as I tried to build a life I didn't even know if I wanted.

"If you're going to be an entrepreneur, Zo you'll have to know what you're good at and what you're not. The stuff you're not great at, you hire out . . . or become good at it."

I slumped back in my seat. "That sounds expensive." Also, I wasn't good at *any* of this, so I was going to be broke in fifteen minutes, if I wasn't already there.

The whole point of this venture was to build a new life and find a husband. The last thing I wanted was to be like Damion, consumed by my work. I wanted to be consumed by my family.

The traffic was mild, typical for this time of day since it wasn't even noon yet. Most of the children were at school and parents at work, living normal lives. Fulfilling lives. Others had a clear path in front of them. Not me.

My phone vibrated in my purse. I dug for it, taking almost everything out of its black hole—papers, receipts, pens, candy wrappers. I finally found my cell and read a text.

Do you want to get together and discuss what we are going to talk about tomorrow night? Reynesh

My hand shook. I shouldn't be excited about getting together with my competition. I should be cautious. I should act constrained and careful. I looked at my phone, then at Tiffany.

"How did my neighbor get my phone number?" I asked.

She smiled. "He needed it."

"Tiffany! It should be my decision whether or not he has it."

She shrugged. Not listening to me again. Never, ever listening to me or respecting my wishes. She flipped on the radio and rotated through stations until she stopped for the traffic light.

My phone rang. This time, Nick's name popped up on the screen.

"You know that Nick guy I was talking to at the meeting?" I took a breath. "He said he could refer me to lots of people. This is him calling now. What do I say?"

"Hold on." My sister slipped into commando voice. "Don't answer that call, for starters."

The phone chirped its third ring.

My finger hovered over the answer button.

"Don't," she snapped. "You aren't ready for *that* conversation."

My eyes started blinking from the brightness of the sun. "I hired him to be my social media person."

"Zoey!"

I caught my breath. "What?"

"You need to vet people, especially in that group."

I twisted my fingers. "I don't get it. You were all friendly with him."

"Friendly, yes, but I wouldn't hire him—ever."

This was all very confusing.

Tiffany stopped at another yellow light. Way too many stoplights dotted the street.

"He's not calling to get you clients or help you build your business. He's calling because he wants to date you," she said. "Offering to do your SEO is his way of getting to know you *and* make a few bucks."

I glanced at the red light, then down the vast, mostly empty street that lay before us. Leafless trees spread out on either side, bumping up next to the sidewalk. I gripped the armrest next to me, feeling its rough fake leather. A cloud slid in front of the sun, and the day slipped into grayness.

Tiffany's face appeared pale and expressionless as she watched the traffic light. Her suit had managed to stay wrinkle-free and appeared freshly pressed. My outfit was wilting, along with my belief in myself that I could do this. How could Nick be interested in me when he could be interested in Tiff?

My phone stopped ringing. I slid it back into my bag. "What makes you say that, Tiff? It's just about me working with him."

She shook her head. "He's a busy bachelor who's dating several women in the group."

Several?

"You're his next conquest."

Heat shot up my neck. "That's ridiculous."

"He was subtly asking me questions about you," she explained. "A guy only does that when he is interested."

My heart hadn't stopped going into spasms. One networking meeting had a way of creating a lot of trouble for a person.

"If he wanted to date me, why didn't he just ask?"

"Guys like him aren't going to risk rejection flat-out. They become your friend, get to know about you, find out how much baggage you have to see if it's going to be worth it to pursue you."

"Baggage? He's evaluating baggage? That doesn't sound good."

Tiffany laughed hard. "Calm down. This is California, after all. Almost everyone who moves here has baggage. That's why they come here. To start a new life. Don't worry about that. Anyone over twenty-five has baggage."

"So, what's he trying to figure out?"

She pulled up to my house, switched off the ignition, unsnapped her seatbelt, and shifted to face me. "In California, the legal system is really screwy. You don't know. You were lucky because Damion didn't fight you on anything."

"What—?"

"Zoey, he signed the papers, I know it was traumatic for you, but you two agreed—eventually. I have a ton of friends who have been negotiating for two to three years, and still end up back in court because the state wants the couples to work it out themselves rather than have the court make the decisions."

She gave me that smug know-it-all expression and declared, "Singles here want to date others who are free of all that."

What my sister was saying was ridiculous. Singles evaluated each other in terms of baggage? Like human commodities. I sighed. My head hurt. It all seemed so impersonal and judgy.

I dug my phone out of my bag and glanced down at it to see the missed call notification. Hopefully, I didn't have too much "baggage" for Nick. Or maybe he'd be one of those people who overlooked it. After all, I liked

Disneyland and so did he. That had to be worth something. It showed a connection in spirit. Like-minded, valuing the same things.

I gathered myself and said slowly, "So how much baggage do I have?"

"It all depends on the guy and what he wants." She flipped her hair onto her back. "Nick has a reputation for not being very tolerant. No girl has made it beyond the second date. So far, *everyone* has had too much baggage for him. Or maybe he doesn't want to settle down."

Disneyland Dad, who seemed so nice and happy and fun, was picky? I closed my eyes. "What's my baggage? Be honest."

She shook her head slightly like it was obvious. "An X-husband who isn't over you."

"I don't have any control over that."

Tiffany shrugged. "Well then, you can understand the guys' perspective. They'll probably be okay with it being in your past, but if you're currently dealing with it, why would they become involved?"

I rubbed my forehead to ease the increasing headache. Finding Mr. Perfect was getting more complicated. And on top of that, I had a speech to prepare with Ray.

Yellow sunlight spilled down onto my small home. The palm trees framed it, giving my place a quaint feeling. Ray's car was parked out in front of his house, spotless and shiny, of course. His lawn lacked the palm trees mine had, but his grass was greener and didn't have the brown patches or bald spots. The bunnies preferred my place for some reason. Maybe that was a destiny thing—I was destined for my grass to be munched on, and he was destined to have thicker, greener grass, and a more successful business.

My sister shifted her attention to me. "We need to talk about what you're going to do for the presentation."

A lump appeared in my throat. "I've got it."

Tiffany's eyes narrowed in on me. "How do you have it when you've never presented before? Zoey, this is serious. I risked my neck and reputation to give you a chance."

Panic was vibrating in her voice.

I placed my hand on her shoulder. "Thank you."

She stared at me. "I need—"

"Going to Ray's now to work it out. I'll do a good job, promise. You don't need to worry. I know you have a packed day."

Tiffany sighed. "I'll call tonight to see how it's going."

That was fair.

Ray's text message burned into my thoughts as I said goodbye to my sister. He wanted to lock down what each of us was going to say. The idea of going on about my subject for more than thirty seconds made me feel like I was on a roller-coaster ride. I could ask Ray what he was going to do so I'd have a clue what *I* should do.

Waving goodbye to my sister, I straightened my shoulders, swiped my hair onto my back, and headed over to Mr. Ray's house while listening to Nick's voice message. He wished me luck for tomorrow's speech and wanted my company name.

Sighing, I thought about it. I texted, *Relationships Done Right.* Feeling a little bit more professional now with a business name, I noticed the sun felt good spilling down on me, encouraging me to take this step. I rang the doorbell. Butterflies swooped around in my chest.

I took in the valley.

Ray opened the door with a smile, still as attractive as ever in his tight-fitting polo shirt. "Hi, Zoey. I have good news."

"Yeah?"

"We just have to prepare a fifteen-minute spiel each, and for the other part, the emcee will show a movie clip from the scheduled speaker. We don't have to do the whole two-hour presentation, even though in some ways, that would be better."

I tried to swallow a sizeable intense knot of panic in my throat. "Better? How could talking for two hours be better?"

He smiled. "Much better conversions that way."

My face must have appeared as horrified as I felt because he laughed.

"Relax. Even if we had to do that, it's not so bad." He leaned a shoulder against the doorframe. "These kinds of things are a great opportunity to build your business. If you do your job right, the more stage time you have, the more clients you get."

None of that made me feel good. Not even a little. When my sister asked me to speak, I should have said no. I was too new. I needed more time to get used to this foreign world I had stepped into.

"Is now a good time to work on it?" Ray asked.

I took in the questioning face of Mr. I-Find-Beauty-in-Chaos. He had a spark like he was egging me on. Fine. Game on.

I smiled, head held high. "Yes," I said firmly.

Fake it till I make it. I could do that. Business was about appearances. All I had to do was look good enough. I had that new outfit, I thought, remembering that very expensive shopping trip I took yesterday.

Ray interrupted my internal pep talk by gesturing to his porch swing. "We can work here and enjoy the nice breeze and the daylight."

I stared at the swing, surprised he wanted to work outside. An advantage of being an entrepreneur was that we could do what we wanted. I suspected his house was probably in bachelor-pad condition, and he didn't want me to see the mess. That was something I could understand, and it secretly made me feel a little better about my own mess.

"Sounds good," I said. "Let me run home and grab some things, and I'll be right back."

I couldn't help but feel his eyes on me as I crossed the street. My flats, a bit loose, caused my feet to slip. Despite that, I kept my head held high.

Once inside my house, I kicked those suckers off so I could run around the place to find a paper and my Rules-Based Relationship binders. Naturally, I hunted in several rooms before spotting them.

For some strange reason, I also double-checked my reflection in the mirror, probably just to gain confidence as I returned to Mr. Chaos's house.

As I crossed the street in my slippery shoes, the sun shone in my eyes, making me squint. When I finally could make out images, I spotted Ray on the porch swing. He leaned back with a broad smile, watching. I pressed my binders and notepad closer to my chest. That man made my nerves flare.

Ray was in a full-fledged chuckle by the time I stepped onto his porch. The laugh sounded somehow inviting, but I also had the feeling it was aimed toward me. In fairness, his lightheartedness about this project induced a calming effect. The knots in my stomach had already loosened.

"What's so funny?" I checked behind me to see if I was missing something. The midday traffic from the highway hummed in the background, part of the beauty of living a couple miles between two highways.

He tipped his chin toward my relationship binders. "You came armed for a very long speech."

I held up the science notebook, proud of my resources. "One can never be too prepared."

His eyes flickered from my response. "If you say so."

My attention snapped on him. "What? Is preparing not important?"

"It's nothing. Just seems like you're going to a lot of effort to control the uncontrollable."

I shifted my weight. "What do you mean?"

"You can't change what's supposed to be."

A warm, gentle breeze blew through my hair as I clutched my binder.

He spread his hands. "What will be will be."

Does that go for everything? "Are you saying that people don't impact their lives by what they do? If you believe that, why are we preparing our speeches? Why don't we just let what will be, be?"

He shook his head. "No, I'm saying you can't change destiny." He waved me to the other side. "Some things you have control over, and other things you don't."

I plopped on the other end of the swing and put my binders next to me. "So, how do you know what you have control over? What determines it?"

He smiled. "Destiny. If it isn't destined, you can have influence."

I wasn't sure why he was smiling. This whole idea that I couldn't control my life, couldn't follow the rules to make things work out, was disturbing, to say the least.

"That's it?" I asked. "That's your entire philosophy? Someone can't control certain things, and they have no idea which things those are. Sounds fun."

He pressed his lips together. "Well, with relationships, if you hook up with someone who isn't aligned with your life path—your suffering—it won't work."

I shook my head. "It sounds like someone who doesn't want to take the time to learn how relationships work and wants to blame something outside themselves."

He shifted to face me. "Not at all. It's someone who realizes they don't have control over everything. It's respecting that there are more laws of the universe beyond one's own self. It's acknowledging one can't control one's life, and there's great freedom in being okay with what is and what is meant to be."

I shook my head in confusion, or maybe anger. "I don't think I like that."

"It's not a very American approach," he acknowledged, as though that would make my perception okay. "Americans like to believe in the American dream and think it's entirely in their control."

"You're American."

He nodded. "Yes, I am, and Indian."

I sat back, picking up my nearly forgotten binders as I considered him. "So, where does that leave you with all this?"

He picked up his notepad. "It leads me to building a matchmaking dating service that blends my American and Indian views. It leads me to spend this early afternoon with my beautiful neighbor, figuring out what we're going to share on the stage together."

Beautiful? *Me?* He'd let that fall from his lips so casually. My lips parted. Our eyes held. The prettiest shade of gold reflected from a speck in his right eye. It was almost impossible not to stare.

I yanked my gaze away and cleared my throat the way Tiffany did. I set all the binders aside except one and started flipping pages as if searching for something. The silence extended, so I turned more pages.

Not letting that slow him down any, Ray asked, "You want to go first in the presentation?"

I snapped my head up. "I don't know about that."

"If you want me to, I can." He shrugged. "It doesn't matter to me. I thought it was traditional for ladies to go first, and you'd want to get it over with since you're so anxious."

He watched me.

Waves of butterflies flew through me. Waiting would suck. "Fine. If it makes you happy, I can go first."

A grin edged at his lips. "Oh, I can see now how this is going to go."

I couldn't help but smile. Working with Ray would keep me alert for sure.

It took about two hours for me to organize my speech down to bullet points. I did check my phone a couple of times to see if Nick had left another message. He hadn't.

Ray didn't seem quite as concerned about bullet points for his speech.

In fact, he slouched back on the swing and waved his hand whenever I got wound up about how our speeches would work off each other. He let me have my way in everything. It was very disconcerting because he always did it with a slow smile. I could almost see the word "destiny" floating over his head in silvery letters.

I closed up my binders. I stared into the murky blue sky and blew out a breath.

"Okay," I said, reviewing things out loud. "I think the most important points for me to cover are the research, the good chemicals, and the fact that healthy relationships are also important for your physical health. That should sell them the island." I leaned back in the swing.

"The island?" Ray echoed.

I waved my hand. "Something Tiff said."

"Where's the island?" he asked playfully.

I tapped the side of my head. "In here." I shifted my weight. "What about you? Have you decided what your most important points are going to be?"

"Not sure. Whatever comes to mind at the moment, but I'll remember to sell the island."

His inviting smile only irritated me a tiny bit.

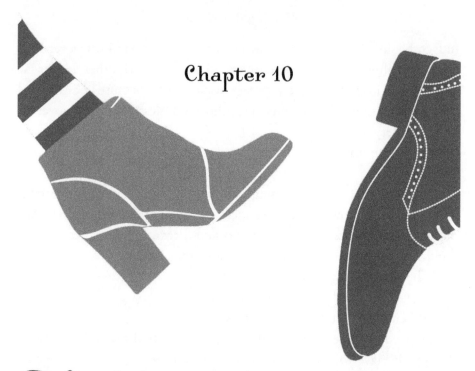

Chapter 10

The endless hours I spent with Ray yesterday didn't do anything to calm my nervous system. I scanned over the growing crowd in the auditorium as they settled in to listen to the marriage expert for the Murrieta Family Day Celebration. There had to be at least a hundred people already seated, and it didn't look like the trickle into the auditorium would slow anytime soon.

I recognized a couple faces from the chamber of commerce, but I hadn't seen Disneyland Dad's face yet. I shifted in my tight pencil skirt and crossed my legs. Sure, it cut into my waist, but it also showed off my legs all the way down to my three-inch heels. I was not yet brave enough to attempt the five-inchers.

The thought of Nick seeing me, watching me, made me even more nervous. A few minutes later, Ray strolled onto the stage. I gave him a little wave, to which he nodded as he approached his seat next to me. I blew out some nervous energy while taking him in, decked out in a tailor-fitted royal-blue suit that made him downright sexy. His gelled hair and the scent of a light woodsy cologne completed the image.

My competition had arrived.

"Hey." I settled back in my seat. After a few seconds passed, I leaned closer to Ray so he could hear me over the noise of the crowd. "Talk about irony. All these people want to know how to make their marriages better. They're getting me, a woman who was divorced this past week, and a guy who's never been married and lectures about destiny."

He laughed.

I smiled weakly at him and turned back to all the people who wanted answers neither Ray nor I could provide.

"Are they going to think we're phonies?"

I searched Ray's face to see if I could grasp a sense of what he really thought.

He touched my forearm, sending warmth down it. "Zoey, they aren't expecting us to be perfect. If we give them one idea or get them thinking at all about something they haven't thought of before, we'll have done our job."

I stared into his deep, calming brown eyes. "That's it?"

He smiled a relaxed grin. "Yep." He leaned into me closer, causing our shoulders to touch. He tugged on his suit jacket. "You look great."

My face grew warm. How to respond? Thank him? Tell him how absolutely attractive he always was?

Nope. That was too close to flirting, and definitely unprofessional. What kind of businessperson flirted with their competition? Their single attractive competition?

I cleared my throat and uttered a simple, "Thank you."

The young blonde program manager hurried over. She came to a sudden stop in front of us. "I wanted to thank you both for doing this so last minute. You really saved us."

"We're here to serve," Ray said with an incredibly inviting smile.

The manager beamed back, her eyes locked on him as her neck and face turned deep red, signaling her clear attraction to him.

He'd just outshone me again, but right now, it didn't matter. My gaze fixed on the crowd. Nothing mattered now but how big this crowd was becoming.

When they called my name, I jerked my head up like a frightened bird. They introduced me as the relationship coach who helped people find true love. I thought of Damion and almost puked.

Ray was introduced as the man who was revolutionizing romance through his new matching service app.

"Let's give them both a big round of applause."

The auditorium erupted as I stumbled straight into the blaring lights. The only good news was that those bright lights kept me from seeing too much of the crowd.

Ray gestured for me to go first. I gulped and picked up the mic. "Welcome," I yelled into the microphone.

The crowd responded with more applause.

I took a deep breath to find the words I had worked so hard to craft yesterday. My ankles wobbled in my high heels. I inhaled another breath. Here went nothing—

"How many of you want more of the feel-good brain chemical dopamine?"

There were a few hoots and hollers as I walked to the front of the stage like Ray had suggested. It was a gesture to physically and emotionally move closer to them.

"Let's put it this way. How many of you would like to lower your levels of stress?"

Some claps. I forced a smile as I took in the people who responded.

"Lower levels of anxiety?"

More claps.

"Want to live longer? And be happy?" My voice grew stronger as I wandered stage left.

A few called out "Yes" and "I do!"

They were listening to what I was saying and responding with enthusiasm. Maybe I *could* do this. My legs stopped shaking and the pounding in my chest eased.

I stared into the darkness, wandering stage right. "You can have it all. You can have *all* that," I said the second time, my voice growing stronger with emphasis.

"You can have a happy, healthy relationship. Scientific research now shows what works in romantic relationships and what doesn't. Dr. John

Gottman has a ninety-three-percent accuracy in predicting which relationships will last and which will fail, and he does this based on scientific data."

I let that land. The crowd leaned forward, waiting to hear more. Maybe they were as excited about a way to win at love as I was. I strolled stage left, hearing whispers and people shifting forward in their seats. A few people made gestures as they whispered to their neighbors.

"The truth is that happy, *loving* relationships are proven to help your health, give you increased longevity, and to lower your levels of the evil chemicals cortisol and adrenaline."

Silence. Uh-oh. My hand grew sweaty on the mic. It was a big black sea of people. "Who wants that?" I asked softly, no longer sure they did.

Maybe my low voice sounded confident instead of terrified because people roared and clapped.

I grinned into a dark sea of faces, feeling the exhilarated energy of the crowd. I could understand why people became performers. Going with the energy, I headed downstage, albeit a little wobbly on the heels. "When you first meet someone of interest," I explained, "your brain is flooded with dopamine—the feel-good chemical. That's the chemical you want."

I wiggled my hips just to throw in a little fun. People laughed.

Their laughter served as a boost for me.

I continued meeting the glints of people's eyes in the encouraging darkness. "The more you're with that person, the more you meet each other's needs, and the more bonding moments you experience. When this happens, both of you release the good chemicals in your brain."

My gaze connected with Ray's. He watched me with a half grin. I grinned back and a little rush zigzagged through my body, almost like dopamine.

Distracting.

I peeked back at the audience while I struggled to remember where I was in my spiel. Recovering, I continued, "Scientists have found that older couples who've been together for a long time are *still* releasing that chemical. The honeymoon stage doesn't have to end."

More clapping.

"Not only is each individual's brain being dumped with dopamine, but they also produce oxytocin, the bonding hormone. All these hormones wash the brain, making each person in the relationship happier and their bodies healthier."

I waited through the applause, then lowered my voice and stared into the darkness. Turns out, I had a showmanship bent in me. Who would have thought?

"The important thing," I told them, "is to find the person you can co-create these moments with. There are a lot of wrong people for you, too. People who will never give you those dopamine and oxytocin rushes. You don't want them, do you?"

The crowd replied in sporadic shouts of "No!" and bursts of laughter.

My hip cocked. "Well then, you'd better come see me."

Another sustained round of applause. They had liked what I said! I had done it. I stepped to the lower end of the stage to give the platform to Ray.

I suspected it'd be hard for him to top my success. He waited for the applause to settle before stepping into the spotlight. Women cat-called and whistled. I pursed my lips. He stood there, solid, not saying anything, just gazing at the audience until they calmed. He rolled the mic between his hands as he waited for the noise to fade and to get the crowds' attention.

"Funny how science is now able to prove what the ancient civilizations already knew. When people form marriages, the family and the community do better."

A trickle of laughter flittered through the auditorium.

"Zoey is right. Healthy relationships are good, but the problem is, there's an epidemic of failing ones. Modern society is hard. It takes more than a few feel-good hits of dopamine to safeguard relationships."

I glared at him. What kind of game was he playing? He had been all buddy-buddy with me before the speech. He even complimented me. Had that been his way of derailing me?

"That's why we at Perfect Destiny have taken the wisdom astrology has used for thousands of years and applied that knowledge to matching people into sustainable relationships."

He paused, letting his point land. There were a few coughs and some uncomfortable shuffling in the crowd.

"Need proof?" he asked.

Of course, everyone here needed proof. Astrology as the basis for a relationship? That was pushing it.

"Relationships that have been formed with astrological guidance statistically do much better. That's why in India, there's a better success rate in marriage than in the United States."

I sensed how the crowd leaned back at the veiled insult.

He didn't seem fazed. Impressive. He scanned the audience until they waited to see what he would say next. "Matchmaking might seem a bit foreign, even old-fashioned, and it lacks the romantic notions most Americans prize."

He paused again as the crowd grew silent. I considered his words. I didn't *want* to believe them, but he was right. I'd had a thousand romantic notions about love when I met Damion, and none of them had been realized, which is why I'd turned to science. And here was Ray, talking about destiny.

And people were responding.

"The practice of matchmaking is a science in a way. It's the skill of the matchmaker, one they passed on to the next generation for centuries. But the practice isn't dependent on one person. The whole community is involved in networking and social media."

Social media? I sat a little straighter, and so did the crowd in the darkened room. The resistance in the air seemed to lessen.

"Almost no couple would ever become married without the help of an astrologer and having the individual's charts read."

I snorted softly. Astrological charts?

Ray's head turned in my direction ever so slightly. Then he went on.

"I know there are going to be skeptics here. Before you criticize too much, I want to remind you that Sir Isaac Newton told a skeptic of astrology, Edmund Halley . . . quote, 'I have studied the matter. You, sir, have not.'"

My fingers twitched at my side. He dropped Newton into his presentation. One of the great founders of science. He hadn't mentioned Newton yesterday.

Ray held up his finger. "I know that even the great Sir Isaac Newton might not be enough to convince some of you. I want to remind you that we live our lives under cycles—cycles of the seasons, cycles of the moon, and cycles of the sun. Our environment affects us. There's a reason why more people end up in the hospital when there's a full moon."

He stopped walking, stood center stage, and looked over the entire crowd, making sure every single one of them was listening.

"These cycles have power because we, as humans, pick up energy from the universe, from planets, from the greater cosmos. It's measurable and observable. That's why there are more computer issues during Mercury retrograde. That energy impacts who we are and how we interface in this existence.

"This is science, and it studies how all this affects people and their journey. It dates back to the millennium BCE. That's a solid foundation for one of the most important decisions of a person's life."

The crowd seemed to hold its breath as he talked.

"At our company, we use this ancient science to study what each individual's possible deepest wounds are. The way they express themselves. What are their profound desires? After that, we search for a mate who has similar makeup and suffering."

That sounded like a good idea.

"It goes beyond the nice relationship skills Zoey talked about. If someone is on a similar life journey and has similar suffering, the way they interact with the world and with their partner is more harmonious. This works on a subconscious level because each person in the relationship just gets it. They get *you*."

He gathered his hands into fists. "That's an excellent way to start a life journey. That's how you achieve continuous dopamine hits to the brain."

As the room erupted into enthusiastic applause, he bowed, then came over and stood by my side with a very wide grin.

I clapped too. He was good. Very good.

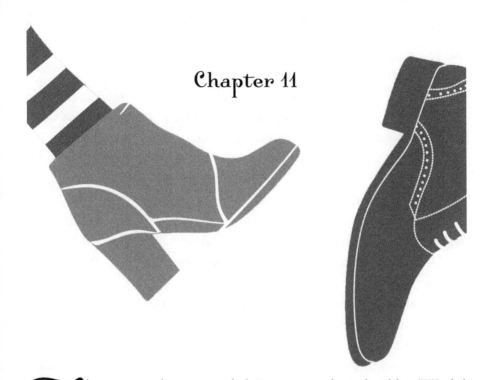

Chapter 11

The moment the event ended, Ray squeezed my shoulder. "We did it." He sounded happy.

I was less sure, seeing as how he upstaged me. I was always being upstaged, usually by Tiffany, definitely by Damion, and now by Ray. I made a noncommittal sound as the noise encircled us. People were talking to each other, others making their way out of the auditorium.

"You threw in a few points that felt like jabs."

He shook his head. "Naw. Never. When in the flow . . ." He shrugged.

"I *thought* I was in the flow," I grumbled quietly. "You got up there and talked about Newton."

His gaze narrowed in on me. "Don't sell yourself short. You were great."

I smiled a little. "Yeah, I was—especially for a newbie, wasn't I?" Heck, I'd almost convinced myself I knew what I was doing.

By this point, his raving fans surrounded us, waiting not so patiently for his attention. Throats cleared as people pressed closer to talk to the man of the hour. Ray turned his attention to the first older lady who waited in front of him, and I moved back a few steps, then a few more.

No one came up to surround me, but I didn't have brown eyes or a ridiculously charming smile.

Naturally, he gave the person he was talking to his full attention. His head bent low so he could hear them. I was unsure why I was disappointed that I didn't get to speak to him longer, but that would give me more time to speak with Nick, if he had come. The place was packed, and I didn't see him. He must have been there, though. He seemed very involved with the community.

I hurriedly said my goodbyes to Tiff and a few others who told me I did well, then slipped into my car. Not wanting to wait for a second longer, I called Nick. When he answered, I said as casually as I could, "You rang?"

"Did. Need to know what keywords you want."

"Key what?"

He laughed. "Never mind. Are you busy right now?"

My pulse increased. "I actually finished giving the keynote presentation, you know, and—"

"Oh, no worries. We'll connect later." He hung up without saying a word about my speech.

Even though I had worn the right clothes, strolled around the stage like I was supposed to, and pumped up the crowd like Ray had suggested, I didn't feel like I made progress toward getting clients or securing Disneyland Dad.

This all might be harder than I thought it would be.

———

My senses heightened to a jittery frustration the next morning. I couldn't get those annoying gawking women fawning over Ray out of my mind. To escape the plague of those disturbing scenes, I grabbed a piece of paper and pen, and sat at my kitchen counter.

Since I had come up with my business name, it was time to come up with the business card concept. I stared at the paper. It stared back with a glaring white glow. I took a sip of my jasmine green tea.

Someone had said at some point in my life, "To beat writer's block, move the pen." Okay, I picked up my pen and moved it. But instead of drawing a rectangle to represent the card, my pen swirled in tiny sloppy dark circles. The more I drew them, the more my pen took over filling the page.

The day, overcast and gray, fit my mood just fine. I was forcing myself not to peek at my phone. It didn't matter that I'd assumed Nick had shown up last night, but he probably hadn't. Or if he had, he had nothing good to say about my speech, so he didn't mention it. More circles, darker this time. It wasn't like we were dating or anything.

The circles consumed the page. It didn't matter that people lined up to talk to Ray and hadn't lined up to chat with me. Circles, circles, circles. It didn't matter that other women found him as attractive as I did. Deepening the swirls to an almost black hue. He wasn't right for me, anyway. None of that mattered.

I squiggled tiny circles around and around until I wore holes into the paper. I thought I had done well last night. I put my all into that dang presentation. I grabbed a new sheet of paper, since the last one was shredded.

A sprint of tiny circular dots burst through my pen. I thought maybe someone would want science-based love advice and dopamine hits.

Not wanting to think about it anymore, I slipped outside to feed the stray cat. The bowls of food and water I left out were almost always empty. I wasn't sure it was the orange cat eating the food, but I hoped he wouldn't have to fight so hard in this world.

Feeling grumpy, and since creativity wasn't happening, I determined the business card could wait. If I could speak to a room full of hundreds of people and not fall while pacing the stage in heels, I could add up my debt and find out just how bad a situation I was in.

I slipped into my most comfortable clothes, sweats and a T-shirt, and turned my focus to adding up my debts.

First, my lawyer bill of $7,503.43. Ouch! I wrote a check, popped it into an envelope, and set it to my right in my "done and done" pile.

Next came the cable bill. Apparently, Damion had us on the Elite Entertainment package. Idiot. Well, I'd cancel that. All I really needed was the romcom channel, and I could stream that. On a mission to do hard things, I picked up the phone and spent forty minutes convincing them that yes, I really, really, really did want to cancel. After an endless time on hold, I finally received their consent. I set the phone down and put the bill in the "done and done" pile.

Pushing up my sleeves, I reached for the next bill. It wasn't so bad. Things kept up like that until I hit the mortgage statement. That's when I saw Damion had taken out a second mortgage.

A second mortgage!! With variable-rate interest.

My heart sank when I saw the monthly payment. $3,340.22 each month? How could he have done that? I had trusted him and let him handle everything. This was the price I paid for it.

No more.

Inhaling slowly, I carefully lifted the paper—it weighed no more than, well, a piece of paper—but my hand shook like I was holding an anvil. My face felt hot as I set it down on my left in the "to-be-paid" pile and picked up the next bill.

Overdue phone bill.

And the next. My credit card. It carried a balance of $1,200 at eighteen percent interest. And all my fancy clothes would show up on the next one, along with the payment to Nick.

My whole body shook. My eyes teared up and my hand moved of its own will toward the phone to call Tiffany. I slapped my hand down on the desk.

"No," I told myself. "You're not calling her. You can handle this."

My hand sat quietly as if it believed me, but my mind whirled because it wasn't sure I *could* handle this . . . at all. I lowered my head and rested it on the wooden table. All I had to do was breathe and take one small step at a time. Breathe and eat, and I'd figure everything out eventually.

My head popped up. Food. There was nothing in the fridge. Seizing on the simple problem, I hopped up, grabbed my purse, and headed to the grocery store for broccoli cheese soup. It'd be cheap and nourishing and comforting. And I certainly needed comfort.

I made it to the grocery store to find only yellow-tinted broccoli stalks on display. Seriously. No fresh, healthy broccoli? How was I supposed to avoid potato chips if I couldn't even make broccoli cheese soup? The lentil crackers weren't going to work.

My phone buzzed, insisting on being answered. I stared at it, not sure if I wanted to.

"Hi, Zoey. This is Nick from the chamber."

The pings in my stomach increased like a pinball machine.

"Have you forgotten me yet?" he asked in a teasing tone.

The sprinkler above the vegetable racks snapped on, watering and refreshing the vegetables with moisture. The same way his interest was refreshing me.

He had a flirty tone. So, what to say to a person I'd just met a couple of days ago who could possibly be *the* Disneyland Dad?

I forced a slight laugh. "I haven't forgotten." I pushed the grocery cart to the meat section to scope out the sales that weren't really sales. I need cheap, cheaper—like, almost free—meat. Steak was definitely out of the question.

"You did a good job last night."

He *had* been there. "Thanks."

Why didn't he say anything about it last night when I mentioned it in our call?

"One suggestion, though. You need to work the room. Walk around more and connect with people rather than just aimlessly wandering around like you have no intention for your movements."

That made sense. "Okay, will do." I hoped I sounded like I could do that—when, in truth, I had no idea if I could—and at the same time remember what I was saying and come off more confident like Tiff suggested.

Nick plowed on with the conversation. "I'd like to schedule our meeting to go over your social media. You're going to need to do a lot of catch-up to match Ray."

I swallowed a lump in my throat and stopped in front of the ground beef.

Nick wanted us to get together and help me outshine Ray. Both of those things smacked of good news.

"Sounds great," I said with enthusiasm, snatching the smallest package of ground beef I could find.

"That's what I'm here for—to save you. I'll show you how it's done."

I pushed my cart forward with more pep. That gave me the courage to say, "I didn't see you last night."

Talking sounded in the background through the phone. "I was there briefly. Had other things I needed to do, so I just dropped by and stood in the back. It seemed like you tried to do your best to stand up to Reynesh. He does have game."

That was true.

I moved the cart past all the frozen meat and frozen desserts, feeling the pep drain away. "That he does," I said, longing for the raspberry pie that caught my eye.

"Stick with me. I'll show you what to do."

Unlike Ray, who thought I was doing well. Nick told me the truth. I needed someone who would be honest, even though it hurt—someone to challenge me to be better than my competition.

"We could do lunch," he continued. "Or, since you're single, we could have dinner." He emphasized the word "single" like there was a message in us both being free.

My ping-ponging stomach flipped into overtime. "Okay." The sound of riffling papers came over the phone line.

"Or wait." He gave a breezy chuckle. "Super busy. Let's start out at five, then we can see where it goes from there."

Disneyland Dad was asking me out and willing to give me a chance.

———————

Time for action, even if I did feel like I was going to puke. I filled my afternoon researching other local events where my involvement could drum up business. After an hour of hunting, I stumbled onto a group that helped people develop speaking abilities. The website said it was a friendly and supportive place. That was what I wanted. That, and making progress without my sister.

I picked up the thousand-pound phone and dialed the massage lady I had met at the chamber of commerce who wanted to make a trade. My heart pounded in staccato before the first ring buzzed through.

On the second ring came a friendly "Hello."

Outside my window stood my palm tree, confident, steady, not wavering. I straightened my back to be more like the tree. "Hi, Tami. This is Zoey. We met at the chamber meeting."

"You have no idea how perfect your timing is. It must be a sign that I'm meant to work with you."

She believed in signs, but she thought I was perfect, not Mr. Perfect across the street.

"Just everything is going wrong," she continued. "This morning, when I tried to leave for work, my car wouldn't start. My battery has been acting funny, but I've been ignoring it for weeks."

"Uh-huh," I murmured so she'd know I was listening. Apparently, I wouldn't have to worry about talking. I mentally noted that working on

taking care of messes and incomplete elements in her life might be important for her so she'd be in a space to allow in relationships.

That was good advice I needed to listen to, I thought, noting all the
messes in my house.

Tami didn't even pause for breath. "And I have lots of leads from the
chamber, but I haven't followed up with any of them. You're so much more
on the ball than me. I can't believe what a slacker I'm being."

I almost dropped the phone. She had leads? Lots of them? Hmm, but
the fact that she hadn't followed up meant she could probably improve the
relationships around her if she had someone like me to hold her account-
able. And the fact she thought I was on the ball was a good thing, I hoped.

"And . . ."

Tami rattled on and on about all these little troubles, most concerning
her love life, as I made notes in her newly constructed file.

I wanted to jump in and start coaching her, but I stopped myself. This
was a sales call, not a coaching one. *Focus on the sale,* like the coaching
school had drilled into us.

Tami kept talking as I wandered aimlessly around my house. She
needed someone to listen to her. I could do that.

"I'm so stressed about dating," Tami said. "I don't know if I could ever
put myself out there."

It was time to take a risk. "It sounds like you're afraid of getting rejected."

"Isn't everyone?"

"But it isn't rejection."

"What?"

"You're searching for what would make your life better. If the guy
would make it worse, that isn't rejection. *That* is being saved."

She laughed.

The knot loosened.

"That's so true. You might be right. I've been approaching it wrong."

Divorcing Damion was saving me, even though it felt like I was going
backward. But I had more possibilities, like Nick.

Crap. Nick.

I glanced at the clock. 4:15. I still had time to get ready and make it to
the restaurant, but I had to bust a move.

Tami kept talking, giving me a long story.

I scurried upstairs to find the perfect outfit.

When her voice waned and I thought she was going to pause, she'd pick back up.

Come on, I thought. *I've got to go.*

She kept talking.

I clenched the phone. "Well, Tami," I said brightly, "I can see you have a lot you want to focus on, and I'm . . ." I searched my brain, thought of what I'd heard Nick say, and finished clumsily, "and I'm here to help. Would you like to schedule?"

"Umm, sure."

As I hurried downstairs to the calendar, my foot slipped out from under me. I crashed, hitting the hardwood floor and yelping in pain.

"What was that?" Tami asked.

I stifled a groan and struggled to my feet. "Nothing." That was going to be a nasty bruise. "How about Monday afternoon at your place?"

We scheduled our dual appointments. After hanging up, I gripped the handrail as I awkwardly hobbled up the stairs to the looming wardrobe crisis. A few seconds later, I stood inside the messy closet, flipping through the shirts and dresses as the hangers clicked. Most of my clothes were really old or tent-like, or both.

Nothing else had been vetted or sister approved, and I was one-hundred-percent positive any of them would make me look awful. I scanned the room, my gaze landing on the tight-fitting outfit I had worn when I met Nick. It was crumpled on the floor. Nick had sure acted like he liked it, although he had questioned my flats.

I shimmied into the skirt, shirt, and suit jacket, then crammed my feet into the three-inch heels that were almost impossible to walk in. There. Nick would be happy, and I felt absolutely ridiculous. But I knew nothing about business, so I needed to trust "them"—Tiffany, Nick. They knew what was best.

Five minutes later, I ran out the door and into the car. I sped down the road with a comb hardly tugged through my snarled hair and lipstick barely brushing my lips.

Mr. Disneyland Dad, here I come.

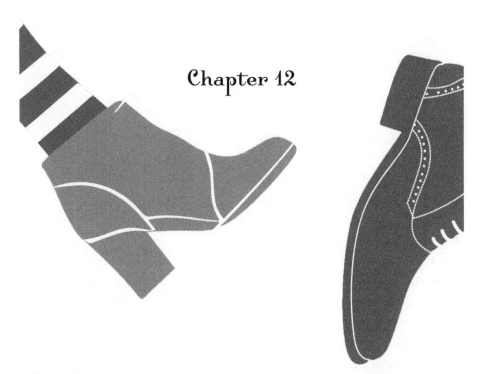

Chapter 12

The car clock announced I was twelve minutes late for my meeting with Nick. I clambered out of the automobile, heels clicking against the cement as I rushed into the busy restaurant. The heavy glass door opened with a *swoosh*, drawing Nick's attention over to me. He stood in the foyer in the midst of a crowd of late twenties and early thirties businessmen, all without suits, chatting with casual lightness.

His eyes caught mine. He tilted his head back an inch as his eyes wandered up and down me. My skin prickled. I might have been making it up, but it seemed like a disappointed sneer crossed his lips for a brief nanosecond before he said, "Hey, there. Glad you could make it."

My ankles wobbled in the high heels.

His gaze skated down to my feet, a smile curling on his face. "Man, I love women who wear heels. You should wear them all the time."

Who knew heels were such a big deal to guys? "Oh. Sure. I'll remember that."

"Do you remember these guys from the chamber?" Nick gestured to his loud guy group.

None of them seemed familiar, but if I was going to be a businesswoman, I needed to get to know people like this, even if it was a lot of testosterone.

"Um, hi," I said, my mind scrambling for how Tiffany would handle this and how she'd manage to fit in the group.

Nick thumbed each of them in turn. "This is Miguel—he's a mechanic. Brayton is the insurance guy. Abdulah is the real estate guy."

He continued through all of the men as I stood there, nodding and wiggling in my outfit that felt tighter than before as it aggressively pinched my sides.

The group stared like I was intruding on the guys' club. I shifted awkwardly in my shirt. "Nice to meet you."

They continued to stand around, looking blankly at me, making me very aware that I needed to learn how to network. I'd add that to the list of skills to work on to grow my business—a very long list of things I needed to learn.

"When are we getting food?" asked the insurance guy.

A *swoosh* sounded from the restaurant door opening behind us. The men burst into greetings and high fives.

"Reynesh!" someone called.

My body froze.

"Now the meeting can start," said the insurance man as he brushed past us to reach my neighbor, apparently preferring Ray over food.

A meeting?

Nick watched me as the men moved around us to talk to my neighbor, my competition, the man I hadn't seen since yesterday when he outshone me on the stage.

"You okay?" Nick asked.

I brightened my weak smile. "Fine!" I said in a chipper voice.

Ray's voice came through the crowd, strong, confident, and sounding way too happy for my mood. "Hey, thanks for waiting for me. Glad to know the meeting revolves around my schedule."

The jeering immediately began as men called back "You wish" and "Not a chance."

Ray was good at this stuff too. Of course.

As that commotion continued, Nick's gaze stayed on me.

"I didn't know we were meeting for a meeting." I flushed. I thought Nick had asked me out for a work date, but it would appear I had flattered myself.

He patted my shoulder. "I just ran into them while I was waiting for you to arrive. Love these guys. Don't worry, I'll get you alone."

The tightness in my chest released a little. "Oh, good," I said. "I thought I misunderstood."

He stepped closer. "You didn't misunderstand anything. You're too smart for that."

Smart. He thought I was smart. More, it felt like he *wanted* me to be smart. Damion hadn't thought I was smart at all, but worse than that, whenever he had to face the fact that I *did* have a point, it made him angry.

I threw off the memories of my X like my sister had thrown away his flowers. Those memories belonged in the trash. Besides, this guy wasn't Damion. He was—or might be—Disneyland Dad. I hoped.

My smile grew more genuine.

"I was beginning to think you forgot about our appointment." His voice had a strong edge to it like I had done something wrong.

My genuine smile froze. I shifted my weight, causing me to wobble again. Taking in his taut jawline, I frantically thought what science taught about turning a situation around. Gottman taught sending bids of love in an argument. But this wasn't an argument, and I wasn't in a relationship with him.

Nick's lips flinched with a disapproving frown that disappeared as a host of men dressed in business casual dress flowed by us.

"I'm so sorry." I spoke in an automatic rush, avoiding his critical gaze. "I got caught up with a client."

He put his hand on my arm, and I jerked my head up.

"Don't worry about it," he said, all charm and ease.

A rush of relief poured through me, cold and spiky. "Oh, okay."

"I mean, who would ghost *me*?" He flashed a hundred-watt smile, then laughed as if he'd been joking.

But really, he was probably right. Handsome, stable, charming—what's not to like?

I glanced over and saw Ray.

"Hey." My neighbor's face lit up.

I nodded, trying not to notice how incredible he looked in a royal-blue business shirt. Not to mention how seeing him lightened the mood.

"Hey."

"Are you here for the meeting?" He waved for the men to continue on without him.

"It's a guys' club that I am not invited to."

Ray laughed. "I understand how you would see it that way."

Nick grabbed my elbow, drawing my eyes to him. "Shall we get a table?"

Ray shifted his gaze between us. It held on Nick's hand touching my elbow, then lifted to my eyes. "Well, it was good to see you. I hope business is going well for you after your great speech last night." He winked. "If you need sugar, remember I got ya covered, *neighbor*." He glanced at Nick. "Good seeing you. Have a great meeting."

Nick didn't respond. He just tugged at my elbow. "Let's get to our table."

It had been a long time since anyone touched me like he had just done. *Act casual*, I instructed myself as I followed him and the young hostess to a booth.

Nick took in the spot and gave the hostess an approving nod as he grabbed the menus from her. "Thanks, Becca. This will work out fine." As she left, a waitress walked up and asked for our drink order. "We'll have two large glasses of Coke and glasses of water with lemons."

"Chamomile tea, please." I forced a smile at Nick. "Coke upsets my stomach," I said as if I needed to make an explanation for my choice.

"You get an upset stomach often?"

If I didn't already have one, him asking gave me one. I scooted into the booth. "Sometimes."

"Sensitive one, aren't you?"

I glanced at the waitress, who waited for us to finish our drink order with a pen poised to write.

"Lemon in water is a great idea." I shifted my attention to Nick. "Did you know lemons help get rid of acidity in your body?" I crossed and uncrossed my legs.

Nick nodded at the waitress. "We need a moment for the food order."

She made her departure.

He sat back in his chair and opened up his menu. "Have you eaten here before? They make waffles and fried chicken that my niece just loves. She covers her whole face with the whipped cream."

Family man! "Aw, that's so-o cute." I pictured in my mind a girl with curly hair, a big grin, and whipped cream everywhere. "I bet she had a ton of fun."

"She *always* has fun with me. I'm the coolest uncle ever."

"She's very lucky to have you."

He closed his menu, acting a bit distracted. "She is."

I leaned toward him, thinking about his relationship with his niece. "I want *lots* . . . a whole pack of children."

"Me too."

We smiled at each other. "My favorite thing here is their blueberry muffin. I love anything blueberry."

That proved the secret sauce was blueberries. Easy peasy. I would swing by the grocery store on the way home and buy him blueberries . . . just in case food truly was the way to a man's heart.

After we'd placed our orders, Nick asked, "Why haven't I seen you before the chamber meeting? I know everyone who's anyone in this town."

He hit the nail on the head. I wasn't anyone yet.

"I'm just starting out." I focused on giving him a confident smile.

This seemed to perk him up. "A new business?"

"A new everything," I murmured.

He reached over and patted my hands. "We'll get your social media rocking so people can find you."

I let his wise guidance seep into me.

"Maybe we could put on a workshop—"

I loved hearing the "we" part. I took a deep breath, soaking it in.

My body froze.

Damion stood across the room.

Crap.

With a woman. A tattooed one at that. She looked tough and stunning in her black leather with her shiny black hair. He held hands with her. Two days after sending me flowers. Jerk.

He glared at me. "Zoey!"

His new friend leaned over to see who he greeted with such enthusiasm. Her eyes narrowed as she scanned me up and down.

Nick eyed us both, his eyebrow raised in silent question.

No one ever wanted to introduce their new X to the new hope on the first date. That was totally not a thing to do in the rule book of dating. I was new to the rule book, but that had to be there.

I glanced between the two men, knowing I had to make introductions, but Damion beat me to it like the sly dog he was.

"I'm Damion." He extended his hand to Nick, cocky and self-confident as ever. "I'm Zoey's former husband as of the past two weeks."

A cold chill shot down my neck. My gaze flashed to Nick as I tried to laugh that point off. "Damion, I didn't think you worked on this side of town."

My efforts of distraction were no good, though, because Damion kept his eyes on Nick. "I'm sure she's told you all about me. Trust me, none of the stories are true. She has quite the imagination."

"Okay," I said, "that's enough. Go do what you were doing." I waved my hand over toward his lady friend.

"We're about to close a big deal with the Anderson Company."

Of course he was. Leave me with a double mortgage, and he gets to pull in the money. That was fair.

"Really?" Nick perked up. "What kind of business are you in?"

"Software development."

"How are you—?"

"Let's go." The lady friend tugged on Damion's arm like they had a super-close connection.

Damion gave her a look of disgust I knew too well. He tipped his chin up at Nick.

"No more flowers," I called after him.

The minute I said that, I knew I shouldn't have drawn attention to baggage that apparently, we—Damion and I—still had going on. To save face, I turned to Nick with a bright smile. "Do you think the food will come soon?"

"What's the name of his company?"

Seriously? Ray had known Damion was a jerk right away, but Nick was clueless.

"You don't want to work with him."

"Yeah, right." Nick looked over toward him. "Sorry. Seems like you two still have some interesting issues going on."

My pulse picked up. "My grandma, when she was alive, would always say 'interesting' as a polite way of saying she didn't like something."

Nick gave a gruff chuckle. "Caught me on that."

I swallowed. "Been married before?"

Damion sat in a booth across the room exactly in my line of sight. Not wanting to see him, I shifted in my seat so another patron blocked my view.

"When I get married," Nick said, drawing my attention back to him, "*I'm* going to make sure it works."

Was that a judgment against me?

"How do you guarantee that?" I challenged Nick, feeling attacked. "No one can make sure they won't get a divorce. There isn't a guarantee policy on marriages."

"I treat dating like I do my business."

That caught my attention. I held my breath, hoping he would explain.

"We go slowly," he said. "We spend a lot of time with each other." He reached out and brushed my finger, sending a jolt of surprise through me. He smiled, warm and inviting. "We learn each other's pain points and search for the solutions we can offer each other."

I could feel my mouth drop. "Relationships are a business to you?"

His fingers grasped two of mine tighter. "Business is relationships. If you take enough time to see all the plusses and minuses and draw up a good contract that both sides understand and agree to, that equals success. The problem with most relationships is they rush the discovery process and never learn about their client or future partner's wants and needs."

My flush doubled itself. The way he was talking about discovery seemed so sensational. It could be a scientific way of approaching relationships. He was talking about really taking time to understand the other person. My whole body tingled.

"We are in the discovery process." He squeezed my fingers.

Swallowing my embarrassment, I said, "Okay, good point. Let's discover something about you."

He laughed. "What do you want to know?" Before I could answer him, he leaned back, fingers sliding off mine. "I work with a lot of big companies, helping them grow their online presence. I actually don't work with many small businesses like yours."

This was a much safer topic. I needed to keep the conversation on his work. Keep it about him, not about me, and the mess of a relationship I had with the man across the restaurant.

"That sounds serious. Hardcore."

He met my eyes directly. "You get it." He tapped the table again. "I have quite a few big companies I work with down in San Diego."

On and on he talked, and I listened. I'd learned if I listened hard enough, people would tell me who they were. With Nick, I learned he was stable, and people liked working with him, and he wasn't afraid to brag.

It was obvious from the way his voice pitched higher and the cadence switched faster that he really liked his work. He was passionate about it. He wasn't going to leave it anytime soon.

It inspired me. I wanted to feel that too, in my own business. I wanted to love what I did and be really good at it. Nick seemed so relaxed. So sure of himself. I tried to ease into his monologue and just listen to him, but I couldn't stop thinking how Damion sat at the same restaurant as me. I fought the urge to look at him, but eventually, I darted a glance in his direction.

He was watching me, not even hiding that fact. I glared at him. He glared back.

"Your face just lost all its color," Nick said.

I shifted in my seat under Nick's gaze that had hardened. "I'm sorry things got weird earlier." I gave a weak laugh.

"Don't let that man ruin our fun."

"Oh, well, sure. I won't. I just—"

"We are having fun, right?"

Well, he'd been having fun telling me all about himself. I'd just been trying to absorb some of his self-confidence. Which, I guess, was fun?

"Sure. I mean, yes," I said firmly. "Fun. That's what we're having."

He nodded approvingly. "I'd like to see your face bright like it was before. You were kind of blushing." His eyes twinkled. "So pretty." His hand rested on the table within reaching distance. "Come on. Be pretty for me again."

No one had ever called me pretty. Well, except Ray, who'd said I was "beautiful."

I smiled at Nick to make myself, I hoped, pretty. From the corner of my eye, I saw Damion sneer. I winced.

"Enough of this." Nick stood, opened his wallet, threw several twenties on the table.

My jaw dropped as I scrambled to my feet. "I'll pay."

Nick turned his head. "Don't bother. You can pay next time." He moved a couple steps away and said over his shoulder, "Wait here."

I reached out to the table to steady myself as I debated whether to go after him. He was making a beeline to my X.

Damion tipped his chin up a quarter of an inch in the cocky way he did when he thought he was better than everyone else.

"You'd better not mess with me, man." Nick's voice filled the restaurant.

"Or what?" Damion drew the attention of the other patrons.

"Or we might have to tango."

A slow, menacing smile spread across my X's face.

Nick did not need that. I hurried over to his side, stumbling in my shoes. Damion was *my* problem, not his. "Damion, stop this."

He threw his arms up in a helpless gesture. "What? I didn't do anything. He came over here."

Nick extended his arm out for me. I grabbed it, reinforcing the message to Damion, to me, to the whole restaurant that we were a team.

Nick leaned toward Damion, hovering over him. "This interesting girl," he pointed at me, "you have lost." Then to me, he said, "Let's go."

Arm in arm, we strolled out of the restaurant as I took in that Nick had just stood up for me. He was moving fast, and I struggled in my high heels to keep up. I'd blown it. Somehow, this was all my fault. Me and my extra baggage. No man would want to deal with what happened at the restaurant. I could understand that. But Nick was still with me. That was a good sign.

He held out his hand. I stared at it. "Keys," he said. "I'll get your door for you."

"Oh. Um, sure." I rummaged through my purse for my car keys while he stood there, waiting. I dug under my phone. No keys. They weren't in the side pocket, either.

He sighed.

Jeez, I never had such pressure when hunting for car keys. It was nice of him and all, but it would've been easier to do it myself without the pressure. I continued to dig until at last, my fingers found them hidden underneath my coaching book.

Nick unlocked the door and swung it open. I slid in. He was a man who loved kids, had a stable business, and would take care of things for me if only I could win him over. That was what I wanted, right?

I waited for him to say something about what he was thinking about us, about the situation, about our meeting ending early.

He shut my car door firmly and said nothing. Nothing at all.

I revved the engine and rolled out of the parking lot, heading to the grocery store to buy the family man blueberries.

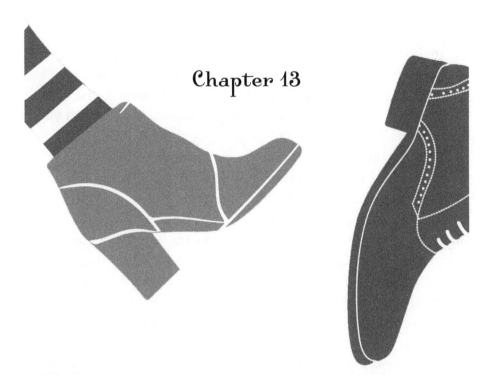

Chapter 13

my foot pressed on the gas hard the moment the traffic broke, jaw set and eyes fastened on the road as the engine ripped. A few minutes later, I rolled the windows down and opened the sunroof to let the elements of sunset and wind bathe me.

The wind roared, flipping my hair in a funky dance like it used to do on roller coasters. I wanted to be taken away from all this serious adult stuff and have that feeling of freedom like I had on a roller coaster. That was where a person could just let go. No one made mistakes while on the ride.

I twisted the radio button, hunting for the perfect song. Bon Jovi or Guns N' Roses would do, but the radio stations did not comply. I finally settled for a silly popular song that repeated three words over and over with a thumping beat. I sang at the top of my lungs, letting the rhythm go through me and my frustration.

Back when I was married to Damion and drove like this, he'd duck his head to avoid being seen and snap, "You're acting like a moronic teenager."

I'd stopped doing it.

In defiance of that memory, I turned the volume way up and sang even louder. I got into a long line to fill my car up with gas. By the time I had finally filled up my car, put the roof back on and washed it, the sun had sunk behind the mountains and blackness spread across the town. I pulled up to the grocery store, tired and not wanting to shop.

What I really wanted to do was go home, put on sweats, and drink hot chocolate. But I would be seeing Nick tomorrow at another networking meeting. It was best to be armed with blueberries.

The day had disappeared into a cloak of darkness as I parked. Raindrops pounded my windshield as I prepared to make a dash to the grocery store in way-too-tight pants and way-too-high heels. All of this because I needed to play this unsettling game to get what I wanted—marriage to a successful family man.

I flung open the car door, jacket held over my head. The rain pelted me like a water gun.

"Nick better appreciate this," I said to myself, my gaze fastened on the grocery store's sliding glass door. I blinked away the water in my eyes as I hurried through the puddles, and then . . . *Boom.* I was on the ground, sprawled out on the cold pavement.

The rain hit my back, seeped into my eyes, and curled down my cheeks. I stayed that way for several breaths, shocked at the suddenness of the fall. I snatched the straps on my purse and scrambled to my feet. My knees, hands, and especially my elbow throbbed.

Nursing my right arm near my chest, I stumbled inside the store to grab those darn blueberries and hopefully my future husband. I wiped awkwardly at my rain-drenched hair, pushing it out of my eyes. Mascara probably puddled under my eyes or down my face, but it didn't matter. I wasn't going to see anyone I knew.

"Are you okay?"

I stiffened, pulling my purse tighter to my body before turning around to find Ray, grocery bags filled and draped from his hands and wrists. He looked dangerously handsome with his hair disheveled and concern in his alluring eyes.

I swiped at my soggy bangs in a weak attempt to appear somewhat presentable.

His forehead crinkled. "You're soaking wet. And shivering."

"Oh, no," I said cheerily. "It's nothing." I ran one finger under my eyelashes. A puddle of black goo came off onto it. Dropping my hand to my side, I straightened my shoulders and peered back up at my neighbor, who waited quietly.

Shifting my weight, I admitted, "I fell coming in." My skin prickled, and I felt like a complete ditz. I hurriedly added, "I didn't see a pothole."

A small, teasing smile lit his face. "An early bath?"

I pressed my lips together, staring at a few smudges on the white tile floor. "Just a little scratched up," my voice cracked.

"Are you going to be okay?"

Using my left hand, I grabbed a nearby cart. "I'll be fine." I pulled the cart to me, which was supposed to serve as a simple, easy gesture signaling the end of our discussion. Instead, the cart jerked in jagged motions every which way. I forced a smile. "The tires on this thing needed oiling."

Ray studied me. "Do you need anything? I can help—"

I tightened my grasp on the handle of the cart. "I'll take a hot bath when I get home."

Ray scanned the parking lot, then took me in. "Are you sure you're all right? You seem like you're in pain."

"I'm okay." My voice wavered, betraying me.

"You wince when you move. Let me give you a hand." He glanced at his watch. "I need to get on a WhatsApp call with family in India in three minutes, but as soon as I'm done, I can help you."

"Don't worry about that. Kind of late to call, don't you think?"

"Not late for them. We're fourteen and a half hours different." He glanced at my shopping cart. "You could finish up your shopping, and I'll help."

"You don't need to worry about—"

"You seem a bit shaken."

"I am actually—"

My purse strap slipped, and when I went to pull it back up on my shoulder, pain shot through me. I gasped.

His lips tightened with concern. "You're having a tough night, huh?"

I pushed at my bangs and flashed him a smile. "What makes you think that?"

He laughed.

I sighed. "Honestly, all I wanted to do was go home and have hot chocolate. Instead, I came here, and now look at me."

His gaze swept my body, sending flashes of heat over my chilled skin. "I think you look great."

I smiled a little. "You have very poor taste."

His return smile was heart-stopping. "Maybe. But I like hot chocolate. Even better," he went on, "I *have* hot chocolate. Want some?"

All I had waiting for me at home was an empty house and an empty bed since we drank all of my hot chocolate the other night.

"I could put on a fire to warm you up."

Maybe hot chocolate by a fire was just what I needed.

"Sure," I blurted. I was single. I was in charge of my life. I could use a little fun. "I just need to grab blueberries."

"You go do that, and I'll be right back to help you through the rain." He darted out the door.

I stared after him, suddenly feeling a little better. I still moved cautiously toward the produce. It didn't take any time to find the blueberries nestled beside the brilliant raspberries that, in truth, were far more inviting. But if blueberries would make Nick happy, it would be worth it in the long run.

I reached for a small container with my right hand, forgetting that it hurt. Sucking in pain, I switched hands and maneuvered carefully to the empty checkout. Ray already stood there, smiling at me and waiting patiently. I doubted he'd rush me across the grocery store in high heels.

"That was a short phone call." I set the berries down on the black conveyor belt.

"Told my family I had a neighbor who needed saving, and I'd give them more time on tomorrow's call."

A rush of warmth splashed through me. "Jeez." I set my purse on the small shelf with the credit card machine so I could open it with one hand.

Ray made a real effort to stay connected with his family. I liked that, even though twice a day seemed a little much.

"I help them mostly with tech issues," he explained. "I'm the oldest man in the house."

I talked to Tiffany often, but not to see how I could help her. Maybe I should . . . No, she'd hate that. She didn't really help me with what I wanted help with either. Her help was more about getting me to do things her way.

"I can't imagine having a set time to talk with family. All I really have is Tiffany. It sounds like a lot of family involvement."

He held open my purse for me. "They're family. That's what you do."

I went again to unzip my credit card holder with my right hand and winced.

"Let me see where it hurts," Ray said as the store clerk watched.

I lifted my right elbow up.

Ray cradled it in his hand tenderly. A softness spread through his face as he examined my forearm and elbow. "I think you're going to be okay. It doesn't appear to be broken. Just bruised. It might be uncomfortable for a few days." He let go of my arm, then stared at my shoes and shook his head. "No wonder you got hurt, wearing those."

My eyebrow lowered. "What's that supposed to mean?"

"They're nice," he said absently. "But not practical. I'm surprised most women don't break their neck wearing those things."

"Tell me about it."

His attention drifted up to me. "If you don't like wearing them, why do you?"

I slid my gaze away. "They're professional."

"And suicidal," he added.

"Okay, doctor," I teased.

He winked. "At your service."

The store clerk interjected with my total.

I stared at the card in my hand, figuring out how I was going to do this.

Ray held out his palm, indicating for me to give him my credit card. "Want me to do it?"

The checker smiled at us. "Have you two been married long?"

"No," we said in unison far too loudly.

"Not married," I reinforced.

I handed my card to Ray to let him make the transaction. After that, he put my card back into my purse and grabbed my bag.

We started out of the store. The rain had finally stopped.

Once outside, I snorted. "Married. Can you imagine? Me with Mr. Destiny."

He chuckled. "And I couldn't marry Ms. Western Romance Science with her belief in limited relationship rules and constructs."

I laughed at how ridiculous the notion was, and Ray joined me in the chuckle.

Marrying him was out of the question. It didn't matter that Ray was attractive, seemed truly kind, and apparently a good person. He was an entrepreneur who risked far too much with his app for my blood and wasn't stable yet. His risks had huge consequences, not only for him but for his nephews, and it seemed like maybe even for his extended family in India. That amounted to pressure!

Two younger Indian guys approached us. One sported a beard. The other was taller, thinner, and clean-shaven. Both attractive, with Ray's same dark eyes and hair.

"These are my nephews." Ray gestured to the taller one. "Sai."

He smiled widely at me.

"And Dhruv."

The bearded nephew bowed his head slightly.

"They live with me," Ray continued. "My sister—their mom—and their dad returned to India, but the boys flew over to go to college here."

"Wow, you're *really* into the family," I said slowly.

"Nothing is more important."

"Except that the Giants win the pennant this year," Sai said.

Ray laughed. "Right. We're going all the way this season."

"You guys are nuts," Dhruv interjected. "It's the Cubs."

Ray looked at me apologetically. "*Dhruv* means 'immovable,' and he likes to live up to the meaning. We usually make him stand in a corner when he talks that way, but . . ."

I smiled at them all, and asked, "What does 'Sai' mean?"

Sai puffed out his chest. "Divine."

His brother laughed. Ray grinned.

"And Ray—" I asked, curious.

"Reynesh," Sai helped me out. "Some people mistake his name to mean 'ray of light,' but it actually means 'one who's like a king.'"

I raised my brows. "King?"

Ray shrugged like there was nothing he could do about it, then slapped Dhruv on the back.

I watched their easy camaraderie, wondering what it was like to be a part of it. Ray was not only attractive, but also good with young adults.

The only thing lacking was the kind of security that came from success or a stable job. Oh, and the fact that he based everything on the stars.

Sai smiled and went on. "Uncle Ray said he was giving you a lift home. Want me to drive your car back for you?"

"What?" I asked.

Ray cleared his throat. "It seems, with your arm hurting, that it'd be a good idea. You seem a little dazed."

That was thoughtful. I surveyed them all, standing around, waiting to help. Ray had gone to a lot of work to make this happen.

Giving in, I held out my keys. "Be careful."

Sai smiled wide. "If we weren't, Ray would kick my—"

"And we're good," Ray interrupted.

The nephews grinned at each other, then headed toward the parked vehicles. "Which one is it?" Sai asked.

I pointed out my car.

The nephews waved as they hurried over to it, teasing each other and goofing around, making a lot of noise.

"They seem wonderful," I said.

Ray smiled at the antics. "They've been great."

"You seem to get along so well."

He shrugged as a burst of the boys' laughter came from my car. I glanced over to see them jostling each other. Smiling, I leaned on Ray's extended arm to steady myself.

"We have our moments," Ray acknowledged, lifting his arm to help me, "but we get through it. We love each other, you know?"

That sounded idyllic.

We headed toward his car, the noise from the nephews filtering back to us.

"I'm sure it's normal for them to be so loud."

"Very." He shrugged his shoulder. "I'm used to having family around. It'd be weird not to have noise. We are always doing something together— pizza night, or ordering an India feast from the local Indian restaurant, to celebrating Diwali or watching Bollywood movies."

"What kind of movies are you into?" I asked.

"Classics *Gangs of Wassaypur*, a gritty crime family feud drama, *Kisi Ka Bahai Kissi Jaan*, a silly action-drama romance, to the moving and inspiring and award-winning movie *Rang De Basanti*."

That sounded like a completely different world, one he was passionate about and felt a deep connection to. I sighed before saying, "I like noise too," I told him. "Kids, pets, all of it."

He glanced at me. "Yet your house is so quiet."

I lowered my head. "Divorce has a way of doing that."

But honestly, my marriage had actually brought the silence. Damion was always working, and I was always home alone. Once, I'd suggested getting a cat, but Damion didn't like pets. Too messy. Too noisy. So, we never even tried pets, let alone kids.

Of course, Damion was gone now.

"You should get a dog," Ray suggested.

I gave a start, shocked. "What are you, a mind reader?"

He laughed. "Nope. You will have a pet. It's written in the stars."

"You're joking."

His gaze stayed on mine, thoughtful and considering. "You seem like someone who should have a pet or a baby. That's all. Something tells me it's right for you."

"Was it the three-inch heels that told you that?"

His gaze slid to them. "The three-inch heels told me you don't like three-inch heels."

"They're in style," I said a little sharply as he stepped between two cars and moved toward a big black SUV. "And anyhow, with me trying to start a coaching business, I can't imagine having a dog. Too much work."

"Maybe a cat." Ray whipped out his car keys.

At the words, a coolness washed through my chest. I felt lighter, more buoyant.

"Yeah," I said softly. "Maybe a cat."

There was no one to tell me no anymore. I was free to do what I wanted.

I could get a cat. Holy heck!

He swung the car door open for me.

I grinned as I slid into the front seat of his SUV. Our eyes met.

"Maybe I will," I said thoughtfully. "After I get my business off the ground."

"Don't delay your happiness, and by the way, dogs are better."

I laughed, enjoying the fact that my new animal choice was completely my own.

It was hard not to notice that I was climbing into an extra-clean black car with an excellent stereo system that thumped into the dark velvet night.

As Ray drove, he kept his eyes fixed on the empty road. He leaned over and turned off the radio. "Can I ask you a question?"

"Sure?" I put my aching hand on the door handle.

His fingers tapped the steering wheel. "You have no problem standing up to me to tell me what you think, but you appear to flinch around your X."

The engine kicked into action and he stepped on the gas as I hunkered in my seat, listening to the click of the turn signal.

"Are you criticizing me too?"

He tapped the steering wheel. "See? No problem with me. Why do you retreat with your X?"

I shifted my weight. "You wouldn't understand."

He took his eyes off the road to look over at me, then snapped his eyes back to the road and maneuvered the car onto the main street. "I probably shouldn't have said anything. Sorry, it's not my business. Forget it."

The landscape changed to mostly dirt hills with an occasional house sitting on top overlooking the town.

"You don't understand Damion, and I don't want to talk about him. You're different. Let's leave it at that."

Silence filled the car until he asked, "How am I different?"

My gaze moved to him. "Really?"

"Yep. I'd like to know."

I pressed my lips together. "You're kind."

He cleared his throat. "I try to be." That acknowledgment filled the air between us. It was the truth. This neighbor of mine was a good man. Someone I might have fallen for in the past, but now I had rules to stick to. Rules that would keep me safe.

I was *not* going to get involved with an entrepreneur. That caused so many problems last time. I needed to keep those things in mind when talking to him because he could be distractingly cute.

"By the way," he said, pulling me from my thoughts, "if you need any help with graphics, handouts, business cards, that kind of thing, my nephews are awesome at it and would be glad to help you out."

I studied his face, not sure if he was trying to drum up business for his nephews or trying to help me, or both. I needed business cards, so it really didn't matter why he said that.

"How much do they charge?"

He winked at me. "For you, nothing."

I needed to be careful here. For one thing, I was starting to wonder if his being an entrepreneur actually had to be an obstacle to romance. That meant rewriting the rules, and that was bad.

I was also trying to stand on my own feet for the first time in my life. Was it okay to accept help? Did I have to pay for business cards to be an independent woman, or was it okay to let someone do me a favor?

Every time I'd been helped out before, I'd ended up feeling controlled by the helper. Damion, Tiffany.

I couldn't let that happen again.

"Can't do that," I said firmly. "I'd have to pay."

He tapped the steering wheel. "They need testimonials and experience, and you need a fun tagline."

I gave him a sideways glance. "Do you always get your way?"

He grinned. "Pretty much."

"Because you're so darn charming."

He considered this for a second. "No, it's because I have darn great ideas."

I laughed and settled deeper into the cushy leather seat. "Hmm. Okay, well, tell me a great idea for a tagline."

"You could do something like, 'Know the rules of successful relationships.'"

I stared at him. "That's really good, but I'm still paying."

He nodded. "Great. I'll have them draft up your cards tonight, and payment will be in brownies."

He smiled broadly, liking that idea.

I had been defeated, but had also won.

Ray pulled up to my house. "I'll get the door. Stay there."

I settled back in my seat, wondering if letting a man be a gentleman was dependent behavior or ladylike. It barely crossed my mind to wonder which I actually preferred.

Ray seemed so intent on taking care of me. I decided I'd err on the side of being ladylike. What did it hurt, letting him get my door, especially with my sore arm?

Before I could give that thought much more attention, the door opened and a commotion immediately started as the nephews gathered around Ray. Sai handed him my keys, while Dhruv joked about his brother's driving. He winked at me so I knew he was only kidding.

Ray shook his head and reached over to take the blueberries from my good hand.

I pulled them back from him. "I got it." I needed to do something for myself. But when I struggled with the front door to let us into my home, he ended up holding them again.

The second I walked into my house, I kicked off my shoes, asked Ray if he would mind putting the blueberries in the fridge while I changed my sodden clothes, and hurried up the stairs as quickly as I could.

The house creaked, shadows loomed, and a wave of shyness poured through me. Should I be going to a single man's house this late at night for hot chocolate? It all felt a bit like I was breaking the rules. Whose rules, I didn't know. So, I shook them off.

Maybe I had been married too long and wasn't used to the single life where I could stay up with a new person at nine o'clock at night. It was new not to worry about what anyone thought. I was free to do whatever I wanted. At the moment, what I wanted was to stay up at an attractive neighbor's house. The whole idea was liberating.

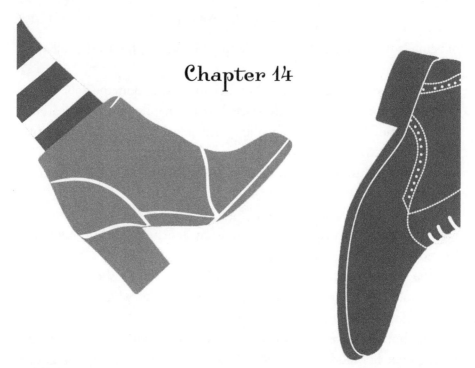

Chapter 14

One peek in the mirror told me liberation had its limits. Mascara was streaked under my eyes, and my hair was both flattened and wet. Not sure Ray would care—I was pretty sure Nick would have—but I set about taming the wildness anyway.

I quickly cleaned up, bandaged my scrapes as best as I could, pulled my damp, flattened hair back into a ponytail, and slipped into sweats. Since Ray was just my friendly neighbor, it didn't matter what I wore. Feeling free from the constraints of the professional clothes, I hurried down the stairs.

Ray, leaning a shoulder against my front door, glanced up. A slow smile touched his mouth. "You look much more comfortable." He pushed off the door. "Ready for hot chocolate?"

I laughed. "So ready." I felt happier than I had for a long time. Must be the sweatpants.

We crossed the road separating our houses and climbed his porch steps. Ray swept open his front door and ushered me inside.

I walked into the cleanest house I'd been in for a long time. An elaborate, highly detailed tapestry covered one entire wall. Gorgeous, colorful paintings in reds, blacks, and browns hung on the other wall, along with art showing images of goddess-like figures and animals with hard-angled lines.

Nothing was out of place, and the house sparkled. "Wow," I said as I glanced around. "So, this is your bachelor pad?"

Ray smiled with an amused grin. "Not what you expected?"

Busted. I gave an embarrassed smile. "Not what I expected."

He winked. "I'm full of surprises." He turned to his nephews. "Would you two mind designing a business card for Zoey?"

Sai shrugged. "What style?"

Ray led me deeper into his house to an upstairs home office. Two computers were set up across from each other, surrounded by piles of books and papers stacked everywhere.

Okay, so there was some mess. It made me feel better.

Sai plopped in front of one of the computers. Dhruv pulled over a chair for me.

"Thanks." I sat on the corner of the chair.

Sai's fingers poised over the keyboard, ready to dive in. "What style did you say you wanted?"

"Um . . ." I took a deep breath. "To be honest, I don't know anything about design."

Ray, who stood at the doorway behind us, nodded like that was normal. "Most people don't. That's why Sai and Dhruv are earning college degrees in it."

"Well, if most people are like me, then I guess you guys will earn a lot."

"That's the dream," Dhruv said.

Ray turned to me. "Teach Sai how to walk you through the process. It'll be good for him to get hands-on experience. Just tell him what you want."

Sai and Ray both stared at me, waiting. Their faces mirrored each other's—patient and a bit amused.

I blinked, taken aback as I realized they wanted to hear my ideas. Even though I'd just told them I had no clue what I was doing, they still thought my opinion mattered. I leaned forward, carefully resting my elbow on the desk so it didn't hurt my arm.

"Show her some examples," Dhruv instructed from over my shoulder, maybe sensing my panic.

Sai went back to the computer and pulled up a page full of designs.

We scrolled through myriad examples, down one page, to a second, and a third. My eyes glazed over—so many options.

From behind me, Ray's voice came quiet and calm. "Which ones are you drawn to, Zoey? Let the colors and shapes speak to you."

I let myself take in nothing but color and shape, like I had with Ray's artwork in the living room. The room was quiet as they waited patiently. Bold reds and electric greens. Hard, declarative fonts and thin, ornate scrolls. Thick lines and thin ones.

"That one." I pointed to a sample that was extra curly and fancy. It gave the feeling of lightness, fun, and professionalism all at the same time. It made me happy.

Ray sat a few inches away from me so he could see the screen too. "Excellent choice," he whispered, sending chills up my arm.

Even though he believed in stars and destiny, there was something really alluring about him.

Sitting up straight, I said to him, "Is your house always this fun?"

Ray picked a book off the floor and put it on the table. "Sometimes a lot more. Our house is Grand Central Station . . . from business meetings to friends to other Indians visiting."

"Wow. How can he—" I gestured toward Sai. "—work with all that noise going on?"

Dhruv, who had plopped in front of the other computer to play video games, said, "Sai rarely does any thinking."

Sai shook his head as he clicked images on the computer. "At least I *can* think."

Ray shrugged at his nephews' banter. "What can one do?"

"I really appreciate everyone's help." I looked straight at Ray. Our eyes locked. My chest pounded harder as I gazed into those eyes.

"What do you think of this design?" Sai broke into our spell. "It's just a mockup."

The design was fine, I guess. A bit angular, rough—maybe "masculine" was the word. I pressed my lips together, not sure what to say. Sai studied design, and Ray knew about business. I certainly didn't.

"It's nice," I offered.

Ray nodded his head to Sai. "The lady isn't loving it."

My eyes widened. "I didn't say that."

"Didn't need to." He moved to sit on the couch facing me. "This is *your* brand. Your company. It needs to work for you."

Sai turned back to the logo. "Is it the shape that isn't working?"

I shrugged my shoulders. "I really know nothing about this kind of thing." The room grew quiet. I shifted in my seat. "Well, um, it feels kind of masculine, doesn't it? Not warm and inviting like love should be."

Sai moved his mouse on the desk like he was taking orders.

Ray asked, "Soft orange? Light purple? Red? What's your favorite color?"

I provided input, and thirty minutes later, I had a dynamic logo of hearts and arrows in reds and gold. Every time I inspected it, a buzz shot through me. "That's *so*-o-o cool," I said.

Sai printed out a handful of cards on their high-tech printer. "Just to get you started," he explained. "Something to have on deck before you take the file to the printer."

I thanked them profusely and clutched the cards like they were jewels. Ray guided me down to the living room for the promised fire and hot chocolate. This night was giving me everything I needed and a few things I hadn't even known I wanted.

The boys stayed in the computer room, engaging in video games. Ray built a small fire in his fireplace, and I watched the snapping orange and yellow flames slowly growing. He gestured to his varied array of handmade blankets, each rich in detail and fabric. "Make yourself warm."

I gasped. "But I wouldn't want to ruin them."

"Don't be ridiculous. Blankets are made to be used."

Destiny Man had a practical side to him. I picked up a sage-green blanket draped over the couch and snuggled into it. It hosted an elaborate pattern of various shapes with an almost dizzying detail and beauty.

I dug deeper into the luxury of the soft blanket, inspired to surround myself with beautiful things too when I could afford to go shopping again.

Thumping and distant laughs spilled through the floorboards above us. Maybe the boys were wrestling? No matter what they were doing, Ray's house felt more like a home than my house ever had.

Watching the newly created flames, I asked, "So, who is 'family' back home?"

Ray wiped his hands as he made his way to the couch. "My ma, nani, and my sister."

The firelight played with his firm jawline, bringing out the sexiness of his midnight shadow. This man was so different from Damion. He really seemed to be there for his family, and also had something more to him. A depth, a deep understanding . . . a concern for the whole of humanity and at the same time, an easiness of being. "They must really rely on you."

He stopped walking toward the couch. "They do," he said softly.

"That's a lot of pressure financially," I said, thinking about how badly I was doing on that end.

"I used to work for my uncle, and he taught me how business works around here. I have a good foundation for business and local networking now after building it for years." He shrugged. "It's in my blood."

"With all that working, did you date much?"

An amused smile flittered across his lips. "You want to know about my dating life, huh?"

I glanced away from him, suddenly feeling really embarrassed. "I-I-I don't have—"

He laughed good-naturedly. "Teasing you. I took a girl out every now and then. Nothing serious. Too focused working for my uncle, building up my own thing, and school. Besides, I always planned on an arranged marriage, and my family kept me very busy helping them out."

"Helping . . . how?" I asked.

He grew quiet, his face paling. "I'm going to make our drinks. I'll be right back."

For some reason, I got the feeling he didn't want to talk about his family in India. Wondering if I was right, I watched him disappear into the kitchen. He seemed to be carrying a lot of weight and responsibility with his family. Maybe that was the plight of being the oldest.

My thoughts drifted to Tiffany and how much she had taken on over the years. I made brownies for us, but Tiff had done just about everything else. Made sure I had clothes as I grew, got me to school when Mom was passed out drunk. I always called my sister controlling, and she was. She didn't just help out a lot . . . she *took over*. But like Ray, she did it out of love. Or at least partly love. Also, partly because that's how she knew to be.

I snuggled deeper into the blanket's fluffy warmth. The room was done in a mixture of dark and light greens, maroon, and tan, rich and expensive, and yet comforting. I felt at home here.

A few minutes later, Ray returned, carrying two steaming mugs. He handed me one.

I reached up for it eagerly. The blanket slipped down my arm to my elbow, baring my forearm. His eyes followed the movement.

"Thanks," I said.

His eyes slid back up. "You're welcome."

He settled on the floor next to my couch, his chin drawn tight.

The silence between us extended to an uncomfortable length. "Was my inquiry into your family too personal? If so, I honestly didn't mean to intrude."

He had hesitation written all over his face like he wasn't sure if he should say anything. After a few more minutes, he said softly, "Just sometimes the pressure gets to me." He stared into the lively fire.

"Talking to the family twice a day would be a lot," I agreed.

He shrugged. "It's not so bad."

"And you have the nephews." I looked up at the ceiling toward the continued thumping.

His shoulders dropped. "They are fine."

"And work."

He pulled his knees closer to him. "And work," he repeated. I detected defeat in his tone.

I tossed over in my mind all that he was juggling and wondered how he could do it. I couldn't even seem to take care of myself well.

He took a sip of his drink. "When my dad died, my mom couldn't handle it here in the States. She eventually returned to India, where she had more support from her family, friends, and a culture she understood."

He seemed so sad when he spoke. It was hard to know how to comfort him. To buy time, I set my cup on the floor to cool. "I'm sorry to hear about your dad."

He shrugged again. "It's destiny. What can you do?" He contemplated the fire with a crease of a frown around his mouth.

"She must really appreciate having such a great son, and all you do for her."

He gave his head a little shake. "It's expected."

I leaned back against the couch cushions. *It's expected. It's destiny.* Maybe, but his beliefs didn't seem to protect him from the sadness of loss or the pressure of living up to others' expectations.

"How do you handle it all?"

Grief filled his eyes. "I just do it. Just like I do with all my life."

Just do it. That seemed to make him miserable, but I might need to have some of that attitude with my business and life. It mostly worked for him. Right now, I needed to think about Ray and get him off the subject clearly causing him so much pain. "You seem like a determined guy. How does that work with destiny?"

This time he put his cup down. He sat on the floor closer to the fire and faced me. "You never know what thing is destined and what is not."

That was confusing. "Do you mind me asking you more about that?"

"Not at all."

"Correct me if I'm wrong, but I thought one of the reasons India has so much poverty and homelessness is because of the established belief system. Each person is experiencing their karma, so it would be hurtful to interfere."

He shifted. "That's close enough."

"But you help out others."

He circled his finger along the rim of his mug. "It's best not to interfere with someone's life's journey. That's dangerous."

"So, why do you—" *help me?* I wanted to say, but couldn't.

He responded with a small, almost undetectable shrug. "What can I say? I'm American too." He studied me for a long moment, not with an angry, set jaw or furrowed brows, but more with curiosity. "Why are you so focused on this?"

I shrugged, but knew he wouldn't allow me to brush it off. "I'm curious about how you deal with two cultures and how you decide what you'll honor and when you'll chart your own way."

In a way, I was trying to do something similar—figure out the business culture and how to make my own way through this world.

He pulled his knees closer to his body again, thinking about my question. "American culture is a lot different than India's culture," he finally said. "I'm a mix of both. I might not have adopted all of the ideology of destiny when it comes to how I treat my fellow human beings. It didn't feel right in my body. Still, I certainly have adopted their ways and views on communities and caring about *our* families."

I stiffened. He was suggesting families weren't important to Americans—*again*. They were important. They were very important to me. They were at the top of my list, and I wasn't the only one.

Disneyland symbolized just how important family was to many people all over the United States. Families worked hard to take family vacations, to make sure their kids had a good education, could do sports and take dance classes. Parents sacrificed a lot for their kids.

"Americans care about their families."

He shook his head. "Indians value their community in a much more profound way. They're bound together in a community fashion."

"I care about my sister a lot. I'd do whatever I could to help her. Just because she's the only family I have."

"I wasn't suggesting—"

"It's easy to belong in *your* family and have a community because you have a big family. Mine is just Tiff and me. That's it. It's not a cultural value that we aren't more community focused. It's a family-you-were-born-into thing."

"What do you mean?" He leaned toward me like he wanted to calm me down.

I stared into the flames and said slowly, "My dad left me. My mom checked out with alcohol, and we had no other relatives that I know about." My voice shook, which I found highly irritating.

He waited for me to go on.

My chest bubbled with emotion. "Did you ever think you might be extra lucky to have a family? Some of us aren't blessed with that."

"Zoey, I didn't mean—"

"And," I rattled on, "I might be living without my sister, but developing my own identity is a good thing. Having too much of your identity wrapped up in your family or culture can be dangerous."

He flinched. "How's that dangerous?"

I stopped short, the words frozen in my mouth.

"How is it dangerous for you?" he added.

"If I had my identity wrapped up with my family more than I already do with Tiff, I'd never have a fighting chance to figure out who I am."

I thought about Tiffany's controlling and determined nature to remake me for my own good. "I'd always be sucked up in other peoples' wants and desires. I'd end up living the life they want me to live, not *my* life."

Ray shifted his sitting position on the floor, brows creased as he thought about my words. "You don't think a person can find their own identity and stay in the family environment?"

"I have no idea," I said honestly. "I just know I can't do it."

He leaned back, arms wrapped around his knees, and watched the fire.

The mystical firelight waved shadows on him. "What do you think about it?" I asked. "You must have some insight."

The crease around his lips deepened. "I was thinking sometimes it's hard to be an American and from India. The contradictions of cultures is a struggle for me to bridge. I value family and the community of India, but I also can see what you're saying. I wonder if I might have allowed my family expectations to overshadow me. I don't want to be too fixed in one way of existing in the world." The fire crackled. "This is a complex issue. I'm going to have to wrestle with it and think about what's best for me." He rubbed his forehead as though he was forcibly keeping something back.

I inched down onto the floor closer to him, feeling his pain. "It seems like something else is troubling you."

His jaw set tight as he stared at the floor.

Not knowing what to do with the silence other than wait, I nursed my drink until the cup was empty, then I set it back on the floor. I glimpsed over at my attractive neighbor.

He glanced at me briefly but then avoided my eyes. "My family is arranging my marriage."

My chest tightened. Ray was going to become a married man to someone clear across the world.

His shoulders bent over as though the reality of what he was about to do pressed on him. "In a few months, I'm expected to fly out there."

My fingers held on to the blanket. "So soon?" This time it was my turn for my voice to crack.

I shifted to stare at the fire. What he was facing was heavy. Our lives and cultures were so different, yet maybe we both understood how a family can consume a person.

"Do you sometimes feel smothered?" I asked.

He observed me with soulful eyes. "Yes."

That we had in common.

"Is your arranged marriage part of that?" I whispered.

"When duty calls," he said so quietly that I needed to lean in to hear, "it must come first."

I didn't understand.

He must have sensed my confusion. "The good of the whole is more important."

I unbent my knees and stretched my legs. "That matters to you."

"It's at the center of my life." His voice fell flat, but his hand inched closer to mine.

"What's at the center of yours, Zoey?" he asked quietly.

I thought about my life, which had no center, just barely defined edges of desperation. The thing I wanted at the center—family, a loving husband, lots of kids—loomed as far away as it ever had.

Fear lay at the center of my life—a lack of control. And a deep sense that I wasn't up to the task of starting a coaching business and wasn't capable of taking care of myself.

"Starting my coaching business, of course," I said firmly, as if it was a perfectly reasonable center.

Ray pressed his lips together, not satisfied with my answer. Like Tiffany. Like Damion. Like myself.

He pushed himself to his feet and said, "Well, we'd better make it happen at the networking meeting tomorrow. It starts bright and early, so you'd better get your rest."

He towered over me. I scrambled to my feet, startled at this quick change of subject. I winced from the pain the sudden movement caused my arm. I placed the blanket on the couch.

Ray walked with me to the front door. "People there are serious about business and are focused on referring to one another. I'd love for you to join in. With me. Want to?"

Was that a flicker of a smile? The meeting had to be the one I had told Nick I would attend, and Tiffany said it wasn't big enough to be worth my time.

"It's seven a.m. sharp."

I hadn't realized it was so early. "Seven a.m. is hardcore." I stared at him and his beautiful eyes.

He stepped closer to me, causing my heart to pound again triple-time speed. "Business is hardcore. You have to hit it strongly if you're going to make it work." He winked at me. "I'll buy you breakfast."

And with that, I left for home.

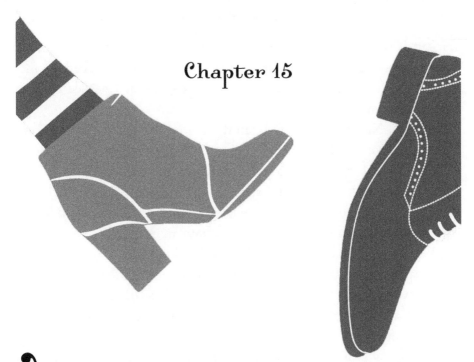

Chapter 15

I stared at the mirror in the early morning, thinking this wasn't me. Being up before the sun wasn't me. The heels weren't me. The presentations-in-front-of-business-people wasn't me. None of it was me. But I was reinventing myself.

It was time for the new me to take myself to the networking meeting and continue building this new life. I lifted my arm to do my hair. Intense pain shot through it. I winced. I tried again and again until sucking in air from the pain, I admitted it wasn't going to happen. A ponytail and a professional smile would have to do. I'd put on a good show like Tiffany always did, and Nick . . . and Ray, in his own way.

Twenty minutes later, I parked outside the orange restaurant. Light had finally trickled through as the air hung still. Despite the stillness, my heart pounded. I was getting so much practice with a racing heart lately that not exercising wasn't much of a problem. I was most definitely experiencing the effects of a workout.

The yellowish light of the rising sun spilled into my car, inviting me into the day as I shook with nervousness. I was on my own—no sister to lean on. That was good. That was what I wanted. I just needed to get my body to stop this uncontrollable shaking. My arm still throbbed, so that didn't help, but I needed to be professional about this. I needed to learn how to chart my own course.

Besides, Nick was going to be in there. I put on my game face, committed to make up for yesterday. He liked confident women. Time to prove *that* was the real me, not the baggage-riddled newly divorced woman.

A bird started up a cheerful song as a dark shadow moved across my window. Before I could figure out what was going on, a bang sounded on my car. I screamed and came face-to-face with an intruder.

Ray gazed down on me with a big goofy grin.

Gasping for breath, I released a chuckle of relief, noticing how handsome he was in his polo shirt that fit too well and his dark, alluring features. Still rattled from my fright, I shakily undid my seat belt with my left hand and attempted to open the door.

Seeing my struggle to maneuver with one hand, he pulled the door open for me and laughed.

"You scared me, Ray."

That made him chuckle more. "It's not hard to do."

I gave him a half eye roll and leaned to grab my purse. I had to stop myself halfway to the console. My right arm wasn't in working condition for even that easy task. Switching my position to grab it put me at a wrong angle, leaving me confused and increasingly embarrassed as to how to nab that dang thing with my left hand.

I grew hot, feeling Ray standing over me, watching.

"Sleep well?" he asked.

I wasn't going to tell him how snippets of our conversation played in my head repeatedly. Nor the fact that the later the night became, the more I thought about what it would be like to curl up in his arms, where I could just be me. We would talk and share ideas and be okay with our differences and maybe even be energized by them.

Not able to extract my purse, I climbed out of the car without it. The plan was to go around the vehicle and snatch it from a direct angle. Once I stood, I straightened my suit jacket and noticed that Ray had moved in the way of the door.

I remembered he asked about sleep. My sleep. "The chocolate worked wonders. How about you? Sleep well?"

He moved me aside, leaned into my car, and picked up my purse. "Not really."

Did he have a hard time sleeping for the same reasons I did? Did he think about holding me? Did he wonder what it would be like to kiss me? I was being silly. He was going to marry someone else. Of course he didn't think of me that way.

He handed me the purse.

"Thanks," I said with an unsteady laugh. "I can't seem to do my hair, open or shut doors, or grab my purse because of the bruise on my elbow. I only just managed to drive here with one arm . . . good thing I don't drive a stick shift."

With a gallant bow, Ray said, "I'll get all your doors today."

I burst into laughter.

He gave me a wink. "M'lady, are you ready to go find clients?" He gestured with his hand toward the door of the restaurant.

I squinted into the rising sun and nestled my purse closer to me. Up ahead, a group of professional people strolled toward the meeting, relaxed faces, buttoned-up suits and high heels, prepared to win.

Well, today was going to have to be about baby steps. I wasn't at the "at ease" level yet. I was going to have to work myself up to that. At least I had Ray as my mentor.

He walked quietly at my side as we headed to the restaurant. I had no clue what he was thinking, but he wore a severe expression. Despite that, my shaking had stopped. It was nice just being with him.

When we came to the restaurant door, a big thick oak one, Ray hefted that thing open like it weighed nothing. I held my gaze at him a tad too long, and stumbled in the process.

He grabbed my left elbow, steadying me. "Careful."

When we stepped inside, I stopped short, scanning the mass of businesspeople crammed in an entry in front of a larger meeting room. There must have been thirty people, all in suits and ties and tight skirts and perfectly coiffed hair, just like me. Well, except for the hair part. I'd learned how to fit in. At least on the outside, I blend in, mostly. I hoped.

"Whoa," I murmured. "It's really crowded."

Ray reached out his hand for my purse, which I handed over. He tucked it under his arm and moved ahead of me. "I'll get you through safely." He held out his hand. "Keep your injury close to you."

Laughing, I took hold of him, feeling like, at least for a moment, I could relax. Just for a second, since my life was messy. I still had to persuade this group I was a serious businesswoman—but right this second, I had a gentleman clearing the way for me.

As he guided us through the crowd, he finally stopped in a space away from everyone else. "My younger sister used to break her arm often in gymnastics. I'm used to opening doors and cutting up dinners."

He gave me a wink like we were sharing a secret conspiracy, but my face fell.

I could hardly even put toothpaste on a toothbrush that morning. I hadn't even thought about the troubles I'd have conquering breakfast food. Crap!

Ray chuckled, his dark brown eyes dancing. "It'll be okay."

Easy for him to say. He had a functioning arm. "I'll start with coffee," I said. "I only need a couple of fingers for that."

Ray laughed. "Sure. I'll get it for us."

Within sixty seconds, I was drinking liquid courage, standing next to my chair. Ray chatted with a group of men a few feet away, doing the networking thing.

Armed with caffeine, I spotted a lady alone dressed in a sparkly gold top and black slacks. She seemed to have her act together and might be someone it would be good to know. I approached her with a warm smile like I had seen so many others do.

She smiled back. "Hi, I'm Elizabeth. And you are?"

I cleared out my throat with a cough. "Zoey. I'm new."

"Welcome. What do you do?"

My prepared speech flashed through my head, and I dove in. "I'm a relationship coach helping people form the romantic connections they always wanted based on the principles of science."

Her eyes widened. "Really? Science?"

She watched me through a few beats while I called on all my training and manuals, and addressed the objections I could see forming in her mind.

"Um, yes. They have done a lot of research about relationships and what works and what doesn't." I paused to let it land, like I had done during my speech. I added, "And the solutions are not what you would think."

"Such as?"

I explained some of the research by John Gottman and what elements predicted divorce. I was on a roll. She leaned closer to hear better. I smiled inwardly. *I was doing it.*

Ray approached us. "Elizabeth, you should work with her." He joined our space. "Zoey has amazing insights, and she'd really help you."

He had no idea how I was as a coach, really. *I* had no idea how I was as a coach. Despite that, he seemed to know how to be "very put together," as Tiffany would put it. Words spilled from him like silk.

Elizabeth's eyes narrowed as she took me in. "Are you saying your app isn't the right choice for me?"

He leaned over to me and whispered loudly enough that she could hear him, "Elizabeth is a lawyer and naturally questions everything."

His breath was warm, minty, and gave me chills. He positioned himself to face her full-on. "She can teach you how to manage that relationship so when you find someone through my app, you'll be ready to make it work well."

Elizabeth's eyes widened from his bold claim, implying she didn't know how to manage relationships.

"Zoey's very straightforward, which you need."

A flicker of approval flashed through Elizabeth as she settled her gaze on me. It was almost like she appreciated being called on her stuff.

I wrestled with the idea of being called straightforward. That was something I was working toward—wanted to achieve—but I held back and took direction from others too much.

There was a long drawn-out pause between Ray and Elizabeth.

Ray winked at me, and I smiled bashfully back at him.

Elizabeth tipped her chin out. "Well." She eyed me up and down. "I'm going to trust you, Reynesh. It better work out. I know where to find you."

He shrugged. "If it is meant to be." He sounded totally at ease.

Destiny seemed like a very relaxing philosophy for him.

The lawyer flipped open her binder. "If Reynesh says I should hire you, let's skip that exploratory session and just do it."

My head spun. A lawyer. Me, coach a lawyer?

"What are your rates?"

Worse and worse. How much *should* I charge? I'd been thinking of charging twenty-five dollars an hour, but . . . I eyed the lawyer, then glanced at Ray.

He lifted a brow, almost challenging me.

"Seventy-five dollars a session," I blurted out.

She nodded like that was no big deal. Confidence zoomed through me, and I lifted my head a little higher. Ray donned an amused smile, like he enjoyed this back-and-forth game of business even if he wasn't the one being bought.

"Where's your office?" Elizabeth, the lawyer, *my first paying client,* asked.

I gave her my home address. So far, I had only coached my one client, the massage therapist, at her house. My house would have to be it, then.

Elizabeth flipped through her mobile's calendar app. "I have time at two today."

I was flabbergasted by her efficiency, and deeply impressed.

"That would work fine." I tried to sound equally efficient. Or at least like I was able to keep up.

She snapped her book shut. "Talk soon. I can't wait to see how you're going to straighten my love life out for me and find me a man who isn't intimidated."

"Me too," I said.

I fished out one of my new business cards and handed it to her with a broad smile, even though I had no idea how I was going to do that. I needed to trust the science. I'd crash-study "intimidating women" as soon as I made it home.

Elizabeth clicked away on her heels—she was clearly much better on them than I. I turned to Ray and I lifted my hand in a fist of triumph.

"One . . . reeled in," I said kind of hesitantly. "Thanks for the bait."

"You were a great fisherman," he countered, then held out his arms for a hug.

I thought of my ridiculous daydreams in the dark last night. Of holding Ray. Of having him hold me. A hug right now would not be anything like what I'd been dreaming about, but it would be really, really nice.

I went to him.

Ray pulled me to him. He rested his chin on top of my head and just held me there. He didn't seem to care about the other people around.

I melted under his touch. The hug was better than I had imagined. Everything about him was better. When we stopped hugging, I stumbled backward, feeling lightheaded.

My injured hand hit against a solid mass of body behind me. I winced, sucking in a breath as I fought back tears from pain.

"Oh-h-h," I groaned, unable to find words.

Ray reached out to steady me, but so did other strong hands.

Nick.

"Hey." I grew hot. Bumping into him hadn't been in my plan for reconnecting with him.

"Hi." He spoke with a calm voice, but eyes slightly wide.

"I brought you blueberries," I blurted.

With his brow furrowed, Ray turned away and held out his hand to someone who was walking by.

I focused on Nick and gave a him a hesitant smile. "They're in the car."

"Okay?" His tone implied I was really strange.

"Yesterday, you said at the restaurant that you loved blueberries," I explained in a rush. "So, I thought it'd be nice to get you some," I finished lamely.

"Oh," he said.

I stood there, my right arm bruised and my tummy roiling. "Oh" wasn't what I'd expected or wanted. Neither was feeling stupid.

I wasn't sure what reaction I thought I would get, but I certainly wanted more than an "Oh." I had hurt my arm for those blueberries. I had run in high heels through the pouring rain. I passed up those beautiful red raspberries so he could have the blueberries, and all I got was an "Oh?"

Probably because he was tired or I caught him off guard.

I pulled my purse strap back up on my shoulder with my left hand and shifted my weight in my dang heels.

As we stood there in silence, a lady in a dark business suit tapped a fork against a glass. "Let's get this meeting started," she called out loud and clear.

This stirred the room into action as people scurried to their seats. Nick nodded goodbye to me before quickly weaving through the crowd to sit between two extremely attractive women.

I watched him join another conversation with his easy smile as the noise of the meeting escalated. Not wanting to watch him anymore, I briefly entertained the idea of bolting out of the meeting and heading back home, where I'd stop making a fool of myself with my silly ideas.

A hand on my good arm drew my attention over to Ray. Although he'd shaken hands with someone else and talked to a few people, he never moved far away. He nodded toward our places. "Shall we head to our seats? I'll clear the way, if you'd be so kind as to follow me."

That made me giggle as I scooted around the chairs Ray pushed in, like a true gentleman, so I could make it to my spot more easily. He was thoughtful. Just friends. Nothing but friends. I studied his thick jet-black hair. It would be fun to run my fingers through it. Of course, I would never do that.

The president walked over to Ray. "When are you leaving us?"

My spine straightened. *Leaving?*

"In two months."

I listened harder. And why was I hurting so much at the thought?

"Are you coming back?"

Ray nodded. "Yeah, but I think I need to stay in India for a while. If that's too long to keep my spot, I certainly understand."

Two months? His business was here. It never dawned on me last night in our conversation that he would have to go to India. A sinking feeling pressed on me. I didn't want to think about it.

"We'll keep your spot reserved," the president assured him. "Don't you worry, you're too valuable to the group."

They walked away together, so I couldn't hear anything else, nor did I want to. What I had heard was plenty. For some reason, I was shaking. I slowly lowered myself into my seat.

A few minutes later, the president called the meeting to order. Ray hustled back, slipping into his seat like a smooth gust of air.

I swallowed a lump in my throat.

He reached out and squeezed my left hand, then glanced away from me.

I swallowed again. "That must be exciting for you!" I said too loud, bringing glances from around the table. "What's she like?" I asked, even though it didn't matter. It made no difference. It was his life—his choice, not mine.

His jaw strained tight for a drawn-out second. His face reddened. "Zoey, it's my destiny. We both just have to accept that."

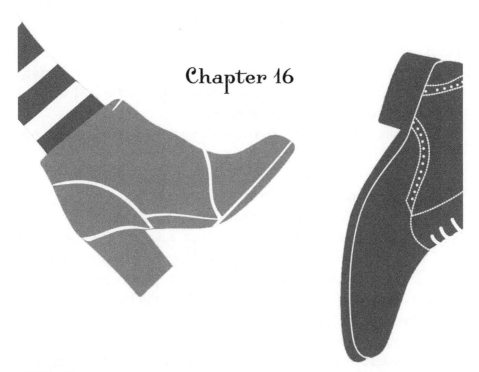

Chapter 16

The Networking Professional Incorporation meeting was a chamber meeting on steroids. The male energy to conquer pulsed through the event. I huddled in my chair like a scared mouse not wanting to be devoured by the lions.

I should like it, right? I wanted a strong male as a financially stable partner with a regular job, and who wasn't so obsessed with his newest dream that he didn't have time for me or the children.

But everything here was about competition, and I didn't know how to do that. Competing seemed to be the name of the professionals' game.

Damion always talked about taking down the other guy. Tiffany acted like she had to dress for war and a game plan. Nick was about strategy and connections. Ray—well, he didn't do that. He trusted everything was going to work.

Mr. Destiny sliced up my egg and sausage.

As the president gave her introductory remarks, Ray went on in a low murmur. "I forgot to tell you this group only allows one person per industry."

The president's rambling continued, but her words faded in the background as I realized the one person I felt safe with in this room was being pitted as my competitor.

I set my fork down on my plate, unable to hold it steady. Keeping my eye on my fork, I said, "I shouldn't be here. I shouldn't have come." I paused. "I don't want to step on your toes."

He shook his head. "No, you *should* be here. We aren't competitors. We're allies."

I wanted to believe him, liking the sound of us being allies. Maybe we could work together and help each other out as he was saying. But, of course, he was leaving. To get married. To meet his destiny.

Ray leaned in closer. The scent of his rich, spicy cologne washed over me. "We go after different crowds of people," he whispered, causing the hairs on my arms to rise and making me think he was pondering our situation as much as I was. "If you want to join this group, think you'd fit, and that it would be good for you, we can talk to them about it after the meeting."

That sounded like the perfect thing for me to do.

The president continued reading with a clear voice vibrating through the room—commanding, but in a gentle way. I peeked around the rectangular table at the people of all shapes, sizes, and ages. Most were well put together and gave her their full focus. I wanted to learn how to do that.

She mentioned the dates of a business fundraiser for a local charity. Ray flipped open his binder, as did a handful of others, to jot down the date and place. The event had something to do with golfing, which I knew nothing about, but maybe it wouldn't hurt for me to help out. I'd like to help the local kids club.

The meeting transitioned into a five-minute training where the presenter claimed, "Relationships are the foundation of business."

If business was based on relationships and there was a solid science to relationships, that meant I just had to learn the rules for business. I sat up straighter. Suddenly doing business didn't seem as daunting. Until I realized, one by one, each person in the room was sharing a one-minute presentation on his or her company.

This time, I needed to focus on working the room like Nick said, and not forget to give the call to action like Ray said, and speak with confidence like Tiffany said. No problem.

I stared at the cold food on the plate in front of me. As I waited for my turn, I learned from one businessman how I needed to clean my carpet or creepy crawly things would wander all over me. I grabbed the carpet guy's business card when the stack passed by me.

Ray took notes.

The chiropractor showed how my neck would give out under the pressure of bad posture. More notes appeared on Ray's notebook pages. I simply sat up straighter.

Finally, after watching Ray's intense notetaking, I tipped nearer and whispered, "What are you writing down?"

He whispered back, "Some general ideas of how I might be able to help them."

This man was so good. "I think your destiny is helping people."

He smiled, his eyes on the next person standing. "I could think of worse destinies."

Unable to hold back a chuckle, I received a warning glance from Nick across the table. I stifled my laugh and plastered on my listening face. A young blonde woman spoke about chemicals in most makeup that were harmful to our health. No notes from Ray, but I scribbled down her name, wanting to learn more. Each speaker mentioned problems I didn't know I had, and I needed to address right away.

By the time the introductions were two people away from me, my heart pounding increased a hundredfold. The man next to me zoomed through his spiel superfast. I didn't hear a word he said.

All eyes shifted onto me. I cleared my throat, forgetting every word I was going to say. Sweat dotted my brow. Panicked, I darted a glance over to Nick for guidance.

He winked.

My throat tightened. That made me more nervous. He'd be sure to tell me what I needed to improve later. Hopefully, that would include the answer for how not to be so nervous.

"Science. Remember, you're about science," Ray whispered up at me.

His words snapped my brain back into gear. "I'm Zoey Woodland." My voice came out weaker than planned. "I'm a relationship coach."

A couple of people in the group bent over their papers to jot down my information. I looked directly at Ray, drawing strength from him. "I help people find happiness."

He gave the nod, letting me know I was on the right path.

I pulled my gaze from him and glanced at various people who listened and maintained eye contact. "I'm standing here to tell you, you can have the love you desire. We all can. All we have to do is learn the science."

Time to work the room like Nick had advised. I surveyed the group, focusing just above each set of eyes that watched me. "I can teach you that science."

With that, I was done, and I sat, knowing I did pretty well. Well enough to get me in the club. I hoped.

"Good job," Ray said loudly enough everyone could hear him as he stood. "Thank you, Zoey." He worked the room, giving attention to each person, but unlike me, it seemed like he actually saw them and connected. When he got to me, I might have imagined it, but it seemed like he paused just a second or two longer.

"She's a guest today, and I'm glad she's here to give us that message of hope. I do believe she's right. We can all have beautiful love relationships. At my company, we take some of the complicated science out of it. We do that so you don't have to work so hard at it in the beginning . . ."

Ray continued his flawless enticing performance that, of course, outshone me again and undercut me again. Maybe I needed to focus and stop shaking. Ray did back me up mostly, so maybe that would be enough for the powers that be to let me in this group.

Nick gave me a thumbs-up.

Okay. A thumbs-up for what? All I was doing was sitting quietly. Meekly, in fact. Earlier I'd been chatty and outgoing and friendly, and I'd gotten the cold shoulder. I found Disneyland Dad confusing.

The meeting continued with people giving their spiels, followed by in-depth presentations about two businesses. After that, the table transformed into enthusiastic round-robin testimonials about one another's work and giving out referrals.

An attractive blonde waved at Ray. "I want to give a shout-out to Reynesh. He's amazing."

My eyes flickered away from her, annoyed for no reason.

Ray blushed.

"He set me up with the most fantastic astrologer who taught me who I am and what makes me tick. He dove into what would be the best kind of match for me." She clapped her hands together. "I'm so excited to let destiny work for me. It's worth every dime."

As Miss Bubbles spoke, I continuously shifted in my chair, unable to get comfortable. My discomfort had nothing to do with the fact Miss Bubbles was flirting with Ray or the fact that she ogled him and his face colored.

Naturally, other women found Ray attractive. Any guy who looked like Ray would draw women. That was just how women were. It didn't matter. He was going to be jumping into an arranged marriage soon enough. In fact, really soon, so these women had no chance, and neither did I.

But that fact didn't stop the women from flocking around him once the meeting ended. It reminded me of the chamber meeting speech night. He was a chick magnet.

Witnessing his allure made my stomach cringe. I tossed my napkin on top of the cold food I hadn't eaten and stood, searching for the president lady to find out how I could join this circus.

I spotted Nick out of the corner of my eye, chatting to the makeup lady. Maybe I could speak to him after they finished. I continued to scan the room for the president. When a group of people moved, I saw her still up at the head of the table.

I weaved between the lingering businesspeople with my hurt arm tucked in safely to my torso. When I approached, the president looked over at me.

I smiled. "Hi. I'd love to find out how I could join."

She squinted at me as she shoved papers into a binder. "You and Reynesh sure went at each other this morning in your introductions." Her eyes flittered over to him, lingering way too long. "It's *clear* you two are competition, so there's really no space for you." She paused, then added, "Sorry."

There went my sense of belonging. The noise of the busboys stacking up the dirty dishes into bins echoed louder. Heat rose on my cheeks. Today was a bust.

"Could she be my substitute when I'm gone?" Ray maneuvered through several people to join our conversation.

The president pressed her lips together. "I'll talk to the membership committee about it, but I doubt it."

The shaking I so proudly controlled in the meeting found me again.

Ray put his hand on my shoulder. The weight of his warm touch seeped into me. "You can be my substitute. Don't worry. We'll get you in one way or another."

I shook my head. "No, it's okay. She's right. I'd be stepping on your toes. Someone has to watch out for you."

Someone tugged on Ray's sleeve. He glanced at the waiting brunette, and back at me.

I waved him on and stumbled backward right into Nick. Again. My eyes widened, taking in his startled face. "Sorry."

I struggled with all my might not to cry. With my arm hurting, I was becoming way too sensitive, or maybe the weight of not getting in bothered me far more than it should.

He paused. "Are you okay?"

"Fine," I snapped.

"No, really. What's wrong?"

I sighed. "I didn't get into the group." I peeked up at his brown eyes. "I really wanted to."

"What? Why not?"

Because I am not good enough, I wanted to say, but managed to keep some pride and not say it. "Ray."

His brow crinkled. "What?"

"Same industry. There can only be one person here per industry, right? And Ray is a favorite. He belongs here."

Nick shrugged. "That's the way business goes sometimes. Ray is a favorite. Well, a favorite in many places."

He glanced over at Ray. His jaw tightened just for a second, then he glanced back at me. "You'll get better. You're all about the rules, right? Learn the rules. Win the fight." His gaze slid down to my feet. "At least you're wearing heels this time."

I stared at my feet, remembering how he had criticized my flats. "I listened to you."

That pleased him.

"That's a smart thing to do."

He tipped my chin up and he scrutinized me. "We can still see each other."

What a weird comment. I took a step away from him, feeling like I was being disloyal to Ray somehow, even though he was engaged, and I was just a friend.

"Want to get together tomorrow night for a date?"

I just told him I wasn't accepted in the group. I didn't belong, and he was asking me out. Was he feeling sorry for me? He waited for me to answer without expression. He didn't seem to care that my arm hurt or couldn't figure out what to say when I was presenting, so I doubted that. Maybe he liked women who struggled to get their act together. Perhaps he liked rescuing.

"Uh . . ."

"I have a good feeling about us."

Nick, the guy who did charity events, the guy who everyone apparently liked, the man who was established in his career, said he had a good feeling about us.

Maybe I was just reading too much into something that wasn't there.

Ray stood in the distance waiting to walk me to the car. My neighbor, for all his smiles and positivity, was not my future. He was someone else's future. Nick was mine, the consummate professional, who loved kids and had a good feeling about us.

I yanked my gaze off Ray's back and smiled into Nick's face. "Sure. I'd love that."

———

Rushing into my house, I immediately took in piles of dishes, trash, and dirt on the floor. Crap! My place looked more like a tornado had spun through it than a professional spot to meet clients. I dropped my purse by the front door and jumped into a panic cleaning sprint, doing my best with only one arm. Elizabeth would be here in less than an hour.

When I made it to the mirror in the bathroom, I couldn't help wondering if Nick liked me because I listened to him. Like I was a good reflection of him. I stared at my reflection with wide eyes and slightly frizzy hair. Maybe not.

I dashed back into cleaning, but all that came to a screeching halt when my doorbell chimed. My eyes darted to the clock. The lawyer who ate people for breakfast had arrived ten minutes early.

"I can do this. I can do this," I said under my breath, serving as my own cheerleader, and threw trash into the overspilling can.

Just because Elizabeth knew the law and courts didn't mean she knew people. And I'd read books about relationships—lots of books.

My mouth had suddenly become very dry as I rushed to answer my future. Hands sweaty, I opened the front door to the star lawyer decked out in her suit and high heels that boosted her up another five inches. She hovered over me like the Leaning Tower of Pisa.

Taking no time for greeting, she barged into my house like a player on the football field aimed for a tackle. Anger radiated off her with such an intensity, I shook in her wake.

The coaching school never covered how to deal with really ticked-off lawyers, but my dad had been angry a lot, and I had managed to settle him down when I was extremely little. My mom used to call me her secret weapon whenever she sent me into a room to climb on his lap and ask to be read a story, or to ask if he wanted a cookie.

He'd glare at me with his tight jaw clenched, and I'd watch him back, just as stubborn. More often than not, it worked. Not enough to make him stay with us . . . but that was a different matter.

The first step was not to address the anger head-on. Give the person space to calm down.

"Come on in." I gestured wide for her to find a seat in my mostly clean living room. It only lacked a dusting—which, judging by how angry she was, I doubted she would notice.

Her eyes narrowed.

My neck throbbed.

"You have no idea what kind of day I have had. I'm going to kill someone."

Hoping that someone wasn't me, I slowly followed her over to my couches. Taking a seat across from her, I grabbed the paper and pen I'd set out, and asked, "Why don't you tell me about it?"

She plopped down on the edge of my couch and set her briefcase on my wood floor with a bang. She forced a smile. "Oh, I'm sorry. I didn't mean to take it out on you. Sometimes it's unreal what happens in these court cases. Justice is an illusion the legal system likes to sell."

I glanced at the basic coaching questions. None of them were going to work. She was mad. I needed to focus on what was going on for her and not the justice system. That would be a distraction from helping her.

Pulling my legs up under me on the couch to radiate calmness, I flipped over my useless paper. I had to wing this.

"I can tell."

She nodded. "Okay, how are you going to help me?"

Good question. I cleared my throat and thought about how I helped my friends over the years. "Why don't you tell me what you'd like to work on? Do you want to talk more about what upset you? Or would you like to talk about relationships and what you want?"

She stiffened. "You're going to turn this on me?"

Okay, that hadn't worked. Maybe start with something she could agree with. "Well," I said, my fingers playing with the tassels on my couch pillow, "Ray said you're working too much."

"Of course I am. That's part of being successful."

I brushed my hand along the pillow. "Is it part of the problem, too?"

She shifted in her seat, clearly uncomfortable. "Don't know," she finally said in a voice so soft, I strained to hear it.

I waited to give her time to think and be with that.

She flopped her hand on the couch cushion. "Oh, this is hard. I'm a professional woman. I'm successful. I shouldn't have these types of problems."

Something had made her hesitant. I decided to stay with it. "Everyone has problems."

I sensed her stifling a growl.

I gave a weak chuckle. "It can't be that bad."

She crossed her arms. "I'm tired of being alone. I want to be in a relationship, but I don't know how."

Me and you both, I wanted to say. "What kind?" I asked.

"A romantic one." Her tone held a "duh" quality.

Well, two could play that game. "There are a thousand different kinds of partnerships to have, and to have what you really want, you have to define it."

That information I spouted sounded really good. I should take notes.

"He needs to be successful in business, but not for the reasons you think." Her eyes narrowed. "I don't want him to be threatened by my career."

I fiddled with my pen. "Makes sense to me." Staring down at my blank paper, I stewed on what could be the cause of all this intense pain. "Have people been jealous of you your whole life?"

She froze. "Yes."

"You were always better at things than they were," I guessed.

Her hands clenched together. "Most of the time. I played volleyball and did student council and debate. I did do a lot."

"And you were still alone."

She swallowed and nodded.

I thought about Damion and my sister. How they were super talented, super knowledgeable people, always at the top of the pack, but that made them all about the performance. They could never just *be*.

"People think it's good to be talented," I said quietly. "It's what society wants. But honestly, I think it must be lonely."

Her eyes swept up to mine. "Very. But I like being on top. I don't want to give it up."

"So, what do you want?"

"A guy *and* a career. Is it possible?"

"Well," I said thoughtfully, "tell me about this ideal guy."

Elizabeth took the question seriously and described how her partner would be tall and strong. What he was like—a man in charge, driven, career-focused, who didn't let anything get in his way, and loved who she was the same way.

A power couple was the dream. In a weird sort of way, it seemed like she was describing Damion.

Disturbing.

Before she left, in much better spirits, Elizabeth hugged me a bit too tight and handed me a check with a five-dollar tip.

"Thank you." I waved the check from the doorway.

"See you next week at the same time." She took several steps toward her car, but spun toward me. "You're a miracle worker."

Huh. I guess I did well, with Ray's help. Three cars were at his place. Maybe they were his nephews' friends. Or people there for his work.

Stepping back into my house, I took one last peek at Ray's home for no reason at all as I thought about how to celebrate my new client and upcoming date. I was finally moving the pieces of my life into place. I put on hot water for tea.

A few minutes later, I sat at my kitchen table with hot peppermint tea, taking in the stunning landscape of Murrieta through the window. The doorbell rang. I took another sip of my tea. Maybe those cars at Ray's house were traveling salesmen and not business.

Someone switched from ringing the doorbell to pounding. I set my cup on the kitchen table, not daring to move. I definitely did not want to answer the door.

A male voice called out, "Zoey, I know you're in there."

A shiver ran down my spine.

Damion.

Oh, my gosh. Why wouldn't he stop coming over? I never saw him this much when we were married. This was getting ridiculous. He had no reason to be here . . . what with that tattoo lady he hooked up with. I needed to take care of this once and for all.

Walking with dread and giving a couple deep sighs, I made it to the door and threw it open. "What the heck do you want?" I blinked up at him in the glaring afternoon light. "We're divorced. You need to stop this obsession."

"Don't flatter yourself." He spoke in that very familiar threatening tone he liked to use to get his way. "We need to go to the bank and get our financials worked out."

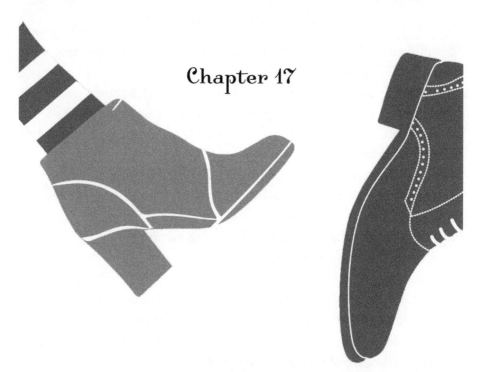

Chapter 17

Pure dread shot through me, but I was court-ordered to sign over his part to him. I found myself staring at a bunch of legal documents with a lot of fine print that looked far too serious.

After I was done here, I would buy the biggest bag of potato chips I could find and binge-watch ex-wives revenge movies.

"You put a second loan on the house," I said under my breath.

He shrugged like there was nothing he could do about it.

My eyes narrowed in on him. "You gave me all that debt."

"You wanted the house," Damion said flatly.

My body trembled. This man who I had thought I loved was nasty.

Air-conditioning gusted, giving me chills. Maybe I should call Tiffany for help. I glanced up at the wall clock. This was her wheelhouse, even though—at Damion's insistence—Damion and I used a different bank than hers.

Red flag there.

This man had set me up. The forms glared at me. If I was going to be independent, I needed to do this on my own. I should be safe. This was pretty straightforward name change and account ownership stuff.

And I did handle it, and since I was on a roll doing hard things to put my life in order, I decided to wait on the chips and revenge movie. Instead, I'd visit the Speech Masters group I googled.

Doubt found me as I sat with the car air-conditioning blasting outside the meeting location in the Temecula Offices on Jefferson Street. After all, I had failed once already today at the breakfast networking group. Did I really want to go for two failures in one day?

The noise from other people gathering in this mostly empty parking lot seeped into my car, bringing with it the old queasy feeling. The goal was to learn how to speak like Tiffany and Ray. Develop a golden tongue to persuade new clients and to capture Mr. Right's interest.

A small group of professionally dressed people passed my car, laughing and jostling each other. That didn't make it any easier to open my door, but I did anyway. It'd be quicker to find where to go if I followed them. They led me straight into a cold-looking room filled with chairs lined up along the back wall.

I stared at the people, who all knew one another. Not wanting to be noticed, I slipped into the closest chair. I got away with it for a few minutes, but then an elderly gentleman wearing a faded plaid jacket greeted me.

"New?"

I nodded.

"Welcome!" He smiled. "I need to start the meeting, but I'm glad to have you here."

He waved goodbye, charged to the front of the room, and started the meeting, explaining they had a new guest and how the meeting would go.

I leaned back into my chair, settling into observation mode. The back door swooped open. I glanced up to see my sister take the seat next to me, appearing harried and tired.

"What are you doing here?" I whispered.

She set her purse on the chair next to her. "I told you that this was a bad idea."

She had. I ignored it. This was my choice, not hers.

"So?" I whispered.

"You need to spend your energy on real networking groups."

She might be right, but I had a good feeling about this group and that was why even after a long, trying day, I was here.

"Can't I make my own decisions?"

She shifted in her seat. "Of course you can. It's just . . ."

I watched the speaker in front of the room. "*If* it's such a waste of time, why are you here?"

She flipped her hair to her back before leaning toward me. "I heard you visited a bank today," she whispered at a fast cadence.

"From who?"

She gave me a crooked smile. "You think I don't have connections with all the banks in the area?"

"It's my life," I whispered and then watched the speaker like I was listening deeply to her speech.

After the speech was over, I whispered to my sister, "The bank reps shouldn't be talking about their customers like that. That has to be a breach of some law."

Tiffany's eyes narrowed in on me. "What were you thinking, signing documents without me there?"

"I am adult, and I don't need your permission."

She gasped. "But signing legal documents?"

"And I handled it." I smiled, a little proud of myself.

A young, thin man in front of the room asked, "Would our newest guest like to do a table topic?"

My sister shot to her feet. "Sure."

Apparently, she was supposed to speak for two minutes without knowing the random subject until she reached the podium. I sank into my chair, waiting for her to deliver a sparkling speech. Of course, she did, even though she thought coming here was a big mistake.

As people clapped for her, and I studied the carpet feeling outshone, I suddenly jumped to my feet.

"I'll go next. Just ask me about love . . . please."

"Love?" he said, his face bursting into a teasing smile. "Okay."

I strolled up to the front of the room, thinking about how badly I had done that morning when trying to please everyone. I also thought about how the networking group's president wouldn't even give me the time of day. Then I thought about Elizabeth and how she claimed I was a miracle worker just for asking a few questions, listening, and being myself.

I clenched my good hand into a fist. Fine. I wasn't going to follow all those directives from others.

The young man gestured at me. "What do you think of love?"

I watched him leave the podium, wondering why I had asked to talk about *that*. Love hadn't worked for me . . . yet.

The room waited for me to speak. Every last gaze rested on me.

"Love is difficult." My voice wavered. Maybe that afternoon was still getting to me.

Tiffany caught my eye, her face expressionless.

"When you see those commercials with a mom or dad holding a child with so much love, it makes a person think love is safe and comfortable, and—" I stomped my foot on the floor. "You have to watch out for that message."

I drew out the pause again, like Ray did. "That's dangerous because when Mr. Wrong comes into your life, he'll seem to be right. It'll feel like home, and that's *really* bad."

Several women nodded.

"These men, or women, who feel like home can reach into your chest and rip your heart out." Feeling my quirky nature bubble up in me, I made a grand gesture, acting out someone ripping my heart out of my chest. "They stomp on it."

I threw my pretend heart to the ground and stomped on it with gusto like I was in an aerobics class. Walking away from my pretend banged-up heart, I looked back at it. "This heartbreak can devastate the victim. It can cause them never to date or believe in love again."

I let that message land. "I was like that for a long time. It's hard to believe that things can work out like the commercials claim. This is sad, if you ask me."

I glanced at my sister as I wiped at bangs that had fallen into my eyes. After being hurt, my sister was guilty of not letting anyone in.

At least I was trying to manage the love thing.

A red light flashed on, signaling I needed to stop my presentation.

As I bowed my head and thanked the crowd, the room exploded into applause.

I heard murmurs.

"That was too funny."

"She was good."

"I loved how she just ripped out her heart and stomped on it."

My sister gave me a strained smile when I sat next to her. "That was interesting."

I gave her a bright smile. "Thanks."

Her face fell.

The rest of the meeting went quickly, with other people giving more short speeches, then a wrap-up with group business. The moment the president banged the gavel, people surrounded me.

Me. Not Tiffany. Not Ray. Me.

"Zoey, you are sooo funny. We would love to have you in our club," someone called out.

"Your sister can join too."

Tiffany whispered to me, "What do you think?"

Heat crawled up the back of my neck. This wasn't one of those serious networking groups. It was a place where people laughed and liked me stomping on hearts.

"I think I will join, but my sister will not. She is this big career woman and doesn't have time for things like this, but I'm glad she came to support me."

She pursed her lips, a tell-tale sign she wasn't completely happy about me saying no about her joining.

The secretary handed me papers to fill out. My fingers shook. I had never stood up to her that way before, telling her I wanted something of my own.

"You are having quite a day," Tiffany said, sitting down next to me.

I shot her a glance. "You don't even know the half of it." I tried to keep a straight face, but couldn't.

"What?" she demanded.

I filled out my address on the signup sheet. "Nick."

"What about Nick?" Her voice sounded hard.

"Tell you later," I whispered, struggling to hold back the exciting news, even though I knew she wasn't completely happy with me right now.

"Tell me."

People hung around, but no one was paying any attention to us. "We're going on another date."

"What?" Tiffany practically yelled.

People glanced over at us. "Shh," I snapped. "He's perfect—good-looking, likes Disneyland, wants children, has a good, solid job . . ."

She shook her head like she was the teacher, and I'd gotten the answer completely wrong. "That's the worst list I have ever heard. How on earth can you think you can teach about relationships when that's your criteria?"

The words bit. I sank back in my chair as doubt swirled around me. I had no idea why I thought I could teach relationships. Despite that, I didn't see anything wrong with my list.

I walked over to hand my paperwork to the secretary, and left the meeting with Tiffany in my wake. "At least my criteria includes *having* a relationship, not hiding and burying myself in work."

She caught up to my side and stiffened. "Some people aren't desperate to have a relationship, but you don't understand that because you aren't one of them."

Our shoes clicked against the cement as we made our way to our vehicles.

"A person can be completely happy on their own," Tiffany continued. "You *should* learn that before trying to jump into another one."

We climbed into our respective cars. Feeling grumpy, I drove home, glad to be done. Still, apparently, Tiffany wanted to continue our conversation because she followed me in her car and pulled up behind me in the driveway.

We climbed out at the same moment, and she picked up where we'd left off, her eyes narrowed. "When did you say your date was?"

I unlocked the front door, and we walked inside. "Tomorrow night."

"So, there's still time," Tiffany muttered, shutting the door behind us. "I just need to figure out—"

"Figure out what?" I tossed my purse on the couch, heading to the bathroom to fill the tub. I needed a hot bath, and it would probably be full by the time Tiffany stopped correcting me.

"Nothing," she said, following after me. "Forget it."

"I'm hoping to forget this entire conversation." I leaned over the tub to reach the knob. "If you can't be happy for me—"

"I can be happy," she retorted.

I flipped on the water. Cold gushed out. "It doesn't seem like it." I flipped the faucet to hot. "I did a good job today, plus I have a date with a great guy, and you think that—"

"He's *not* a great guy."

I felt the water again. "How would you know?" Cold water still rushed out.

"You don't listen to me," Tiffany said, like that was a sin.

Really, really cold.

"And then you call me in a panic to rescue you."

I flinched. There might be more truth to that than I wanted to believe. "Not today, I didn't."

"You just don't get it," she said. "Nick is not the right person for you. You'll regret getting involved."

This was my life, and I was going to live it my way, mistakes and all. I felt the water again. Freezing cold. I glanced up at Tiffany. "My hot water heater is broken."

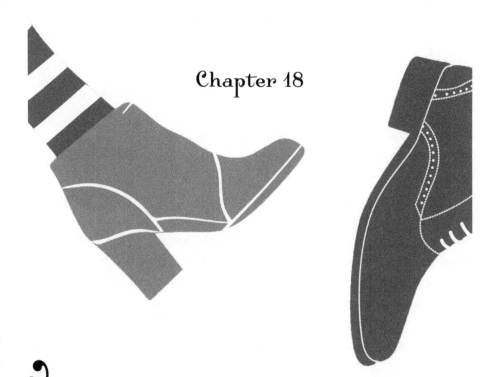

Chapter 18

I raced out of the bathroom to check the water in the kitchen. I flipped on the sink water to hot.

She followed behind me and again said something about there still being time. I realized she was up to something suspicious. She kept hinting like she wanted me to figure it out, but I really didn't want to know what was stirring. She would, for sure, let me know when she was ready.

Clearly, she was jealous because she didn't have any guy in her life and hadn't had one for years. But that was her life, not mine.

"Sorry, sis. You're wrong about Nick, and I need to figure out my hot water issue." The kitchen sink faucet ran cold water. "Do you know how to fix water heaters?"

"No." She straightened like my question insulted her.

A loud pounding banged on the door. We both jumped.

I sighed. "I'll get it."

The door opened to Ray with an empty brownie pan and cup. I brushed at the ratty hair falling into my eyes and wished I hadn't driven home with the car windows down.

"Hi."

He held out his white foam cup. "I saw lots of lights on, so I hope you don't mind me coming over so late. Hey, I know I have been offering to lend you some sugar but it's me that's out. Could I get a cup?"

Tiffany made it to the door by this point. "Reynesh!" she called out. "Come in. Just the person we need right now. Zoey's hot water stopped working, and we aren't sure why."

Ray entered the house on a mission to help. "Where's the water heater?" His gaze remained strictly on me.

I gestured to my sister to answer. She stared back at me like I would know or should know as the homeowner. In theory, I would agree with that.

I brushed at the rat's nest of my hair again, as though that would help anything. Putting on a fake confident smile, I peeked up at Ray, feeling a bit shy. "I could take you several places it *might* be."

Ray stepped up close to me, and his aftershave tickled my senses. "Lead the way."

The hairs on the back of my neck bristled as I led everyone to a utility closet that housed a lot of pumps. I looked back up at Ray for confirmation. This was the right spot. His dark eyes watched me, maybe a little too closely.

It took me a moment to stop staring at him to find my voice. I pointed at a big cylindrical metal thing. "Could this be it?"

Ray peeked inside. Our arms brushed each other for a much-too-brief second. I gasped at the jolt of sensation from our touch.

"Do you have a wrench?" he asked.

Tiffany piped in, "I'll get it."

Apparently, she knew what a wrench was and where it might be located.

As she hurried away, I assessed Ray, who examined the water heater. Tonight, he wore a T-shirt that snuggled against him tightly, drawing attention to muscles that flexed and rippled as he moved.

"You're strong," I said with a low voice.

Ray laughed, eyes dancing. "Not as strong as galvorn."

"What?" I glanced up at his midnight shadow of a beard.

He stood straight and stepped so close to me I could almost feel his breath. "Galvorn is a metal. In Middle-earth."

I laughed at the geeky side of in this man.

He continued with his Tolkienesque lecture. "Some people mistakenly think steel or titanium are the strongest metal. Those who know a little more will argue that mithril is the strongest, but galvorn actually is. Tilkal comes close, but galvorn wins every time."

I laughed with a bubbly chuckle at his treatise on metals.

He elbowed me in my arm. "You're thinking I am a geek."

I elbowed him back just to brush against him. "Maybe."

We were knocking against each other in a mock fight, laughing, when Tiffany cleared her throat and waved the wrench.

We leaped apart.

"You guys done?"

Face hot, I said, "We were just waiting for you."

My sister gave me an "oh, sure" expression as Ray fiddled around with the equipment and took off an outer shell of one of the pumps to reveal the inside workings. "Can I get some matches?"

Inspired to be a good assistant and away from Tiffany's prying eyes, I hurried to the kitchen to grab one, then rushed back to watch the master at work.

A few minutes later, Ray stood. "Should work now, though you won't have any hot water for a while."

"What was wrong with it?" I asked.

"The pilot light went out."

Hmm. That made sense and seemed easy enough to fix. "Can you show me how you figured that out so I know what to do next time?"

He proceeded to show me as Tiffany watched for the next few minutes.

When he finished imparting his wisdom, Ray asked, "Anything else need fixing?"

I kind of wished something else was broken because it was fun watching him work.

"No, we're good. Thanks for your help. It was very kind of you."

"Naw," he said, brushing aside my comment. "I needed to earn my cup of sugar."

"That's right," I said. "We haven't even gotten you that yet. Just a minute."

Tiffany held out her pointy finger. "I'll do it." She hurried into the kitchen, leaving me and Ray standing there alone.

A banging and whirring sound came from deep in the kitchen. I had no idea what my sister was doing. I twisted my fingers against one another, not willing to leave Ray's side.

"Thanks for the lesson."

He shoved his hands into the front pockets of his jeans. "Thanks for being a good student."

I smiled shyly at him and gestured down the hall toward the kitchen as Tiffany rushed out and met us in the front room.

"Here's your sugar." She handed him his foam cup. She also held up a baggy with brown seed-like granules in it. "And I have a special coffee for you tomorrow morning."

He took it happily. "Hey, great."

"You need to drink it tomorrow or it won't taste as fresh. I just ground it. I was going to walk it over after visiting Zoe, but now I don't need to."

"Since when are you a coffee fanatic?" Ray asked.

"I'm investigating a coffee business for the bank. Try it out. It's really yummy."

Ray gave her an odd look. "Okay."

"I need to get your feedback on it, if that's okay."

"Sure." He took the bag from Tiffany, stepped through the door, and waved goodbye.

"Night," Tiffany and I replied in tandem as he sauntered down the sidewalk.

Back in the kitchen, I tried to hide my quickened breath by wiping counters that didn't actually need it because of today's earlier efforts. I noticed a couple of dishes I'd missed, though.

Tiffany watched me like a hawk. "There's something going on between you two."

"What?" My spine stiffened. "Of course not." I folded up the kitchen towel. "Just friends. Nothing more. We don't want to be more. We're too different."

Her lips pursed.

"Do you want some chamomile tea?"

"What?" she snapped.

"You seem like you need to relax."

"You've got to be kidding. A VP position is opening up at the bank. I don't need to relax. I need to hit it."

She moved over to the coffee grinder, grabbed the washcloth, and used it to wipe the machine.

"And why else is Ray not a possibility?" she asked suggestively.

I stacked plates on top of one another and moved to the sink. "Because he's Ray."

Tiffany circled to face me. "What's that supposed to mean?"

I washed a dish glad my arm was starting to feel better. "Ray is Ray. You know, he's a stars guy. Also, he's almost engaged to someone else." I fussed with a dish towel, avoiding Tiff's eyes.

I could almost feel her gaze boring into me. After a moment, she turned away to prep the coffee machine for tomorrow. "So?"

"So, his business is not stable—I'm not making the same mistake twice." I let the cold water wash over my hands. "He isn't as steady as someone like Nick."

"Nick!" She turned on me.

I set my jaw. "Yeah, Nick. He's a family man."

"Ray is a family man too."

She wasn't understanding. "It's different."

"How?"

"Ray's not Disneyland Dad."

Plus, he would soon be attached to someone else.

"Nick, on the other hand, shows he is into *kids*. He takes his nieces and nephews out on adventures. He likes Disneyland. He wants to take his own family there."

Tiffany closed the lid to my coffee machine.

I peered over her shoulder. "What the heck are you doing?"

She dragged a towel across the counter. "Helping you straighten up."

I turned off the sink water. "I don't need you to help. If the place is a mess, it's *my* mess."

"Fine, fine." She held up her hands in surrender. "I need to go."

As I hustled her out the door, she turned back to me, her face lit by the porch light. "You're always wanting help, then rejecting it when it's not exactly what you want. You know what I think?"

"I'm sure you'll tell me." I hoped the heater had warmed the water enough for that bath I had planned on an hour ago.

"I think you're scared to live life on your own."

"Ha," was my great comeback.

My older sister waved goodbye in that knowing way of hers. I returned the wave, ready to prove her wrong. I was already focused on building my new life. Tomorrow, I would reach out to five potential new clients and really sell myself, even though I hated doing the performance thing. I also had a trade session with my massage client. After our session, I would drive to the local print shop and have my snazzy new cards made up, even though I didn't have the money for it.

Also on my list for tomorrow was to contact that mortgage lady from the chamber meeting and listen to her talk about mortgages. I *really* didn't want to think about mortgages, but I needed to do something about mine. Plus, I wanted to buy a new pair of heels for my date with Nick, the kind I hated, but he liked. I needed all the leverage I could get with him.

I was going to do all the things I didn't want to do to get the life I wanted.

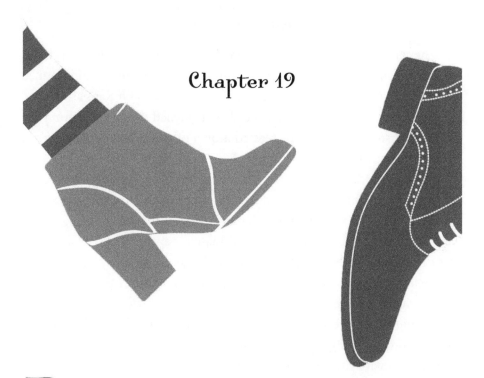

Chapter 19

D espite my big plans the night before, my first thought when I woke up the next day was one hundred percent on Ray. Still in a half daze, I remembered how his warm fingers heightened the awareness of my skin, the touch of his breath caressing as we elbowed each other.

Tiffany would never have gotten in an elbow match with the self-employed guy across the street. She'd have signed him up as a client. I had to stop being distracted by what I *wanted* but wasn't possible and focus on what I *needed*, which might be possible.

I kicked my red blanket and sheets off me, leaving nothing between me and the empty, looming house. I stumbled to my closet to find the best "put together" outfit I owned for my date with Nick tonight. I blinked a few times at a short row of worn-out shirts. I sighed. They certainly weren't qualified candidates to be in the "put together" outfit for Nick. It mattered with him. I needed to go for an outfit he would approve of.

The smell of coffee floated up to greet me, thanks to the timer Tiffany set last night. Unable to figure out the perfect outfit yet, I turned from the closet of confusing clothes. I needed coffee for this.

The coffee tasted different, perhaps with a little burnt flavoring, which was odd because it was a fresh cup. Odd-tasting or not, the heated liquid warmed my insides with a comforting sensation, almost like being in Ray's arms.

As I stood there, my senses came alive. I smelled the lavender from the dishwasher soap and the rich, roasted aroma of my coffee, reminding me how nice Ray had smelled last night.

Thinking of last night, I hurried to the front of the house to see his home, to be closer to him, wanting to be connected to him. Fortunately for me, he stood outside, mug in hand, gazing out on the day.

His chin tipped up in that rugged masculine way of his, making me want to take in his beautiful brown eyes. The need for touch, the craving to inhale his spicy cologne, the yearning to become lost in those rich deep-brown eyes of his overcame me.

Taking one more sip of the rich coffee, I could fight my longing no longer. Forget getting dressed or running a comb through my hair. My body pulsed with the need to get to Ray.

I secured my bathrobe belt tighter around me and hurried out the door, not worrying about closing it. No time. Could do that later. Nothing was more important than to get to Ray. My slippers flopped against the sidewalk and the blacktop as I shuffled across the street.

A car screeched to a stop to avoid me. I waved, thanking them for not hitting me, but I didn't bother taking my eyes off Ray. He was just feet away. Entrepreneur or no, arranged marriage or no, I had to be near him. With him—

As I stumbled across the street, I wondered how his full name was pronounced? I didn't know. I hadn't learned it. I needed to say his proper name. Needed to feel how the sounds formed in my mouth. How it felt against my tongue, and I didn't know how to do it.

Shame washed through me. Even if he said it was okay to call him Ray, people close to him would call him by his real name and learn how to say it right. It was time for me to show him that respect. I don't know why I never thought to do it before.

I needed to accept him—all his mixture of cultures.

"Ray," I called loudly to him.

He swung toward me on the porch and held up his coffee mug in greeting.

My gaze zeroed in on him and his textured sky-blue shirt. I should've figured out earlier how much he must be into texture if he had a bathrobe like he wore the other day. It suggested a sensual nature. Of course. He paid a lot of attention to the smallest details.

What a fabulous quality.

I shifted into a jog with my lime-green bathrobe flopping open and my feet sliding everywhere in the slippers like I was running in slippery sand.

Too much distance lay between us. "Ray!" I called out louder.

He made his way toward me. "You got my attention," he called back. "Ray."

His brow crinkled. "You can stop yelling my name."

I panted as I came to an abrupt halt on the sidewalk a few feet from the porch—the idea to stop yelling his name slowly made it through my thoughts. I didn't want to stop. I liked how the sound of it rolled forth from my mouth. I never noticed before how it released air, free and light. His name felt like it was a part of me. I really needed to know how to say it right.

I wiped at my bangs, fallen down over my eyes again, and stood there, letting my breath return.

"Yes?" He waved his coffee mug as though signaling my turn to talk.

Two people walking their dog had stopped to stare in our direction like we were the morning entertainment. I regarded my bathrobe and cleared my throat.

He must think I was a freak standing near his porch like a crazy possessed woman suddenly obsessed just to be near him, but I really, *really* wanted to be near him.

"How do you say your full name?"

He paused, likely taken aback by my sudden morning urgency, but he didn't treat me like I was nuts. He didn't criticize me or tell me I was embarrassing him.

"Reynesh."

"Ray-ish," I rolled over my tongue.

"Ray-nuh-ish," he corrected me.

I said it wrong again, and he corrected me again, not looking at me until the dog walkers started moving.

I tried it over and over until he finally said, "Yes, that's it."

I gave him a big, huge grin. "Your nephews said it means 'king.' I love it. A person's name should represent who they are, and that really fits you."

He crossed one arm under his armpit, and kept the other arm extended, holding his coffee. I didn't see any steam circling upward. It must be getting cold.

"So," he said matter-of-factly, staring at my face, "I'm sure you didn't come here to learn how to pronounce my name. What can I do for you? I have a call with my family in five minutes, and I have a full work schedule."

I shifted my weight in my fluffy slippers. What did I want?

"You, of course."

"Wha-at?" he choked.

"I want you." I blinked. I had never ever said anything like that before. But it was true, so why hold back?

He swallowed. "Okay."

I didn't like how wide his eyes had gotten.

"Um, yeah, I was standing there in my kitchen drinking my coffee when suddenly I knew I had to be with you."

He uncrossed his arms. "That must've been a big knowing, since you left your front door open."

Not wanting to take my eyes off him, I didn't even turn around to see if that was true. It probably was. I gave a goofy laugh. "Coffee can do that to you." I gestured to his mug. "What do you think of the coffee? Is that the stuff Tiffany gave you last night?"

He made a face. "It tastes a little odd."

I nodded, glad for any excuse to keep talking. "I thought so too. Not sure I'd recommend that her bank loan any money to that company."

He sipped another mouthful. "Agreed. And yet, there's something about it . . ." He drank again.

I watched his throat move as he swallowed. "Just something about it," I echoed.

A phone rang inside his house. "That's probably my family," he murmured. "I should get it." He half turned to go inside.

I stepped on the porch just to stay close.

What was going on here?

We stared at each other. His phone kept ringing. "I really need to get that," he said vaguely and took another sip. "Really need to get that."

For two beats of my heart, we stared at each other. Then, as if it was a dream, he reached out and moved a strand of hair away from my eyes.

"You're beautiful, Zoey. You know that?"

My heart felt as if the sun shone on it.

"What are your plans today?" he asked in that slow, intense way we both had going on.

Mortgage Lady. Client. Future clients. Business cards. High heels for Nick.

"Nothing," I said.

"Good. Want to go for breakfast?"

My whole body felt warm from the inside out. "Oh, yes," I said, not so much whispering, but more breathing the word. *Yes, yes, yes.*

"And then lunch," he went on, his finger resting against my cheek.

I tipped my face up to his touch. "Yes."

"And then maybe . . ."

"The beach."

His hand slipped to the nape of my neck as we stared into each other's eyes. "It's a date."

I laughed, and he followed suit.

"I actually have a ton of commitments today," he said, still laughing.

"So . . . do I." The words broke with my own laughter.

"It's sort of nuts."

"Agreed," I said.

We grinned stupidly at each other.

He licked his lips. "What's going on?"

I giggled again, fingering my ratty hair. "I don't know."

"We need to be together."

I couldn't have agreed more.

Ray peered intently into my eyes. "I just . . . I just need to be around you."

I laughed again, relieved he felt the same intensity and desire. "I know that feeling."

"Crazy." He brushed my loose hair out of my eyes again. His fingers lingered on my forehead, sending goose bumps through me.

"Yep, crazy." Our eyes met. "Maybe it's destiny," I whispered.

He set his coffee down on the rail and cupped his hands on my hips. A flood of heat washed down my body. "I don't know what it is, but let's ride it out today, okay?"

"Okay," I whispered back, trusting his wisdom.

"Let's have one perfect day."

I blinked up at him, the sunlight creating tiny stars in my eyes.

He tugged me to him for a hug. "Breakfast. Pancakes and toast to make up for all the bad networking breakfasts we choked down this week."

I chuckled. "They have been terrible." Squeezing his hands, I said, "Let's go now."

He picked up his empty coffee mug. "We both need to change our clothes. Let me get into something more comfortable and you . . . well, tell you what, let's meet out here in five."

My head nodded like it had a bouncy spring in it. "Okay," although it wasn't okay. I didn't want to be away from him even to go across the street and put on proper clothes and comb my ratty hair. There was something pulsing and electric between us. It felt like being away from him would make me wither.

He wrapped me up in his arms again. I laid my head on his chest, smelling his cologne. It was a bit exotic, but the scent had spice to it I had smelled before. The scent was perfect for him and made my head swirl.

He ran his hands through my hair. "See you soon."

I nodded into his chest.

He tipped my chin up so I could gaze into those eyes. "Baby, we can be apart for a few minutes."

I hugged him tighter, breathing him in. I needed to have his scent on me while I was gone from him. It'd give me strength. I let him go and stepped back, then took off running.

His voice trailed after me. "Five minutes."

Crossing the street, I stumbled several times before entering the house. I also tripped on the stairs. On the last fall, I kicked off my slippers. "I have to hurry."

Once in the closet, I grabbed my old funky sage-green summer dress I used to love so much but hadn't worn since I married Damion. I loved that thing. Why had I stopped wearing it? Today, I'd wear it for this funky adventure. I snatched my black sweater too. It was extra soft and made me feel feminine.

After that, I yanked a comb through my hair and opted for a ponytail and one swipe of red lipstick. That had to be good enough. I snatched my purse and headed out the door, this time shutting it before running straight into Reynesh, who sat out front on a motorcycle.

"A motorcycle?" I called out with surprise.

He held out a helmet. "My nephews are always talking about how fun it is to ride their bikes. I haven't gone out for a while. Let's try it."

My eyes widened. We were both stepping out of our normal behavior today.

"This way, you have to hold on tight to me the whole way there." Reynesh arched his eyebrows.

A full smile filled my face. "That's so romantic." I took the helmet.

He slapped the back of the bike for me to climb on.

The pulse in my throat took off, beating at full pace. I never, ever before wanted to be on one of those death machines. But today . . .

"Zoey," Reynesh said, "get on." He held out a helmet.

Something in his voice made me listen to him. Weird. When I heard him, it echoed as a voice inside myself. He offered an invitation to go on an adventure I had no control over, no science rules to guide me, no advice from experts.

The machine rattled. Reynesh extended his hand. His palm swallowed mine, sending currents up my arm.

I stepped forward, but stopped when a loud honk blared from behind me. Both Reynesh and I pivoted to see my sister in her convertible pull up next to the sidewalk with the top down.

"Zoey, why are you getting on a motorcycle?" she snapped. "That's not safe. We need to talk."

Ray and I made eye contact.

"Do you want to stay and talk to your sister?" he asked quietly.

"Do you want to stay and talk to *your* family?" I questioned in response.

A corner of his mouth crooked into a smile. "Nope."

I pulled on the helmet and swung a leg over the back of his bike tucking in my dress. "Me neither." I gave Tiffany a little wave. "We're heading for breakfast," I yelled to her.

The bike roared to life.

"Hold on," he yelled over the rumble.

A shiver rippled through me as I circled my arms around his waist.

"Wait. . . You can't!" Tiffany yelled. "Motorcycles are deathtraps."

"Not always," I whispered, holding on tighter to my sexy neighbor. My sister had a flash of panic in her eyes. She was worried. "It'll be okay," I said louder. "Reynesh will take real good care of me."

"I'm a great driver." He nodded. "I used to drive these bad boys all the time in my college years."

Tiffany stared, not listening to Reynesh. "Zoey, I just wanted you not to be with Nick—"

"What?" I laughed again. I was doing that a lot this morning. "This has nothing to do with you and your worries."

"But I didn't intend . . ." She caught her breath. "I thought *he'd* be reasonable, levelheaded."

I glimpsed Ray through the shields of our helmets. "Who's 'he'?"

"Don't know."

I laughed out loud again and waved to my sister, standing in my driveway with her arms out.

"Tiff, for once, this has nothing to do with you."

I tapped Reynesh's shoulder.

On cue, he revved the engine.

"How does this fit with your rules?" Tiffany shouted after us.

"Who cares?" I whispered into the helmet.

Reynesh glanced over his shoulder. "Do you want to stay or go?"

"Let's go," I said.

He gunned the motor. We took off down the street away from my second mortgaged house, away from Tiffany, away from the rules, away from everything. Just me and Reynesh.

My sweater and dress flapped in the wind like it did on a roller coaster. I felt freer than I ever had. I held my hands out, letting the wind brush against them with hard force. This was truly living. As we turned the corner, I saw Tiff's mouth fall slightly open as she stared after us. Poor Tiff.

The early morning sun was doing its job rising in the sky. The wind blew against my face shield, and it whipped my hair around my shoulders. I let out a big, "Who-oo hoo-oo!"

Ray let one out himself.

We continued the yelping and the ride all the way to the first stoplight. While still stopped, I hurriedly tucked my dress more snugly underneath my legs and hugged Reynesh tighter. He leaned into my touch.

"This is my first time ever riding a motorcycle," I called out loudly.

I was on an adventure with a lack of rules and Tiffany telling me what to do.

The breakfast house was a cozy joint. The booth seat was designed for one person, but with a sly smile, Reynesh asked me to sit next to him. I snugged up to him as a thrill zoomed through me. The touch of our shoulders sent electrical currents down my arm.

Reynesh leaned into my arm with his biceps against mine. After a few minutes of staring at the menu together, he grabbed my hand closest to him and circled it around his forearm.

I sucked in my breath. He was every bit as strong and solid as he appeared. I pressed my cheek into his biceps. "I like being with you."

He stroked my face. "I like being with you, too."

My skin felt alive with his touch. "Let's do this more."

"Whatever you say."

After the waitress refilled our coffee, I tugged on Reynesh's arm. "What caused you to develop an app for love?"

He took a long sip of coffee before answering. "I don't know. I grew up my whole life hearing how important it was to have your charts read before you jumped into a relationship."

He ran his fingers up and down my forearm, causing the goose bumps to chase. "I've always been obsessed with technology, so why not combine the two?"

Suddenly, I found myself wondering if my suffering was similar to this attractive mystery man next to me.

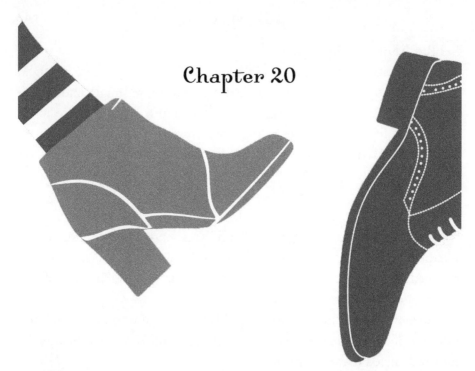

Chapter 20

After breakfast, I held on tight to Reynesh's waist as we wove through Southern California traffic. Cars were backed up for miles. He navigated the motorcycle in and out like an expert. We flew down the Avocado Highway lined with acres of avocado groves, stately palm trees, rolling purple mountains, and occasionally a sighting of a distant house. There was no chance to admire the trees, mountains, or splendid display of pastel sky as we rushed by.

The wind whipped at my clothes with a fierce intensity. I'd be a mess once this was all done, but Reynesh had to be getting used to that.

"Ah-h-h," I yelped when he swerved unexpectedly to the left.

He didn't seem to hear, or he had nerves of steel because he kept tearing down the pavement without cringing.

"Hold on tight!" he called to me as he revved up the engine and road straight on the white dotted line in between the two lanes of cars.

Not having the courage to witness this risk, I closed my eyes and trusted, actually trusted, that he could get us through alive. I knotted my fingers together as I hugged his middle.

By the time we pulled up beachside, I was smiling wide. The beach appeared to be mostly empty, but the side streets for parking certainly weren't. With the sun kissing my shoulder, it took sixteen minutes of hunting to find a parking spot for a motorcycle.

Once we found it, Reynesh flipped off the engine and tugged his helmet from his head. "We're here."

He climbed off the bike as my fingers shook, struggling to unlatch my helmet. I couldn't seem to grip the straps.

He stepped close. "I'll do that for you."

My face was on fire, not a little flame, but a completely red-hot one. Wind burned? Sunburned? I didn't know. I didn't care.

He grabbed my hand, his thumb rubbing with affection over the top, causing all my senses to light up. "It has been so long since I held your hand."

He continued to caress it, and I took in his touch. My breath sped up. It *had* been an awfully long time. When his stroke slowed, I squeezed his hand back, feeling his strength. He pulled me toward him, and I fell into his arms. Hints of his lingering cologne washed over me.

He held me firmly rooted with my feet on the hard dirt until my shaking lessened to a tremor. A soft wind picked up and blew between us. He drew me in even tighter and squeezed as he held me.

He gently kissed the top of my forehead. His breath tickled me as he whispered, "Let's stroll the beachfront."

It didn't take us long to ditch our shoes. The bitter-cold ocean brushed against the bottom of my legs. Every time a wave roared in, I squealed, and Reynesh chuckled.

"This is lovely." I swung his arm with mine. I could almost imagine us coming here with children and building sandcastles and splashing in the waves . . .

But he was going to marry someone else.

I kicked at the sand. That thought depressed me more than it should. I should be happy for him. Him marrying in his culture made sense. He was American too, though.

To stop my endless, painful thoughts, I asked, "Do you wish you lived by the beach?"

He shook his head. "I'm fine wherever destiny takes me."

"Back to India?" A twinge of irritation surged in my chest.

He shrugged. "We'll see."

My hand gripped his more firmly. Today he was with me. Today his hands were in mine. I sighed.

"Do you want to live near a beach?" he asked.

"Yes, yes, yes, yes."

Reynesh smiled. "Wow, that's a lot of yeses."

"I love the beach. Always have. I used to dream of moving here. But then honestly, I always worried that when I had kids, if I lived near a beach, they'd wander into the water. I worried about mold. About the fog." I watched the endless waves. "So much worry."

"Hmm." He scanned the expansive ocean. "Those are concerns." His hand squeezed mine, letting me know he was there. Another ice-cold wave splashed in on us. The chill stopped me from talking, and the sun comforted me.

A stroll on the beach with the sand slipping between my toes and holding hands with a guy was idyllic—like a romantic scene in a movie. I closed my eyes to take it all in.

Had I been denying how much I was attracted to Reynesh? That would be crazy. I never really felt a strong attraction to him until this morning. I mean, yes, I liked his eyes, but that was about as far as it got. Well, except that one morning when I thought about what it would be like to be in his arms—briefly. Other than that, I hadn't thought about it. And maybe I'd thought about how strong his arms were when he was fixing my heater, but other than that, not at all.

Why did I, all of a sudden, find him irresistible to the point of making a complete fool of myself?

Our feet sank into the wet sand, leaving perfect imprints. Reynesh and I strolled the beach together. The imprints melted away until one would never know we had been there at all.

"Did you like it?" I asked to forget our disappearing footprints.

His grip tightened on my hand. "Did you know the weather in Delhi is almost exactly the same as Arizona?"

"I didn't." I took several more steps and gave that thought. "That sounds dreadfully hot."

He reached out and grabbed my hand into his. "It's like a warm hug. You get used to the heat and the dryness."

I shook my head. "I doubt I could."

"Ohh, a princess."

No one had ever called me "princess" before, but the way he said it didn't come across as negative. He smiled at me, and I returned the smile. Beyond him, I noticed our feet charting a path down the beach sand.

"Princess?" His fingers rubbed mine. "Perhaps. Or maybe a queen."

"Ahh," I said, not sure how to take it, but somehow, I wasn't offended.

He kicked at the wet sand. "You're a quirky one."

"A quirky princess?" I tried to wrap my mind around what he was saying.

"Yep. Beautiful and becoming a queen."

My grasp on his hand tightened. "Do you think I need saving?"

"Sometimes," he answered way too quickly. He squeezed my hand. "Don't worry. That's getting less."

"What?"

"You'll find your way. Someday you'll make your way to stand on your own."

I caught my breath.

This man believed in me and *saw* me. Why did he have to be spoken for?

"What else was it like where you grew up?"

He gave that question thought. "Lots of wildlife. Tucson is a living desert, and of course, we have our clusters of old people and snowbirds. It's a lot more laid back there."

We started strolling again.

"Yeah, probably because of the heat. It's too hot to move."

He shifted his attention to me. "How about you?"

We took in the beachfront that spilled on for miles. Reynesh wanted to know me, and I wanted to share at least a part of who I was on our one perfect day together.

"As I think I've mentioned, my father took off when I was young." My voice cracked. I seldom talked about this stuff, and I didn't know why I wanted to open up about it now on this wonderful, happy day.

"My mom dealt with it with booze."

Reynesh bent and picked up a seashell. He brushed it off on his pant leg. "That's rough." He handed the shell to me.

I moved the white shell around in my hands, feeling the smoothness. "Tiffany and I practically raised ourselves." I stared at the imperfect and yet magnificent shell.

Memories flashed in my mind of our fights, our giggles . . . us staying up late watching movies and doing each other's hair and makeup while Mom lay passed out in the other room.

"We busied ourselves with watching shows, reading, and craft projects."

"Doesn't sound half bad," he said.

I have never thought of my childhood like that. "Yeah, maybe."

He squeezed my hand. "Maybe that's where you get your spontaneity and free spirit from."

I squeezed his hand back. He might be right about that.

He was so easy to talk to. I felt like I could tell him anything, so I did just that for the next couple of hours.

He told me stuff about him too. We were regular talk-a-holics going on and on about who we were and what got us here.

As we headed back to the motorcycle, I knew Reynesh had really heard me. Heard me deeply and hadn't judged me. Not once. He didn't necessarily understand me or my culture, but he had heard me.

And that, to me, was a gift.

———————

An hour later, I stood at the grocery store with Reynesh collecting food for an impromptu barbecue on the beach. My bruised elbow had made a near recovery, leaving me free to grab him by the arm. He leaned into my touch like we were an old married couple whose world revolved around each other.

As I took in all the colors of the food, I said, "We have to roast marshmallows."

He patted my hand. "Very American."

Now that he said it, I guess it was. "Want to squeeze it between a chocolate bar?"

"Naturally. S'mores it is."

This was going well. "Hot dogs?"

"Vegetarian style."

No meat? "You're a vegetarian?"

"I am."

Okay, I had inserted my foot into my mouth. "What do you eat, then?"

His face lit up. "Plenty of things. Beans, salads, rice, quinoa."

Healthy, maybe. Okay, definitely healthy, but it didn't sound like it would be filling. "I'd get hungry, and like a lot of work to prepare."

We rounded the corner. "In India, it is mostly the women who make the food, and it takes them hours every day," Reynesh said. "My father never cooked once in his entire life."

"You're not like that."

He shrugged.

I stared at the man who carved his own path and didn't always do what was expected. I liked that side of him.

Once we made it back to the beach, we loaded up our supplies and hauled them out onto the sand to make a beach fire under the sinking sun.

The twilight sky and small fire glow made Reynesh even more captivating. Vegetarian hot dogs actually worked and were probably a better choice for my emerging healthy-eating lifestyle. However, I couldn't see myself ever buying them on purpose.

The smoke followed us around the fire. We laughed as we moved from one side to the other. Often, I'd tug on his arm to lead him to go from the smoke as the impulsively moody wind changed directions.

We laughed as we danced away from the smoke. When I accidentally bumped into Reynesh on one rotation, I looked up to apologize. He stared at me with a penetrating gaze. When his expression shifted to determination, he pulled me in for a hard kiss.

As our kiss deepened, the passion that flowed between us made my body ache. I realized this could be forever and not just for this one strange and magical day.

When we finally pulled apart, his eyes sparkled in the firelight.

We continued to kiss, talk, and watch the fire dwindle until we finally admitted we needed to head back home. Not long later, we packed up. Soon after, we were zooming up the freeway in the crisp evening air. The traffic had died to a low roar.

As we traveled, I snuggled up to Reynesh and laid my head against his back. It took a little more than two hours before we rolled up to my home. The cold of the ride had chilled me to my bones, and I couldn't stop shivering. I wasn't sure how Reynesh was faring.

Not wanting this day, this freedom, this fun, to end quite yet, I whispered to him, "Roar the engine. See what this baby is made of."

He shook his head. "This is a residential area."

"What happened to the one perfect day?"

His back straightened under my grasp. "Okay." He gunned the engine, which roared into the night.

Both of us burst into laughter as lights flipped on in the house across the street next to his. "Shh." I took in all the lights turning on. "We're going to get in trouble."

Reynesh quieted the engine and put his feet on my driveway to settle the motorcycle and to say goodbye.

I climbed off the bike and immediately circled my arms around my body. The cold intensified once we stopped moving.

"Thanks for the wonderful day. Are you late for your call?"

He took off his helmet. "I missed that hours ago." He slipped off the motorcycle.

"Will you get in trouble?"

He stepped close to me. "Yes."

I tipped my face up to him. "I'm sorry."

He pulled me closer. "Don't be."

We stood inches apart, and I found it impossible not to stare at his lips.

"Why not?" I wanted to kiss him again. Maybe I wanted to kiss him even more than before because now I knew how wonderful it felt. I smelled the campfire smoke on him.

"What I did today was my choice," Reynesh said in his stern lecture voice. "What you did was yours. Today, I chose you over my family, and I'm happy."

I felt giddy and bright and hopeful. My gaze slid to his. "Right," I said slowly. "Your choice."

"You made a choice today too, Zoey. Are you happy about it?"

The heat from being near him sank into me as we moved closer toward each other, and our lips met. I let the action serve as my answer.

We stayed pressed together for a long time before he stepped back. I walked away slowly, watching as he crossed the street and stowed the motorcycle, waved a hand at me one last time.

I blew him a kiss as I stared up at the stars dotting the evening sky.

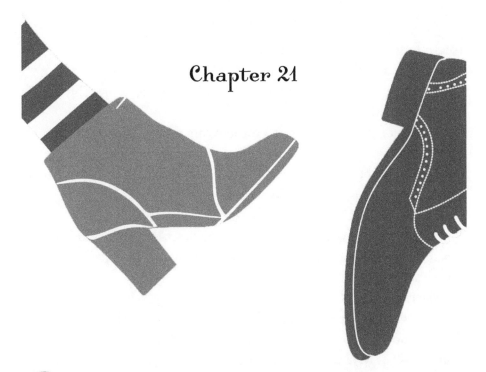

Chapter 21

Sleep embraced me with its wonderful hug until heat lapped at my face with a raging fierceness that woke me up. My legs shared a similar state of burn. It took me a few moments to figure out I was sunburned. Plus, my legs ached from walking barefoot on the sand, twisting and turning for miles.

As I flinched in pain in bed, a feeling that I had forgotten something haunted me. But since I wasn't even sure what day of the week it was, I wasn't sure if I would figure it out.

My phone beeped.

I carefully moved my sunburned body over to the end table and reached for my phone. I found texts from Tiffany. They started out bossy. *Get off that motorcycle right now!* Moved to worried. *Where are you?* Then a hint of scared. *Are you okay?*

I had expected this, especially after I climbed on the motorcycle and said what I had about Nick.

Nick!

I had totally forgotten about him and our date yesterday. How could

I have forgotten Mr. Perfect Family Man? He had been dominating my thoughts, but suddenly, yesterday I completely forgot him?

My breath came hard and loud. What had I done? I probably ruined any chance with him.

Flashes of yesterday flickered through my mind—me running out of my house, leaving the door open behind me, racing across the street in my old lime bathrobe and Mickey Mouse slippers, smiling goofily at Reynesh, and wanting so desperately to be with him.

I relived us loading up on a motorcycle. Me pressing my body tight to him as he ripped down the street with so much reckless abandonment. The beach. The ocean splashing freezing water on our legs, and deep conversations gazing into each other's eyes.

What the . . .?

I couldn't make sense of any of it—me or him—or our actions. He was the neighbor, the soon-to-be engaged Indian, with a match in a different country. What were we doing, and who thought it was a good idea?

I sat up fast and flinched in pain. Sunburn. Ow!

My phone beeped again.

Whoever was could wait. I needed to take baby steps to make sense of things. Figure out what had happened yesterday, who I'd been, and *why.*

I limped over to the bathroom to find bottles of aloe vera. I poured the tonic on my burned-to-a-crisp body. As I did that, something snapped in my mind. I had kissed Reynesh. A lot, if I remembered right.

The butterflies from the kissing fluttered in my memory. I had liked those kisses. A lot.

My doorbell rang.

The doorbell rang again . . . Tiffany? No, she'd always just barged in, using her key.

I focused on brushing my teeth as the person continued being a pest.

A salesperson? I stared at my reflection in the mirror. Did I have to get fully dressed for them?

More pounding on the door.

Damion? My chest clenched.

Reynesh? Why would he come over here today? And so early? I eyed my lime-green bathrobe hung on my closet door and grabbed it. I slid on my slippers before going down the stairs and performed a balancing act as I descended in pain, in the slippery slippers, and with anxiety flashing through me.

Boom. Boom. Boom.

"Coming," I called.

Not taking the time to look through the peek hole, I opened the front door. The sunlight spilled straight into my eyes, so I could only decipher a vague outline of a tall person.

"You look awful," the person said.

I bolted up straighter and pulled my beautiful raggedy lime-green bathroom closer around me. "Thanks," I said irritably. "And you ring the doorbell a lot."

The voice sounded familiar, but I wasn't able to place it right away.

"Reynesh?"

"What?"

It wasn't Reynesh.

Irritation resounded in the voice.

I stepped out on the porch, out of the sun's direct light, and closed the door behind me. My eyes adjusted enough to see the doorbell ringer was Nick.

Embarrassment flooded me. "Oh, hey." My voice came out timid.

His face settled into a hard-drawn outline.

I offered him a shy, flirty smile. "I'm so-o-o sorry about yesterday. I totally messed up."

He breathed deeply. "Care to explain?"

Yes, yes, explaining why I stood him up would be a good idea. I needed to do that. I sucked in my belly to hide the fact that this bathrobe made me look huge.

"Well—" How did I explain yesterday when it didn't even make sense to me?

Shifting his weight, Nick scanned me up and down. "Are you hung over?"

I brushed back my knotted hair. "No," I said, although my head pounded like it, and I was struggling to think clearly. "I'm so sorry. I really am. It's not like me. I kind of lost track of time," I admitted. "And this thing came up that I had no control over."

That was true too, sort of. I mean, I was in my kitchen drinking coffee, then next thing I knew, looking like a hot mess, I was throwing myself at my neighbor.

Nick shook his head. "You're a mess. You really need help to pull your life together. I can show you what apps you need to use. How to put better structure to your schedule."

I felt my cheeks flame with heat. Reynesh had never said that to me, even when I raced over to his house in this lovely bathrobe and left my front door wide open.

I blinked up into the sunlight at Nick dressed in a nice business shirt and pants. His blond hair had gel in it, and not one strand of hair appeared out of place. So unlike mine. I found my shoulders slumping even more.

"You just need clear, firm guidance."

He extended his arms like he wanted a hug.

My body didn't melt toward him like it had done so naturally with Reynesh yesterday on the beach. And on the motorcycle, sitting at breakfast . . . actually, like it had done for that entire day. Possibly, if I was going to be honest, like other days too.

"You need to put systems in place so you don't get so lost and scattered."

I moved back from him, bumping up against the front door. "Systems?"

He nodded. "Systems make people successful in businesses and in their personal lives."

I didn't like the choking feeling that word gave me. "That sounds so confining."

He puffed out his chest. "That's why you're lucky. I'm here to help you."

I blinked at him. He was saying all the right words, but they weren't feeling right. Something wasn't settling well. Maybe it was the hangover from yesterday, or maybe it was something different.

"First thing we need to do is get you looking better. Then I'll teach you how to keep the house clean using an effective system of sprint cleaning. Then you can use the same system to make great meals every day . . ."

Suddenly, I couldn't hear anything he was saying because, as he talked, I started figuring out what was bothering me. Even though it was different, he sounded a lot like Damion and Tiffany. He was telling me what to do.

Reynesh never once said I had to look a certain way. He never told me I was wrong. Instead of that, he always supported me. He gave me suggestions, yes, but he also listened to me and didn't attach strings to what I did. He just believed I would figure it out.

I was tired of people telling me what to do and making me into what they wanted.

I held up my hand in front of Nick's face. "Stop right there."

He flinched, but he quickly covered it up.

"This isn't going to work."

He waved his hand at my bathrobe. "What, you want to look like this all the time?"

"Nick, I can't do this. Send me the bill for the work you did with my social media, and we'll call this good."

His face fell. "What?"

"I just can't. You're too much like, like . . . like everyone. I refuse to be put in anyone's mold anymore."

He shook his head. "You're making a big mistake."

I shrugged. "Maybe I am."

He went to leave, then turned to me and snapped a derisive glance at my bathrobe. Then he glanced up at my frizzy hair before meeting my eyes with a coldness I'd never seen before, yet seemed oh, so familiar.

"I'll give you one social media tip for free. Don't ever post a picture of yourself like that. You'll never get another client. Or a man."

I crossed my arms over my chest in a protective reflex.

Reynesh's front door swung open. He stepped out onto the porch, no coffee mug in hand this time, wearing his business slacks and a light-green polo shirt, looking incredibly handsome. He watched Nick's car peel around the corner, then turn his focus over at me.

Shaken from having to stand up to Nick, I hurried across the street to Reynesh. The neighbor I had kissed yesterday—kissed a lot.

He called out, "Everything all right?"

"Yes," I called back, hurrying over to him.

I smiled up at him, but he didn't return the grin. That stopped me short as I stood there waiting to see what he would do or say after . . . well, *after.*

I shifted my feet.

He stood there, emotionless. Cold.

"Can we talk?" I asked, not wanting to endure the silence anymore.

His lips pressed together. "About . . . what?" He spoke carefully. "Yesterday?"

"I'm sunburned. I didn't know Indians could get burned."

I forced a light laugh, brushing off the edge in his voice. "The Southern California sun is powerful."

And so was whatever had happened yesterday. But from the way he acted, I didn't think Reynesh wanted to talk about it.

He finally broke the silence. "I've been getting complaints from the neighbors all morning."

Complaints? "About what?"

"The way we were riding the motorcycle and yelling."

I felt sucker punched in the gut. People had complained. That would explain his strange behavior today. "The revving engine probably didn't help," I said, feeling regret for my part.

"The police showed up at my door last night."

"Sorry," I whispered. "It's all fuzzy in my mind, but part of me remembers how wonderful it all was—"

"I can't be doing that," Reynesh snapped, speaking over me. "I have too much at risk."

My shoulders dropped like I was a little girl getting scolded by my parents. "I'm sorry." What all did he have at risk? His face reddened. "Is it because of your arranged marriage thing? Did I—I—?"

He sighed. "Not arranged yet. It's not really your fault."

"If you aren't . . . together yet, maybe you just don't do it."

He stiffened, back super straight. "Zoey, don't." His voice came out firm and distant. Not as cold as Nick's, but not as warm and affectionate as it had been yesterday.

Did he feel nothing I'd felt? None of the happiness? "It was nuts. But also—"

"I don't shirk my responsibility. It is my destiny."

I choked back tears, then wiped at my eyes.

His face softened as he whispered, "We had one perfect day, and that needs to be enough."

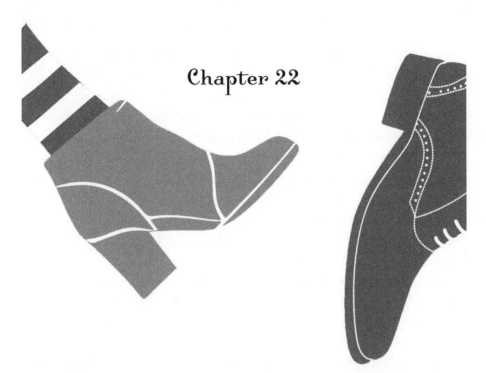

Chapter 22

After reapplying cream to my sunburn and slipping into a quirky dress my sister would hate, but flounced with cute ruffles, I climbed into my car. Through the whole process, I fought back tears. Time for Tiffany . . . *now*.

I rubbed my throbbing head. Shock hadn't made it all the way through me yet. Reynesh had ended our friendship. I hadn't seen that one coming. I should have. The man was marrying soon. We couldn't keep on like we had been.

But . . . I wiped at my stupid tears. But . . . I liked him. Heat rose on my face as I thought about that. I had figured out my feelings for him only yesterday, and *poof*, it was gone. That seemed incredibly cruel. We had one perfect day, and no more.

It felt like a monster had reached into my chest and pulled out my heart, leaving me as a shell of a person struggling to go on. I had no idea how to patch up that hole, but my sister would.

My breath came out in ragged, shaky gasps as I pulled up to Tiff's mid-size bank. Fortunately, not many people seemed to be visiting right now. I saw only a few people in business suits stroll out the front door, deep in conversation.

I tapped my fingers against the steering wheel, listening to the same old songs playing on the radio all summer. The repetitiveness of the music didn't help with my agitated state. The car had grown incredibly hot, partly because my sunburn was killing me. I got out of the car still shaking as I headed into the bank.

It only took seconds to find Tiffany tucked in the mostly glass walls of her office. I spotted her sitting at her large mahogany desk staring at an open file with focused concentration. Judging from the extremely hard expression on her flawless face, disturbing her day had not been the best idea.

As I watched her, I definitely caught a glimpse of the cold bank executive. It was clear she didn't hesitate to make brutal bottom-line decisions, not factoring in any human sympathy. To see my sister that way took me aback. I'd never thought of her as an ice queen, just efficient and smart. But with her hair slicked back and yanked into a tight bun, and her spotless gray suit with a single ray of light via her orange blouse, my heart sank.

I was in her territory now.

Hands cold despite the sunburn covering my body, I reminded myself that this was my sister who I had grown up with. She'd been my playmate, had helped me with homework, and often took my side, standing up for me against all the playground bullies. I didn't need to worry about her looking so "professional." She was my big sis. My go-to rock.

She saw me, and the harsh lines on her face loosened, replaced with rapid blinking.

I gave an uncertain wave. She gestured me inside. The moment I entered the room, she rushed to me. "I've been so worried about you."

That caught me off guard. "Why?"

"You didn't answer any of my calls, and you took off on the motorcycle. Did you have a nice time? You weren't home the couple of times I swung by, and I waited for hours to see if you were okay."

Avoiding her eyes, I sank into the closest chair. "Sorry. I'm having a rough day. Nick came over and was such a jerk." I waited for her to tell me she told me so.

She curled her fingers into fists. "What did he do?"

I shook my head. "I handled it. You don't need to fix it. He just didn't accept me for who I was. He was trying to remake me into some version of a woman he wanted."

Tiffany sat next to me. "What did you expect?"

Some sympathy from my sister.

"But what about Reynesh? How are things going with you two? You seemed happy on the motorcycle, and you were out late together."

"Reynesh . . ." I wailed.

Tiffany jumped up, closed the door, and grabbed tissues out of the desk drawer. She quickly made it to my side. She handed the tissue over as her desk phone rang. She swung her arm behind her and picked it up, still scrutinizing me.

A panicked voice sounded on the phone.

"Do not let him leave the bank." Tiffany rose to her feet. "I'll be right there." She hung up the phone. "I'll be back." She hustled out of the room, going to war like her heels were nothing. Wow, she was good.

The sunburn on my legs prickled, and my face flared with heat as I waited. Unable to sit still, I shifted in my seat, calculating if I'd have enough time to dash to the bathroom to coat aloe on the burn and dash back before Tiffany returned. I didn't want to make my busy sister wait.

The clock ticked loudly, signaling I was only wasting time sitting here trying to decide whether to go or not. I stood and wandered to the hallway, searching for the ladies' room. By the time I found it, my nose had started to run, causing me to step into a stall to nab toilet paper.

The bathroom door opened as several women came in talking. Feeling caught being in the wrong place and embarrassed at my puffy eyes, I nudged the stall door closed and locked it with care.

"Rhonda, have you played the game yet?" came a bubbly voice.

"I don't have time," came a younger voice.

"Make time. It's life-changing. I'll leave the secret phone number on your desk. Don't tell anyone, though. It's important not to let the word out."

I leaned closer to the stall door to hear better. Hands in purses rustled, compacts clicked, and a few coughs uttered as the women talked. They obviously came in to primp and chat.

The younger voice countered, "What's so special about it?"

I held my breath to make sure I could hear them.

"It helps people get over themselves to actually find love."

The younger lady laughed. "Sounds too good."

"Yeah, it's a modern-day love potion. People don't even know they have been hooked up. All you do is drop the formula into someone's drink or food."

"But how does it connect a person to their love interest?"

"You go onto a dark secret website called Hooked-In Corp. There are thousands of singles on it, which means you can handpick the type of person you want to hook up someone with."

My eyes widened. These people sounded crazy.

"Why would someone want to do that?"

The main voice laughed. "I did it to get my X-husband off my trail."

"And it's safe?"

"Oh, yeah, sure," the first lady said. "It works differently per person. One is never quite sure how long it lasts or the effects. It's just a liquid. You can put it in anything—a drink, food, even right on the tongue."

"Could you put it in something like this?" the second lady asked.

I craned my neck to see through the door crack. She was pointing at her coffee cup with her lipstick tube.

Coffee? I recalled Tiff messing with my coffee right before she left the other night, and insisting Reynesh drink the special "coffee" the next morning. Could she have—

"Could I use it for myself?"

I didn't hear the answer to that as the bathroom door closed, leaving me with my blood boiling. My sister had really done it this time. I stormed back to her office, wanting to pull all the hair out of her head.

By the time Tiffany returned, I was huffing steam. "Tell me about the game," I blurted out.

Her face colored ever so slightly as she calmly asked, "What game?"

"How far are you willing to go to control me? Seriously, Tiff, a love potion?"

She bolted toward me with a finger to her lips. "Shh." She scanned the room like someone might be listening. "Not so loud. It's a modern-day love potion where you can endorse two people. There are rules. You can't break up marriages, engagements, or committed relationships. Also, you cannot endorse anyone against their natural sexual inclinations."

I wiped my hands on the top of my dress.

"You used it on Reynesh and me," I almost shouted.

Her face turned blank. "I don't know what you're so upset about."

"He's engaged!" I yelled.

Her face crinkled. "No, that can't be. It won't work on engaged people. A lady in the office already tried that."

I sneered at her. "Well, he will be extremely soon. Tiffany, what were you thinking?"

She crossed her arms over her chest.

My throat tightened. "Why?"

She shrugged. "You were determined to ruin me getting with Nick."

"So? It's none of your business."

"Oh, but it is."

"How?" I demanded.

"Zoey, why did you come here today?"

I was almost hyperventilating with anger and confusion. "Why? How can you ask *why*? You used a love potion—"

"You came here for me to save you."

I stopped short.

"Like you did with Damion. Like you would have done with Nick if it hadn't gone south so fast. And I'd drop everything and swoop in to save you. And that's why you are here right now. You were upset, and things were melting down, so you dumped your troubles on me. For me to . . . what? To fix them?"

I sank back in my seat, shaking my head. "No, I—I don't know. I thought maybe—"

"Maybe I'd fix things. Save you. Like I always do. So, I saved you with the love potion. Again, from yourself. And now you're mad? You're always mad when I save you, but it never stops you from asking the next time."

"Tiff," I slapped at my armchair, "this is my life, not yours."

She leaned into her desk, staring at me. "Your poor choices affect me, and I'm tired of it."

"What?" I practically screamed. "You said you messed up my love life because of how it affects *you*? Are you insane?"

In a slow, almost mechanical voice, she said, "Zoey, that's enough."

"Tiffany," I said, voice strained, "maybe I don't make the same choices you do, but that doesn't mean they're bad ones."

"I don't get all swept up with someone just because they said *one* thing I want to hear."

My spine straightened. I thought about Damion and Nick. She might have a point there, but it didn't give her the right to take over my agency and Reynesh's. Poor Reynesh. He was probably as confused this morning as I was. And, in response, he'd turned his back on me.

"I thought if you could experience a healthy connection," Tiffany said, "it'd change things for you. Help you to raise your standards."

"Standards like yours, where everyone is too good for you?"

She flinched, but that didn't stop me from asking, "Why are you so against Nick?"

Tiffany gave a disgusted laugh. "That guy is the biggest creep in the whole business world. He has a reputation with women that's not pretty." She paused, eyes narrowing. "And of course you were drawn to him like a moth to a flame." She shook her head. "I don't have the energy for it."

I stood. Talking to her was going nowhere. "You don't have to spend any energy on it."

She glanced away. "I wish. Even casting a love potion on you with a nice guy doesn't seem to snap you out of your destructive ways."

"Stay out of my life. I'll live it the way I want to."

My sister grabbed the file she had brushed aside. "You got it. Don't ask me to save you again."

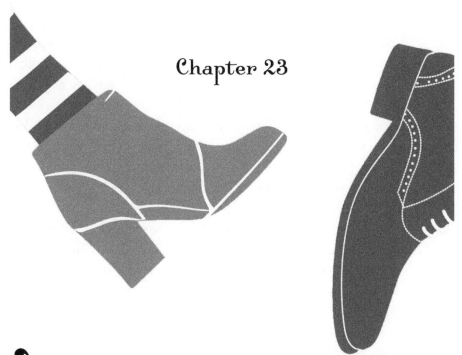

Chapter 23

I should've been happy. My sister wasn't telling me what to do. It had been three days, and no word from her. I had wanted this. I wanted to be independent and to be on my own.

The house was uncannily quiet. And creepy. The days dragged on, long and lonely, but I didn't cave and call my sister. She didn't call me either.

So, no sister. No neighbor. Rarely friends.

Not feeling right about not telling Reynesh about the love potion, I wrote him a note requesting we chat and taped it to his front door. It disappeared by the end of the day, so it was on him if we did or didn't talk.

———

Days passed in thick heat. I coached the few clients I had. I also spent hours on my coaching course so I could finish it up faster. I tried to network a couple of times, but without Tiffany, Reynesh, or Nick, the clients didn't pour in like when others recommended me.

Instead, I heard, "Isn't that nice."

To make things worse, the massage client I was trading with suddenly became "too busy" to meet. A bit depressed about that, I chose not to think about Reynesh or Tiffany, or how messed up my life was, or anything, really. I just existed.

Wednesday arrived a lot faster than expected. A major coaching day. My first client was scheduled to call in at seven in the morning, which was dreadfully early, but I was armed with tea, not trusting coffee anymore.

The phone rang at one minute after seven. I love punctual people.

"Sheryl, how are you doing?"

We'd been working together, trying to spice up the romance in her marriage.

"I'm really good," she said with an enthusiastic voice. "That's what I want to talk to you about. My husband just booked a three-month trip through Europe to celebrate our anniversary."

"Congrats!" I said, stunned. That was a complete change from last week. "When do you go?"

"Well, we leave tomorrow, so today all my attention is on packing."

Enough air left my lungs to make my head spin. "Okay, so when do you want to reschedule?"

The phone line went dead for what seemed like forever.

"Well, here's the thing. You have been a great coach, and I appreciate all the help you have given me, but I'm not going to be able to continue with you at this time. Maybe in the future, but right now I don't need one."

My head swirled. "Okay."

I didn't have enough clients to lose this one. I was supposed to be all cool about this and supportive, but I didn't feel cool and supportive. I felt like ripping a Barbie doll's head off.

"I have to go," she said, her voice full of too much excitement. "Don't worry, I'll send you a check in the mail for this session. Thanks for all your help."

She was going on a romantic getaway like I had always wanted to do with Damion. How could I coach others to find the happiness I was unable to find for myself?

She hung up, and I decided that losing a client deserved at least cookies or a potato chip party—something to calm the pain. Fat always did the trick. I had no fat in the cabinets. Why had I been so committed to a diet? Today was not the right kind of day for diet food. That would be tomorrow.

I glanced at my clock. I had exactly one hour and forty-four minutes until my next client called. I tried to console myself with this. I still had a client.

———————

My next client showed up to the phone call in tears. "My husband says I can't coach with you. He doesn't like who I'm becoming when I talk to you. He says you are a bad influence, and we don't have money to waste on silly things like paying someone to hear me talk."

Wow. What does a person say to that? Controlling husband? Yep. Glad I wasn't married to him. Yep. You needed to make your own decision and not let some other person tell you what you could and couldn't do in your life. Absolutely.

All things I needed to tell myself.

Did I blurt out anything like that? Nope. Instead, I said, "I can understand. Would you like to use this session to bring closure to the work we've already done?"

That was what we did for that hour, even as I cried inside. I'd lost two clients in one day. Two clients. What were the chances of that?

Now being a good coach for Elizabeth today was more important than ever. She was my one remaining client, and my highest-paying one. I needed to prove I was helpful to her no matter what. Make myself indispensable.

I had thirty minutes. I could clean or eat Cheetos.

The doorbell rang, deciding the matter for me.

I opened the door to find Elizabeth in a power suit standing in the doorframe with all her tall glory in the afternoon light.

"Hi." She brushed past me. "I hope you don't mind if I'm early. I just can't wait to begin our session. Is now a good time?"

I thought about my Cheetos bag and sighed. "Perfect. Please take a seat." I gestured to where she'd sat before, then hurried out of the room to find her file. Once armed with my folder, I sat on the couch, bracing myself to hear more bad news and about the battles she was fighting.

"So, how's it going?"

"Great." A red flush spread across her face.

Great. Did she say *great*? How could she say that? She was so full of negativity last time. Why was she blushing?

"Tell me." I leaned forward. This was going to be juicy.

"Zoey, can I just tell you what an amazing coach you are?"

That was good to hear, especially today.

"Last week, I was so miserable, and you really pried to get me to open up and voice what I wanted. I never believed in the law of attraction before, but since we did all that work, the most perfect guy has shown up in my life."

I couldn't help staring. "Really? Tell me all about it."

The rest of the session was about this amazing guy, how he fit her description of what she was wanting. She wanted to know if I thought they were going to make it. How could she tell if it would last?

Seriously? Like I knew any of these answers, but she hardly listened to me anyway. I had the real impression that all she wanted from me was to have someone to talk to and be happy for her latest development. If that was all she wanted, and she was willing to pay, I could do that.

"You deserve to be happy," I said, thinking how hard she'd worked in her life.

She gave me a funny look, thought about it, and said, "You're right."

That session flew by. I sighed with relief when she gave me another check and scheduled her next appointment—my losing clients' streak was over. Good riddance.

I followed her to the door to find Damion standing on my porch. His hand was raised as though he was about to knock. "Elizabeth?" he queried. "What are you doing at my X-wife's house?"

Her eyes grew large. "X-wife? What are you talking about?" She glanced back and forth between me and Damion. "You two weren't . . ."

I nodded. "We were."

Her eyes were still wide as though that was giving her the ability to take everything in. "Oh, I see."

I didn't see. "Damion, what are you doing here?"

He shifted his weight. "My accountant was going over the books, and we messed up the health insurance credit, I owe you some money."

I extended my hand. It didn't matter what the circumstances were. I wasn't going to pass up the money.

Damion glanced at my hand, which seemed to snap his mind back into place. "Oh," he said, checking his pockets. He pulled out an envelope and handed it to me.

While I opened the envelope to verify it held a check, Elizabeth said, "Zoey, this was who I was telling you about earlier," she said softly.

"Wha-a-at?" I glanced between them until it clicked. "*This* is the guy you were talking about?"

Damion flopped his arm around her shoulder and pulled her toward him in the crook of his arm. He kissed her on the top of the forehead. For my benefit, of course. Fine. Whatever. I didn't need the front-row show.

"Dear, what are you doing at my X-wife's house?"

He called her dear!

"You shouldn't call her the same nickname you called me," I said. "Show Elizabeth some respect and come up with something different. Have a unique relationship. Don't try to replace me."

His eyes narrowed. "Stop being jealous."

He pulled Elizabeth out from under his arm and grabbed her by the shoulders to face him. "Dear, please explain to me what you're doing here."

"Zoey is the coach I was telling you about."

Damion choked. After catching his breath, he said, "Well, obviously you mean she 'was' your coach because there's no way that's going to work. This is unethical."

Elizabeth shrugged. "Of course. Sorry, Zoey."

I stared at her. Seriously? She tossed our relationship just like that for *him*.

"But we were doing such great work together."

She nodded. "That's true, but Damion is right. It's a conflict."

Damion smirked as I realized everything I'd just heard from Elizabeth in the session was about *him*.

That was enough to make a person sick. Very, very sick, and the fact that I didn't pick up on the reality that Elizabeth was with a jerk meant I might be harming people with coaching, not helping.

"Elizabeth," Damion asked in the take-charge voice he liked to use when situations became sticky, "would you like to go for dinner?"

Her whole face beamed. "Sure."

"Great," Damion said. "Go get in my car, and I'll be right there. I need to finish up some business with Zoey."

Elizabeth peered suspiciously between us.

Please! What did she think I was going to do? Try to steal my lousy, no-good husband back as she waited in the car to go out with him? Did she really think I'd be stupid enough to do that to a lawyer—or anyone, for that matter?

Damion gave her a peck on the lips. "I'll be right there."

That was disgusting to watch.

My X stepped closer to me. I backed against the front door.

"You stay away from me and the people I date. You got that?" He spoke in a deep, threatening voice.

I bumped against the front doorframe. I swallowed a lump. "Stop chasing away my clients, then."

He took a breath, paused, then peered at me. "Leave me and Elizabeth *alone.*"

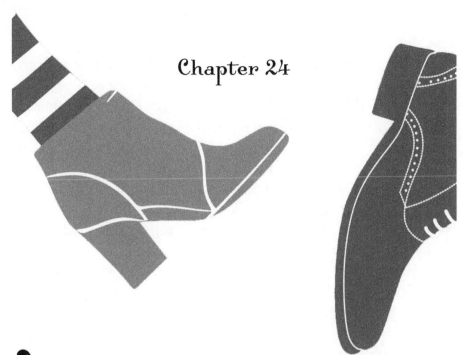

Chapter 24

I hadn't left my house for a long time—a very long time—days. Out my window, Reynesh's house stood quietly with two cars parked in the driveway and the motorcycle parked at a funny angle.

A four-door car drove by, letting me know there was life out there that waited for me to join, even if I couldn't control it.

I stared at my messy silent house. Too silent. Too messy. I hurried out the front door, needing to hear the rustle of the wind and maybe a distant dog bark—anything not to be completely alone.

Midway down my driveway, I stopped to listen to the distant sounds of life floating through the afternoon air. Kids a few blocks over laughed. A car passed by. A voice called out, and another voice responded.

A mailman drove by, puttering away from the community mailboxes. It had been days since I'd gotten my mail. There might be bills in there—bills I had to pay. No one else would do it. I was so bad at this life thing. I had to handle it better. It was all up to me.

Maybe Tiffany had a point, though she never should have done a love potion—that was wrong. But so was dumping all my problems on her, expecting her to fix them, then getting angry when she tried.

My feet felt encased in cement as I dragged them down the asphalt to the community mailbox. A light breeze caressed my face as I opened my box. It burst with mail and more problems. As I gathered the stack into my arms, I saw an official letter from my bank. With a sense of foreboding, I shoved the rest of my mail back into the box and opened the "official" one.

A notice of foreclosure. The letter stated they had sent me repeated mailings. That might or might not be true, but time had run out.

My legs weakened.

I collapsed onto the sidewalk, sitting on the curb with my head between my knees, having no strength to do anything else.

Pebbles crunched underfoot. Fancy blue shoes appeared before my eyes—familiar royal-blue running shoes.

With a heavy head, I squinted up to see Reynesh.

I wiped at my tears, not even trying to hide them. No use pretending at anything with anyone. This mess—with my eyes swollen, hair disheveled, and failure surrounding me—was the *real* me.

Reynesh slumped down by me. "Are you okay?"

I sniffed, wiping at my nose. "I don't have to worry about the stupid grass patches on my lawn anymore, or the fact that your lawn always out-shines mine." I lifted my gaze to his again.

"Why?"

I cried harder. Reynesh put his arm around me, his warmth pressing against my shoulder. I leaned into him, feeling his strong arm settling me.

"It'll be okay," he murmured.

I gave a broken, sobbing laugh. He didn't know that. None of us knew that. "Why are you even talking to me?"

He stiffened. "What?"

I sniffed. "I thought you weren't talking to me."

He tugged me toward him. "Why wouldn't I talk to you?"

"I don't know." I tossed my hands up in frustration. "You've been ignoring me, and you didn't respond to my note."

"Note?"

"The one I left on your front door that said we needed to talk."

"I didn't get it." He sighed. "I would never purposely ignore you. What did you want to talk about?"

I gulped. "The fact my sister put a love potion in our coffee, so that explains . . . explains . . ." I buried my face in my hands.

Reynesh chuckled.

This caught my attention. I peeked up at him. "It's true."

He shrugged. "It actually makes a lot of sense."

"But . . . what?"

"Destiny works that way."

"You're not mad? Upset? Baffled?"

He shook his head. "No. Your sister thought we belonged together. The truth is, us coming together helped our dharma. I'm okay with that."

My head tightened with pressure. I had to talk to someone or I was going to explode. "I lost all my clients in one day!"

His eyes widened. "That sucks."

"And an eviction notice."

He shook his head. "Two things. One, in this county, it takes two or three months—sometimes six—for an eviction to go through, so you have time. Two, destiny has other plans for you."

I frowned. He put everything into that category. "I'm tired of destiny being against me."

"Destiny is never against you. It's always aspiring for our good."

I waved my hand with my eviction notice. "Losing all my clients, getting kicked out of my house, is all for my good?"

Reynesh pressed his lips together, giving that thought. "Yes."

I struggled to my feet. "That's crazy."

He reached up and put his hand on my arm. "Hear me out."

Our eyes connected, and I sat back on the cement curb. I had nothing to lose by listening to him. The late-afternoon sun touched our left shoulders as a final goodbye for the day. He had a stain the size of a dime on his shirt. It was close to the bottom of his rib cage. It comforted me. At last, at least once, he didn't look perfect.

His hands rested casually on top of his knees as he leaned closer to me on the cement curb. Tears filled my eyes. This man was incredible, beautiful, successful, kind—even though he was full of bizarre ideas about destiny.

"Maybe all this is meant to help you get on the right path," he said softly. "Maybe you were going in the wrong direction before, and maybe that's why it isn't working."

I stared at him, annoyed, and a flicker of anger sparked. He acted all smug about how destiny was working for me, but he wasn't understanding how it was working for him. I curled my fingers into fists. "Like your right path is to marry someone you don't want to?"

It was his turn to appear gloomy.

We sat, side by side, staring at the paved road.

"I hope I'm not destined to feel this crappy my whole life," I said after a few moments, a lone tear escaping.

Reynesh leaned over, and with his index finger, he traced the drop down the side of my cheek. His touch was gentle and stirred a storm inside me, reminding me of the one perfect day I had with him on the bike, eating breakfast, strolling the ocean, building a campfire, and lots and lots of luscious kisses.

All because of a love potion.

More tears.

Reynesh put his arms around me.

I sniffed and nestled into his chest, staying that way for a long time—enough time for my tears to dry. I leaned in closer to him. Close enough to kiss. I tipped my head up, nearing my lips to his.

"Zoey," he said. "No."

I laid my head on his chest, hearing his heartbeat. "Why? We acted like a couple once."

His body stiffened with a brittle rigidity. "That shouldn't have happened. I'll be engaged to someone else soon." He gently pushed me from him. "My path is charted, and it isn't with you."

I leaned from him. "It doesn't have to be like that."

He barely shook his head. "It does."

Tears rose. "We get along so well. We have a dynamic relationship."

"Even if I wasn't committed to someone else, you aren't ready to be in any relationship. You're still kind of a mess."

My cheeks flamed at his first criticism of me. "Just because I was crying from being evicted and losing my clients doesn't mean I'm a mess. I have good things to offer. I'm funny and insightful, and I—" I sniffed, my voice catching. "I have a lot of heart."

Reynesh trailed his fingers through my hair. "All of that's true. You need time to get on your feet, that's all. Give yourself that gift."

"Okay," I whispered.

I sat up and grasped for a way to send him back to his house, but didn't say a word. I didn't want him to leave even if I couldn't have him. And maybe Ray was right. Maybe, right now, I shouldn't have anyone but myself. Terrifying.

Our eyes met.

"You'll agree with me too, one day. To do this . . . between us?" His voice trailed off.

"Not our destiny?" I suggested in a whisper.

"Not mine." His voice sounded flat and hard. After a long moment of silence, he said, "You know there are divorce recovery groups, right?"

"What?"

"Yeah, divorce recovery groups. I know someone who runs one. She's great. You'd like her."

I lifted my head a little. Recovery from divorce?

"I'd feel better if I knew you had a safe place to talk and someone to help you through . . . everything."

———————

If I didn't start doing something, I'd be homeless.

Step one, do a local job search. On breaks, feed the orange cat that still comes around.

Step two, apply for anything that might be possible.

Step three, try with all my might not to become too discouraged with the fact that I most likely would not hear from any of the jobs I applied to. I petted the cat one stroke before feeding it.

Step four, figure out another step and name the cat "If," just because.

An overwhelming sense of helplessness settled over me. The only break from it was watching the cat come slinking around for more food.

Two weeks later, forty job applications submitted, and hearing nothing but "no," and silence, and more silence. I opened the back door.

If rushed into the house his tail lifted high.

I chased after him, but he hid from me.

185

Giving up the chase, I sank on the couch, tired from all the packing. If peered around with his curious cat eyes at the packed box. "All my 'science' and my rules and my planning haven't worked."

He remained still.

"Now all there's left to do is pack and shrink my life to a more manageable size alone."

If stared at me.

"I tried so hard to find someone who'd take care of me."

He hopped into my lap. I stroked his soft, newly thickened coat.

"It didn't work." He sank deeper into my lap. "They didn't value me."

Silence penetrated my house, my life, my bones, my thoughts. The occasional roar of an engine of a car driving by was the only thing that broke the absolutely suffocating stillness.

I had nothing to do except to shove my former life into moving boxes, apply for jobs, and value myself. At last, I valued me, and maybe If.

As if on cue, he purred.

Later that day, I bought a litter box for my new cat. He used the box without fuss. That gave me the little flame of hope to move on to step five, hunt for an apartment.

After that, on to step six—be willing to take any job, even if it meant flipping burgers.

My throat tightened at that thought. Damion would laugh, but it didn't matter. Taking care of myself, no matter if it meant a low-paying job, was important.

My phone pinged.

From Reynesh. I had texted him, asking for the name and phone number of the divorce support group. He shared the contact.

Before I lost my courage, I called the group's leader, hands shaking.

"Hello?" said a friendly female voice.

"Hi-i." My voice shook. "My name is Zoey, and I think I might need your group."

———

My stomach tightened hard like it always did before I entered into some new event. I had practice going into the unknown, but the nerves always came. Taking a deep breath, I climbed out of my car and pulled my old purse tight to my free-flowing dress. I could do this. This was easier than a business group—no high heels, no pinching suits, no trying to put on airs of importance. I showed up as myself—mess and all—and it felt better than being all gooped up.

Swallowing a lump, I headed to where the people gathered. No one was dressed up—mostly jeans and T-shirts and the occasional shorts. Some people walked slowly, their shoulders slumped, but others laughed and talked with coffee in their hands.

I slowed my pace when a short motherly type of woman, pleasantly plump, love oozing out of her, dashed up to me.

"Are you Zoey? I'm Cassandra. We talked on the phone."

I shifted my weight. "I am."

"I'm glad to meet you."

"You too."

Others surrounded her and greeted me, telling me they were glad I had come. After they waved goodbye and went into the meeting room, Cassandra focused on me.

"I think you're going to find it helpful here."

For some strange reason, I believed she was right. "At least I don't have to wear heels."

She laughed. "Nope, not here. We're not like those dreadful business events."

The pressure I didn't know I carried eased in my chest. This felt more like a place where I could be me.

Cassandra headed toward the building. "If you want, after the meeting, we can go for coffee and talk."

I gave her a wide grin. "That would be nice."

The meeting was filled with informative training on how to emotionally process a divorce. They covered the stages of healing a person needed to go through. Stages? That was surprising.

One lady asked, "Am I the only one who can't sleep at night?"

Sitting up straighter in my chair, I blurted out, "No, I struggle with that too."

A guy laughed. "I gather my pillows around me like it's a body."

Another lady piped up, "I do yoga for sleep and then play soft music so the house doesn't feel so empty and creaky."

Those were actually all good ideas. I glanced around at these people who were like me and suddenly didn't feel so alone.

When the meeting concluded, Cassandra hurried over to me. "I so see myself in you when I was going through my divorce. I was nervous about facing the world on my own. The pain of a failed dream stifled me."

She had summed it up much better than I could.

Flipping her keys in her hand, she asked, "Still up for coffee?"

"Sure."

Thirty minutes later, we had our piping hot teas in hand at a coffee shop. I would probably never look at coffee the same. I didn't know if I would ever be able to drink it again.

Cassandra said, "It's going to be hard for you to get through all your suppressed pain and learn how to stand on your own." Her eyes never left mine as she spoke. "But you can handle hard things, right?"

Could I? I mean, I *endured* them, but I didn't think that's what she was talking about.

"It's not some complicated endeavor," she went on. "Just be willing to tolerate the emotional hard times, keep doing what you know is right, keep moving forward, and you'll get through it. You got this."

She was right. I would. It was nice to be with someone who thought I could do it. Reynesh was the only one who'd ever truly believed in me before this, but until I believed in myself, none of the other people's beliefs mattered.

I grew hot—with hope this time.

———

The support group gave me enough boost that packing became easier. I applied for at least five jobs a day. I added to my daily routine, walking around the local blocks and going to Speech Masters.

Every day passed a lot like the next until late one afternoon. Reynesh showed up at my doorstep in his business casual clothes, looking sexy as ever, stirring up a lot of those old feelings.

"Came to check on you. Can I come in?"

My heart did more skipping than it had for a long time. I couldn't help but think about those kisses that made my head spin. That wasn't the real us. Not real chemistry. It was drug-induced.

I swallowed.

He stopped in the doorway of my house.

Startled, I shifted around to see what was up.

He scanned the place with the half-filled boxes lined up everywhere. "You're moving?"

"Oh, yeah. I am." I shrugged. "Eviction notice and double mortgage. What can you do?"

A deep line edged on his forehead. "I'll be sorry to see you go."

I flipped my hair onto my back as I laughed nervously. "You might appreciate not getting in trouble with the neighbors."

He gave that thought. "You have a point there."

I shook my head. "And having a neighbor who can do something about the brown spots on my lawn might be a good thing for you."

"That's an excellent point."

I rolled my eyes as I wandered over to the green couch. He sat so we faced each other.

He smiled, and those quivering feelings sparked alive again instantly. The man was cute, whether I was under a love potion spell or not.

"How's the divorce recovery group going?"

He was holding my feet to the fire. That was something a friend would do, what someone who cared would do. I needed someone in my life like that. I had wanted to be independent, but all this silence of not having anyone seemed overrated. Maybe interdependence would be a better option if I could manage being involved with something like that.

"Casandra wants me to take responsibility for my part of the problem with Tiffany," I blurted out.

"And?"

"I will do it. I need to figure out how. How are you doing?"

He shifted in his seat. "Fine. Busy growing the business. We launched."

I looked over at him. "Congratulations! You seem to have a gift for that."

He shook his head. "You know the reality of something is always harder than the dream. It's going okay, but definitely hitting snags."

I sighed. "Sorry to hear that." Maybe a lot of businesses were like that.

Looking better and more successful on the outside. For some reason, Nick flittered into my mind. Maybe that was the truth for him. He did like to talk big, but maybe I had fallen for an image that was a front.

"Zoey?"

There was something to Reynesh's tone of voice that caught my attention. "Yes?"

"Can we be friends? I know it might be awkward because . . . because of everything, but I miss having you in my life."

I gave a sniffling kind of laugh. "Does 'everything' mean the love potion?"

He laughed a little too. "Yeah. That."

Our little laughs faded away. "It *was* just a potion, right? I mean, all that couldn't have been real." I paused. "Right?"

He paused, swallowed, then nodded firmly. "Right. No way it was real."

I nodded too, less firmly. "Yeah, no way. Not our destiny."

"It's hard to know what our destiny is, but it always moves us down our path. I thought about what your sister did, spiking our coffee like that. She needs a shakedown."

"What about just accepting it, like you said before?"

He shrugged with a guilty smile. "That sounded good, didn't it?"

I couldn't help a side smile. I nodded glumly. I shifted, stretching out my legs. "Tiff and I are kind of not talking right now."

His gaze sharpened. "Kind of not talking?"

"We argued, and I . . . we both said things maybe we shouldn't have said. Or . . . I don't know." I threw up my hands. "Maybe they were things that should've been said a long time ago."

"Wow," he finally said. "That must've been hard for you, setting those boundaries with your sister. It used to be you and her against the world, right?"

I kept my face turned away because tears pricked at my eyes. I nodded. "You're right, it was hard. It *is* hard. It's scary and confusing and lonely."

"Sounds like you could use a friend."

I gave a gasping sort of laugh. One tear leaked out as I turned to his kind, caring eyes. "Yeah, I could really, really use a friend."

He smiled. "I'm here."

And there we were, smiling at each other like old friends.

I kept the smile on my face, even though I was breaking inside. I wanted so much more than friendship with Reynesh. But I kept smiling because I was growing up, and it wasn't up to Reynesh to fix my heartbreak. Not even if he was the source of it.

We were friends. That would have to be enough.

"Honestly," I said, "I don't even know what you miss about me. Is it my glittering speeches or the way I stumble on high heels?"

Reynesh didn't miss a beat. "What's not to like? You're funny and open."

My jaw dropped.

"I love how real you are."

"You—you do?"

He nodded. "You give your all to everything you do. You're earnest. You wear your heart on your sleeve."

He was listing out these things as if they were *compliments*. As if they were a good thing, not the character flaws I'd been told throughout my life were going to ruin my chances.

"And you do it so honestly," he finished, turning his hands over like what he was saying was obvious. "You inspire me."

Speechless, I stared at him so long that he finally laughed.

"Don't believe me?" he asked.

"I—I'll try."

"Deal," he said, his smile warm and happy.

I sniffed and wiped the back of my hand under my nose. "Well, Reynesh, you know one thing friends do?"

His grin turned a little mischievous. "What's that?"

"They help friends move."

He broke out in laughter. I did too, and now it was even better—and even worse—because we were laughing together, me and my friend Reynesh.

"Deal," he said. "If I get paid in brownies."

"Deal," I promised. "Lots and lots of brownies."

He looked around at the space. "When are you moving?" He sounded quieter now.

"Not sure yet. Not sure when or where, but I know it's coming, so I'm just facing it. I'm not avoiding it or burying my head in the sand anymore. I'm going to do things differently now."

Our eyes met.

"I'll help."

"Thank you," I whispered. It was good that I stood up from the couch and started moving boxes around or I'd have broken down in sobs.

I really, really wanted Reynesh. I really, really wanted to bury my head in the sand and demand someone save me from all these feelings. Still, I was crafting a new Zoey, the *real* Zoey, and I had to find my way, even with a broken heart.

He shrugged. "Just being around you makes me feel significant."

I blinked at him, feeling myself blush. It was too bad that it was not "in the stars" for us to be something more. I could jump on him and kiss him for saying that. I could hear things like that every day and be completely happy.

"I'd like to be friends, but there's something we have to talk about first."

It was Reynesh's turn to squirm. "Okay?"

"So, how do you feel about our whole relationship being fake . . . a spell, a chemically induced delusion?"

Reynesh looked at me with sadness. "Our relationship isn't that."

"But it—"

"Zoey, there was always something between us. It must be prarabdha. That means our previous actions affect what happens to us, and we have no control over it. It was part of what was meant to be."

The sunlight shifted in the living room, casting a dark shadow.

"For some reason, we were meant to have that perfect day. It'll always be a part of me. It has enriched me and made my life better. It changed who I am, and from what I can see with you, it changed you too. I'm okay accepting the gift and accepting it as part of what was meant for both of us. We were destined to have that time together."

I fiddled with my fingers. "And now we are not?"

"We could have different experiences together now, if you and destiny are willing. It won't be as lovers."

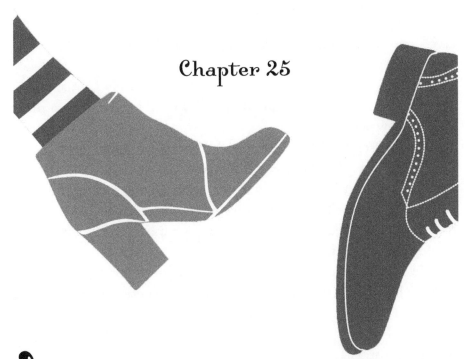

Chapter 25

I sat on my swing on the front porch enjoying the perfect afternoon weather. My journal lay on my lap, waiting for me to explore anger— this week's divorce group homework assignment. But instead of exploring my internal landscape for that elusive emotion, I became absorbed in listening to the crows talk and the rustle of the leaves in the gentle wind. The sun sank in the background with a display of pastels.

I had been missing all this splendor, too consumed with my goals. Goals that weren't truly mine. Goals fueled by fears festering deep inside me. It was taking a lot of work in the divorce recovery group to yank them out. But now, even though it wasn't glamorous, I was taking care of myself. I leaned back on the porch swing, listening to the birds, feeling the breeze, and wasn't stressed even though my business had failed, I was losing my house, and I was very single. A deep calm engulfed me.

My friendship with Reynesh had raised the bar on what I wanted in a man. The bar was now no longer set on how I could fit into *their* life, *their* wants, and *their* desires. If I ever was going to be with someone, they would have to truly see me and treat me with respect. My future partner would accept me, no matter how I looked, and it would be without heels. I wrote that down in my notebook—my new, improved list.

Feeling inspired, I jumped to my feet and placed my journal on the swing. I dashed inside and grabbed my old list and hurried to compare it with my new one.

The old list started with Disneyland Dad.

The new list . . . No, maybe I shouldn't say "list." Instead, "requirements." Mine started with someone who respected me, had family values, and enjoyed me for the way I am. I wasn't going to conform to some standard I was supposed to meet workwise, shoe-wise, or otherwise, and I would give him the same acceptance.

My sexy neighbor across the street popped into my thoughts. I was lucky to have had him in my life to show me what was possible. I ripped up the old list to let go of the old expectations.

Reynesh stepped up on the porch with his sly smile. "Somebody has a grudge against that paper."

I shoved the pieces of paper into my relationship binder, gathered all my stuff, and set it by my feet to make room for him on the swing.

"Sit." I gestured to the space next to me, glad for his interruption. The swing creaked under his weight.

I smiled over at him, loving the fact we had become so comfortable around each other. "I'm sorry to disappoint you, but I have no clogged sinks, broken fridges, or flat tires that need help today."

His smile widened. "Now, *that* is disappointing."

Despite the fact we weren't a thing, Reynesh had made a habit of helping me get on my feet. Not only did he fix the home repairs, but he also insisted on teaching me how to handle it myself. That, in my book, made him a true friend.

To my complete surprise, I'd enjoyed it. I liked to know how to fix a hot water heater and a flat tire, and how to use a level.

Better yet, I could do it. I was competent. I was handy. I didn't need anyone but me. And the local hardware store.

"Does that mean no dinner?" Reynesh asked.

I shook my head. "Sorry, I've been focusing on other things."

He sighed. "Any desserts left?"

I laughed at his puppy-dog expression. "Tomorrow, I'll bake your brownies."

He rubbed his hands together. "Yummy."

As the sun set, the marine layer floated inland to create a perfectly overcast sky. It shielded everything from becoming too hot. In fact, I was itching to start my nightly walk. I loved strolling through the cool, empty streets all by myself, with the mountains in the distance and the wind blowing over my face.

Turns out, I enjoyed being alone. Who could have guessed?

I also really enjoyed being with Reynesh. So, I smiled up at him. "Join me for my evening stroll?"

"You don't have your divorce support group this evening?"

I shook my head. "Got canceled because the leader had a conflict. I'm actually going to miss it."

He raised his eyebrows. "Really? You acted like I was crazy for suggesting it."

I rolled my eyes. "Fine. You were right."

He folded his hands behind his head with a cocky grin. "About what?" he prodded even though he knew actually about what.

"It's helpful."

The people there were all different ages and colors and had different lifestyles, yet we were all there because we were hurting. Some people felt as scared as I was. Some of the participants echoed thoughts I'd had, like, "I don't know what to do," "I thought it was going to be so much easier," "I feel so alone," and "I hate the nights. I'm okay during the days, but the nights . . ."

Some people cried every time they came, and others seemed to have their lives together, and they still came. People talked to me before the meeting and after, and no one ever said I was doing things wrong. Several times, people thanked me for what I'd shared and told me I was brave. I didn't feel brave, but maybe I was becoming that way. I had just asked Reynesh to go on a walk with me. I had never been that assertive before, except under a love potion.

He stood. "That's all I get for being right?"

I nodded. "Yep. Walk?"

"Absolutely."

The days seemed to collapse onto each other, all blurring together. The temperature had dipped to the fifties as autumn settled in, causing most of Murrieta's residents to resign themselves to sweaters and leather boots.

For me, it meant digging out my go-go boots and lightweight fake-leather mid-thigh jackets despite the eye rolls I'd earn from Tiffany if she saw me. Not that she would have these days. We hadn't talked for a long while.

The foreclosure process continued its slow grind. I mostly talked to people on the phone. Still, the bank wanted me to come in to discuss the procedure, during which I learned I had a month left before officially being kicked out.

The trip to the bank highlighted my pain of not talking to my sister. I felt so out of touch not hearing about her big merger or about how stupid the newest employee was or which movie I just had to see. If I was going to be honest, I also missed her very strong opinions. She was always so alive about everything. I missed listening to her and watching her take off in the business world.

I reflected on the fact that I used to feel envious of her. Now I was just glad she had a path. One that worked for her so well. I wasn't sure if the sentiment would be returned, though. I didn't think she would be impressed with my regular visits to divorce recovery, or Speech Masters, or my friendly walks with Reynesh almost every night.

She'd definitely not be impressed by the fact that I had taken a job flipping hamburgers. Or the fact that I had adopted a small orange furball cat. Or did If adopt me? More likely, he did. He had never left the house after barging in that day, which made me love him even more. Often, when I was on the phone working out details, I'd find myself stroking his fur.

The best part about watching romance movies was feeling the warmth of his little body huddled up in my lap. Sometimes he would perk up and watch the screen more intentionally than me. If was absorbed by the show's drama, or maybe the movement television offered.

He was fattening up, probably from the regular food I fed him, and he spent most nights tucked up next to me or on top of me, ending the pain of lonely nights. Who knew a cat would be better than a man? I had spent many days and nights with just me and If.

Tiffany didn't like animals. She would never understand the simple joy I had just being with my kitty. That was my sister's loss, I concluded—a big loss.

Maybe Tiff was on my mind because it was the first day of winter. She and I always shared a ritual of gathering around the fireplace. We would bring our hot tea to welcome in winter, saying out loud all the good things we wanted winter to bring us—our way of dealing with the gloomy cold days pending.

My fireplace lay empty of fire, light, or warmth these days. I thought about Reynesh and I talking so intimately in front of his fireplace. I had liked how alive a fireplace could be. The orange flames had reflected into the dimly lit room, offering warmth and easing my worries.

After the morning visit with the bank, I stared at the darkness of the fireplace, preparing to welcome in winter. It might be better if I waited until evening instead of doing the ritual so early in the day. That way, there would be a mood from the moon, but the mood would be limited to me doing it by myself.

This riff with my sister could continue for years if we weren't careful. I stuffed the sadness bubbling up. There must be something I could do. My mind tore through possibilities. Calling her hadn't worked. She hadn't responded to any of my texts, so that wasn't an option. She had a habit of not being home after work. That left one alternative. I pulled out my phone and called her bank branch.

"Yes, I'd like to schedule an appointment with Ms. Woodland, if possible, today. Maybe in the next hour, if she's free."

"Let's see," the phone receptionist said. "Today in forty minutes would work."

Twenty-two minutes later, I stood in the foyer of the bank with the shiny floor reflecting up at me.

After a few minutes of standing there, I was escorted to my sister's office. She was parked behind her large desk, eyes focused on paperwork like nothing had changed. Still perfectly dressed. Still beautiful. Still extremely serious and focused.

"Hi."

Her head lifted up, and her mouth opened slightly. I shifted weight. She plopped her pen down onto her notepad, then steepled her fingers together.

"Could I have one minute?"

Her jaw tightened as she gave that request thought.

"Please. I'm not going to ask anything from you."

She gestured for me to sit on a plump leather chair in front of her desk.

I moved slowly, struggling to find the courage to do the thing I came here to do. I sat, crossing my legs as though that would keep me together.

"I came to apologize." My voice choked, sounding rusty like it hadn't been used for a long time.

Her face wore a hard expression. I uncrossed my legs. She said nothing.

"I miss you." My voice was quiet, but she softened a smidgen, so I knew she'd heard me.

"Zoey."

I looked up at her. "I've gotten help." A flicker of shock race through her face. "It wasn't okay for me to dominate your life with my problems. I'm sorry."

Tiffany eased back in her chair. "I might have made some mistakes too."

That stopped me short. She thought she made mistakes. "Like what?"

My sister shrugged. "Oh, I don't know. I might have gotten too caught up in the parent role, and I might have taken it a bit too far."

"You gave me a love potion! That's what's going really far."

"That I did." She tipped her chin up. "But I have to admit, Zoey, I wish someone would care for me enough to go to that length."

"Tiffany, I care about you."

She patted her desk. "I have never doubted that. It's that I get tired of the responsibilities of being the oldest."

I wasn't sure the right way to say the next part. "You don't need to do that anymore if you're back in my life."

She shifted in her seat.

My jaw clenched. If she wasn't ready for me to be in her life, I needed to respect that. I was the one coming to her, not the other way around, but I had to see if it was possible to make it work.

"I've changed. You no longer need to take the parenting role. Just a close friend role. One where I give back to you."

The clock on the wall ticked the seconds away.

I silently rose to my feet. "Whenever you're ready, I'm here." I headed to the door.

"Wait."

I shifted back to face her.

"You have needed a lot, Zoe, but you've also given a lot to me."

"What?"

"You believed in me when no one else did—in college, or when I applied for this job, or when I was going for a promotion."

"Yeah," I said quietly. "I remember."

"You were the only one who stood by me. And honestly . . ." She fiddled with her pen. "You always thought I was great. And you listened to me."

I took a deep breath, wanting to receive what she was saying.

"You have this skill to listen and really uncover the truth of what's going on for someone. Elizabeth talked to me about it too, and Tami. Elizabeth was so impressed with your coaching. She even talked about wanting to hire you someday if the opportunity came up."

"Wow, I didn't know." I blinked. "I'm glad I was helping her. If you can call hooking up with *him* a help." I smiled ruefully.

"Who she hooks up with is not a reflection of you. If she found help from what you did, that's all that matters."

An excellent point. I was going to have to think more about that. "Thanks for telling me. It is helpful to know at least I wasn't a complete flop at being a coach."

"How's the business going?"

I twisted my fingers on my lap. "It's on hold for a while."

"What?"

I glanced at the picture of a mountain on the wall behind her. "I needed to learn to be on my own."

She chewed that over. "Makes sense. I've been doing a bit of that myself. Well, the focusing on me part. I've got the being on my own down."

I felt the familiar temptation to spill my guts about what I'd learned and all my current fears. Instead of indulging, I let my smile linger as I stood.

"Well, thanks for letting me talk to you, Tiff. I wanted to check in with you and see if you were doing okay and to apologize. I know I was a strain on you and I'm learning how to fix it."

I pulled my purse strap back up my shoulder. "I don't want to keep you. Know my door is open, and you can call anytime. I'm here for you. Maybe a coffee sometime."

Tiffany rose to her feet. "Maybe I'll swing by your place after work one of these days."

I stopped midway to the door. "Ah, that. Actually, I'll have to get you my new address. I'm moving in a few days."

Her voice rose an octave. "What?"

"I'm still looking for an apartment, but I should have that figured out in the next couple of days, and I'll text you the address."

"But why? You love the house and the neighborhood—"

Time for me to confront things head-on. "I'm going through a foreclosure."

She gasped. "Hang on. I can probably help. I could—"

I shook my head. "No. It's less stress this way."

She was quiet a second, then sat down. "So, no house, and no coaching. Do you have a job at all?"

I refused to blink or be embarrassed. "Flipping hamburgers."

She gasped again, this time louder.

To cut her off, I said, "It's perfect, Tiff. Really, it is. I need something low stress and stable right now. Something simple and basic. Something to give me time to . . ." I shrugged. ". . . become me."

Her mouth closed as she blinked. Noise from the hall filtered into the room.

Maybe this was a test for Tiffany, too.

A smile tugged at my mouth.

"Well," she said, glancing at me with sad eyes, "your life has certainly changed."

"It has, but it's better. Maybe not as fancy or comfortable, but I like myself better."

A smile touched her face. "Good." Then her face fell. "Please don't tell me you're still dating Nick."

I gave my head a single vehement shake. "No. He was too obsessed with shoes."

Her brows crinkled. "What?"

I laughed, realizing that sounded bizarre. "He always commented on my shoes. He wanted high heels all the time. The higher, the better."

Tiffany gave me a blank look like she didn't understand the problem with that. She loved high heels. It was her, every day. It was *her*.

"High heels, no matter how great they look, are not me," I explained. "Him trying to seduce me into wearing what he wanted was his way of remaking me. If he did that before we were even a 'thing' . . ." I shivered. "Been down that path. Not going on that journey again if I can help it."

Tiffany nodded her parental approval. Apparently, old habits die hard. "Good for you, Zoe. Very, very, good."

My sister just gave me the approval I had been working for subconsciously all this time. And I felt no different than I had before I received her approval, other than relieved we were talking. Her opinion about my life really didn't matter. I mean, it was nice and all that she approved and saw growth. That was just extra with me being happy with *me* and doing what was best for *me*.

"I am with no one."

My sister's eyes widened. "Are you okay with that?"

It was a fair question for her to ask. I never would have been okay before. "Dating would be a distraction."

She nodded. "Yep, time to build your career. It does take intense focus."

I sighed. Here it comes. "I'm only focusing on myself and healing—not a career, not guys, not friends, nothing but me and healing and my new cat."

"Cat?"

"You wouldn't understand the cat."

"Probably not. Cat hairs."

I laughed. "It would do a number on your outfits. My cat is a shedding machine."

She looked baffled by my words. "How's your life better, flipping burgers and losing the house you love?"

"I was over my head with the mortgage and bills. I don't want the pressure anymore."

She took a half step around the desk to stand close to me. "But what about your coaching? You were making so much progress."

I shrugged. "It blew up in my face. Turns out, I'm not good at many of the things relationship coaching requires."

"But maybe if you—"

I put my hand out. "Tiffany, stop. This is exactly what I don't want. I don't want you to feel like you have to swoop in and save the day. These are my problems, and I'm making my way through them. It's not your job to save me."

She clenched her hands into a fist. "Come live with me."

"You like your own space."

"It would be fun. Like old times."

The old me would have completely jumped at that offer. But that was the old me. "Tiff, thank you, but no."

"But—"

"If I moved in with you, our problems would start all over again."

She waited for me to explain.

"You'd become controlling, and I'd become dependent. But . . ." I reached out and touched her hand, "it means a lot to me that you offered."

"I like this new you," she whispered.

I squeezed her hand.

"Are you welcoming in winter tonight?" she asked.

I nodded.

"Can I join you?"

My sister was back. And this time, I was going to let her be my sister and friend, nothing more. And I was going to be me. Nothing less.

"I'd love it," I said firmly. "Come at seven?"

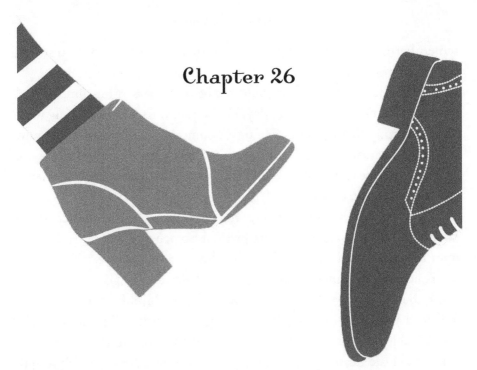

Chapter 26

Unpacking my boxes and setting up the apartment gave me a lot of time to remember the day Reynesh and I traveled to Moonlight Beach. I relived it a lot.

Thoughts flooded me as I cleaned. He helped me so much around the apartment—moving boxes and helping me disassemble heavy items—his scent lingered when he was gone, teasing me.

I also thought of that perfect day while waiting for the next customer to order hamburgers and fries at work. At the divorce support group, thoughts of him flooded through me. By the way, those thoughts were completely off-topic, except for maybe when we talked about relationships and all the ways we lied to ourselves.

Reynesh had been right. I wasn't ready for a relationship. But it sucked when a great guy was right there at my fingertips. Well, a guy soon-to-be-married to someone else. So maybe it wasn't just a timing issue.

But I thought of him the most when I struggled to go to sleep at night. That happened when If decided playing with a loose bottle cap was more entertaining than lying next to me. I wanted to stop remembering that one magical day because it amounted to nothing but a love potion.

Maybe the thoughts of him increased because I was losing him. He had flown out for his wedding yesterday. He'd be starting their week-long wedding ceremony in a few days. He didn't come to say goodbye to me now that I lived across town. I could've gone to him, but pain choked me up, and I had no idea what to say. The truth was, I was losing my best friend, and in some ways, that was harder than losing a husband.

They had talked about the importance of rituals in the divorce group many times. They said it often helped release pent-up emotions. I didn't want to let him go. I really, really didn't, but I had no choice.

Following the guidance of the group, I decided to go back to "our" beach to have my own private ritual of saying goodbye. It seemed fitting. I imagined almost tasting the salt air, feeling the slightly chilled sand squishing through my toes, and my hair raising as the wind tickled my neck. I could also taste Reynesh's salty lips against mine and the way it felt to pull his strong body against me. He had held me that day with so much love and tenderness. Even now, with only the memory, tingles still flowed down my spine. It was hard to believe it was all just a love potion. Impossible, really.

Almost as impossible as having Reynesh gone and becoming a married man. That thought just messed me up inside as I drove without much awareness to our beach. Our spot. It didn't take me long to reach the beach that had no restrictions, just waves, sand, birds, and clouds. I found a parking spot in front of a tiny wooden beach home and climbed out, tugging the hood of my jacket up over my head.

I strolled the narrow sidewalk path toward the ocean. Fallen leaves crunched under my tennis shoes. November. That would be cold in most other places in the country, but it was slightly breezy here.

Once I reached the sand, I looked over the water and watched the waves crash. Damion had called last night to inform me that he and Elizabeth were engaged. The only surprising thing about that news was I felt nothing. Not bad. Not good. Nothing. Maybe that was what healing looked like. No more big reactions.

Damion was cute and asked me to marry him. I'd gone there. I thought I'd make a good coach. Went there. I had grabbed randomly at whatever, without figuring out what was best for me. I was done with that. No house now. No fancy job. No boyfriend. But I could look in the mirror and know who I was—a quirky, imperfect girl who put her all into things even if she didn't master any of it. Also, I could make a mean brownie. And that was something.

Five feet ahead of me, a surfer in a slick black wetsuit strolled the beach with a surfboard tucked under his arm, ready to take on the endless waves. He understood the freedom of what this place offered.

I followed his lead and kicked off my shoes. The wet sand oozed between my toes, letting me know I was alive. The wind picked up in a gust, and I strolled on the squishy sand. Peace settled into my chest as the salt air tickled my nose. I lifted my chin and let my hair blow back.

The air felt electric and snappy. The sun sank, streaking the sky with rosy pinks and subtle orange hues. Simple and gorgeous. Like my new life.

I kicked cold sand between my toes and kept walking. In the distance, a figure headed my way on the beach. He or she walked with a lazy, confident stride. I liked the combination. It reminded me of Reynesh. Easygoing, confident.

How I would miss him. Things would be so different when he returned a married man. I took a deep breath and moved to detour around the oncoming person, but stopped short. I'd recognize that sexy, determined walk anywhere. It couldn't be, but it was. I burst into a jog toward him as he hurried toward me.

"What?" I asked as I drew up to him.

Reynesh, barefoot like me with his hair damp from the incoming fog, smiled his gorgeous, sexy smile.

My stomach burst into a flutter. "I don't understand." I looked up at him as a cloud crawled over the sunlight. "Aren't you supposed to be on a plane right now?" I fought to keep my voice steady.

He shrugged, still sporting that smile. "Didn't make it."

I blinked up at him, seeking to make sense of his presence here. Why would he miss his plane? He wasn't the type of person to blow things off, especially like that.

"Your sister said you'd be here."

Tiffany? I vaguely remembered telling her last night that I might stroll on the beach on my day off. "Why would you talk to my sister about where I was?"

He gave me a sheepish expression, but didn't answer. Instead, he leaned into me. "Do you remember the last time we were here?"

Goose bumps chased down my neck from the touch of his breath, attempting to forget the magnetic pull of the love potion. The pull of Reynesh. Forgetting that day was like trying not to remember my own name.

It was impossible to deny the bolt of connection we had when we touched. The magnet that drew us together. The laughs. The thrill of being near him and having him look at me with such longing. I peered into those brown eyes that tempted me to wish for something more between us.

"I remember," I whispered.

"That was something."

That was one way of putting it.

"I've been thinking," he said.

I kicked my foot at the wet sand. It stuck between my toes as I waited to hear news about his new wife.

"Being with you rejuvenates me."

I blinked several times.

"Every time we're together, I feel alive. It'd be a shame to lose that."

My sadness lifted a smidge. "You want to stay friends," I said flatly and swallowed. I was committed to putting my life in order. I had to do this. I had to get the truth out in the open. A seagull squawked, and waves splashed. "We were both deluding ourselves because of a potion."

"You are boiling down our connection to a potion?" He forced a laugh.

"If you think about it, it is really the only plausible explanation—"

"Zoey, there's more."

I stopped talking.

His gaze held mine. "You don't believe it was just a potion, do you?" he asked softly.

I swallowed a lump in my throat. "Yes, I do," I whispered. "I have to believe it. Because if it wasn't just a potion, then—" My eyes stung hot with tears.

He took a step closer. "Then what?" His words were soft and gentle, but pushing me.

Suddenly angered, I glared at him. "You're leaving the country and getting married, so there's no 'then.'"

"I—"

"Why did you drive all the way down here to tell me this?" I backed up, my foot depressing the cool sand. "I've been putting my life back together. Patching it up, rebuilding. I might look like a mess on the outside, but I am happy on the inside. The first time in a long time. So, why are you messing with me by asking me 'then what?' You have your destiny, right?" I hated how I sounded so hurt. But it was the truth, so I let it float in the space between us.

He neared me and then firmly held both my shoulders. "What if I'm your destiny?"

I gasped a laugh. "Would you stop being hard on me? I'm letting you go, despite how I feel for you. What else do you want from me?"

He reached into his pocket then sank to one knee and held out a diamond ring. "I want you to marry me."

My jaw dropped. "What? Marry you? What about your fiancée in India?"

"We talked for the first time last night."

I swallowed.

"And—?"

"And she is very tied to her family and her community. Somehow the information about her moving to the US wasn't communicated to her."

I swiped at a strand of hair that blew into my eyes.

He grimaced slightly. "She was mad."

He wasn't telling me everything. "Just about the move?" I prompted.

"And the fact that I am so Americanized. And the fact that she has a boyfriend her parents don't approve of. And the fact that I have strong feelings for an American woman."

My hope surged. "What?"

"I have a responsibility to myself to be happy too, like you said you're doing for yourself."

I sucked in my breath. "Is your—is she okay?"

"I don't like hurting her, but if we got together, it'd be even worse. We both agreed to that."

He was right. Rough marriages were not pleasant. He leaned closer. "It has been in front of me all this time. *You* make me happy. *You* are the one I want to be with."

My face flamed. "But your family?"

"I will deal with that. This isn't about my family. It's about us—you and me. And I've learned that's all that matters. It'd be perfect timing. The sun is about to dive into the edge of the ocean, and we could have our first engagement kiss with the last moments of this beautiful day."

I did say yes to Mr. Destiny, and I would tell him about our relationship's scientific rules later. But for now, though, I just had to claim that engagement kiss.

Epilogue

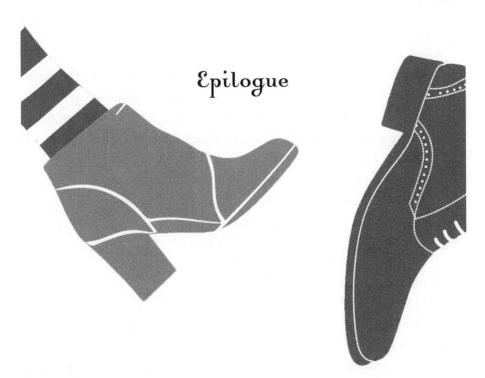

Six Months Later

I barely heard the doorbell ring over the noise of the household. Reynesh's nephews had university friends over at our house playing video games. Right now, their competitive playoff included a lot of yelling and stomping.

The noise filled me. I couldn't keep joy from vibrating through me. Reynesh's very noisy house was exactly what I had always dreamed of. I had spent my day off baking brownies and buying bowls of fruit, potato chips, and dip for their party. The food disappeared faster than a person could inhale a breath. It didn't take long to figure out we were going to run out. I texted Reynesh to pick up more goodies on the way home. I also sent him a complete line of kissing emojis.

The doorbell rang once again. I opened the door to Tiffany, who looked as perfect as ever. Buttoned-up suit and skirt, heels, each hair in place, but no smile graced her face. In fact, black smudges pooled under her eyes against her pale skin.

"Sis, come on in." I swung the door wide.

Instead of stepping in, she gestured for me to come outside on the porch. I did as she requested, taking a quick glance across the street at my old house, which still had the bald spots on the lawn. It was rewarding to know the young Asian couple who'd bought my house hadn't had any better luck stopping the rabbit nibblers than I had.

I shut the front door behind me, blocking out the noise from inside.

"I'm so glad you came," I said to Tiffany. "It seems like since I hooked up with Reynesh, you've become a stranger."

Me being in relationship was hard on her.

"I'm here as a messenger," she said.

I squinted my eyes in the sinking sun. "Okay."

"Do you remember Elizabeth?"

"My X-husband's new wife who used to be one of my best clients . . . that Elizabeth?"

Tiffany nodded. My sister wasn't the type of person to idly bring up anything remotely connected to my X. Something was up.

"She's not the type of person to forget easily. Why?"

"Well," Tiffany said, looking away, "I ran into her at a networking meeting, and she couldn't stop talking about what a great coach you were and how this new position opened up at her office . . ."

I shifted my weight. What was my sister rambling on about?

"Elizabeth wants to know if you're willing to work for her as a coach for her lawyers' office."

I stared at my older sister, who had become much less sister and a lot more friend over the past months. Tiffany had to be kidding. As I tried to take that all in, Reynesh zoomed up the driveway on his nephew's motorcycle. Both my sister and I watched the most handsome man in the world slip off the bike with a bag of groceries draped around his wrist.

He strolled up to me in his tight-fitting polo shirt that made him extra hot. My heart did its familiar racing dance. I doubted it would ever become old, seeing him.

Taking off his helmet, he bent over to give me an explosive kiss. It lasted far too long, especially in front of Tiffany.

I pulled away, embarrassed. "Reynesh."

He drew back, but my whole body continued to tingle.

"Did you get it?" I asked about the deal he was working on.

He shrugged in his casual way. "If it's destiny."

I shook my head at his very bad joke.

He gave me a quick kiss. "Sorry, babe, I couldn't resist. It's looking really good."

I turned to Tiffany to explain. "Reynesh met with Romance Inc."

Tiffany nodded her head like she was impressed. "Oh, I know them . . . the most popular local online dating service today."

Wanting to brag more, I continued, "They're in discussion about using Reynesh's services on their site."

My sister's lips pressed together as she absorbed that, then glanced up at Ray. "Well done."

He shrugged. "All in a day's work."

"You'll most likely need coaches with a gig like that," Tiffany said.

Reynesh tapped me on the shoulder. "See. I told you."

I shrugged as Tiffany gave me an expression that communicated, *Well?*

Reynesh put his arm around me. "She's fighting me on it."

"Why?" Tiffany turned all business.

There were so many things my sister didn't get about me. This, most likely, would be one more thing.

"I haven't said no yet. I'm still thinking about it. I don't want to lose myself in Reynesh's business. A lot of relationship books say working together kills romance. Not to mention, I have my own dreams I want to follow too."

He kissed me on the top of my head. "I always support that. Zoe can do what Zoe wants. I just want her happy."

I beamed at him. This man was a good man. I was very, very, very lucky to be with him even if his family didn't like me for not being Hindu. According to him, it was destiny to be together and to have our troubles.

Tiffany glanced back and forth at us. "Elizabeth is offering Zoey a position too. She's a hot commodity."

Reynesh pulled me tight. "She will always be that."

This was getting downright uncomfortable. "All right, then." I slapped my hands together. "We have a group of boys inside anxious to have more food."

"Yes, yes. We do need to get in there," Reynesh said. "Just one thing." He held up his index finger and focused on Tiffany.

"Tiffany," he said casually, "I've been thinking about that love potion you cast on Zoey and me."

She swallowed visibly. "Yes?"

"Well, it turned out so nice for us, Zoey and me, we'd like to return the favor."

About the Author

Anastasia Alexander doesn't have the answers to life's love questions but knows love in the twenty-first century is complex. There are no easy answers, and there is richness and juiciness in exploring all the complexity that love brings. She is the author of the bestselling and award-winning *Millionaire Romance* series and *Silent Cries*. She is currently flirting with her hubby in the Southwest.

A free ebook edition is available with the purchase of this book.

To claim your free ebook edition:

1. Visit MorganJamesBOGO.com
2. Sign your name CLEARLY in the space
3. Complete the form and submit a photo of the entire copyright page
4. You or your friend can download the ebook to your preferred device

Morgan James BOGO™

A **FREE** ebook edition is available for you or a friend with the purchase of this print book.

CLEARLY SIGN YOUR NAME ABOVE

Instructions to claim your free ebook edition:
1. Visit MorganJamesBOGO.com
2. Sign your name CLEARLY in the space above
3. Complete the form and submit a photo of this entire page
4. You or your friend can download the ebook to your preferred device

Print & Digital Together Forever.

Snap a photo

Free ebook

Read anywhere